Bloodline

Secrets

Avery Thorne

CONTENTS

CHAPTER 1

I woke up today.

As I lay in my bed, I can hear the clock on the wall, tick ticking away, and the sound of my own breathing interrupting the otherwise silent room.

I don't remember getting into bed last night or going to sleep for that matter. It's as if I've been stuck on autopilot for the longest time. Days, months, years? I'm not even sure anymore. Every day seems to blend together as if I'm experiencing the same day and night over and over again.

Sweat slowly begins to drip off my forehead as the temperature of my apartment gets hotter and hotter as the sun starts to rise higher in the sky.

My thin blanket softly pressed against my cheek as I lay with one arm outstretched and one hand holding the blanket tightly underneath the side of my face.

It's so peaceful when I first wake up, before I remember my reality, and every memory rushes to the forefront of my mind again.

I start to wonder what the day holds for me.

The sun had just barely rose an hour ago, but the heat is already becoming a bit unbearable and suffocating, so it's just not possible for me to sleep any longer this morning.

I stood up and headed to the bathroom finally, and I caught my reflection in the mirror.

My long brown hair fell just below my ribs, the weight of it straightening out the majority of the natural wavy texture, my skin is soft in appearance, and more of a tanned color. It's almost like a caramel color, thanks to seeing the sun more often this summer.

My almond shaped green eyes seemed to perfectly fit on my round face. My nose is an average sized button nose, and my lips are more on the slightly plumper side.

I never thought I looked dull necessarily, but I also have never seen anything too special in my appearance, just simply a normal girl overall. Though I do see some of my dads features in me sometimes, which is very comforting.

It's been a very long three years since my dad died, and at this point, I just wish I could at least get closure from his mysterious death.

I was only sixteen when he was murdered, so unfortunately, the police didn't feel like they could tell me everything, and they didn't handle things very appropriately at the time. Not that there was much to tell anyway as far as I have heard. All in all, it seems to be nothing but a mystery to everyone who was involved.

He was a scientist and enjoyed his job. He was also an incredibly kind-hearted man, and I admired and loved him so much. I honestly don't know who could've possibly ever wanted to hurt him, but I miss him beyond what words can describe and think about him every single day.

After he died, I was left all alone because I had no other family, unfortunately. My mom left us when I was about two years old, and I haven't heard from her since. I don't have any other relatives that I know of, so in the end, it was pretty much just me left.

I lived in a foster home for a short time, and luckily, I found a job soon after, and I was able to take a test so that I could get my diploma early.

Then, I was able to find a judge who allowed me to get emancipated and found a private renter who was willing to rent to an emancipated teenager.

It's not a perfect apartment, but it's what I know to be home now, and I'm happy that I at least have what I have. My life is nothing special, but I've gone through so much, and by some miracle, i'm still here. I can only hope that better things will come my way with time.

Todays my day off, so I decided I'm going to head to the park to read and relax for a few hours before time gets away from me, and it gets too late. It's cooler there anyway, under the big trees, then it is at home with my broken air conditioner.

On my way walking down the road I remembered that there's a short-cut through a near by alley, and I would much rather not have to deal with all the people on the main road if I can avoid it.

I'd normally avoid alleyways, but today, I just really want some peace and quiet and dont want to walk through crowds of people who just talk for the sake of talking or just to hear themselves speak.

This city is always so filled with people, so much talking, noise, cars, and I just want to enjoy the quiet for once.

So, I began to walk down this short-cut that I once heard about. It's not a straight shot through, so I'm going to have to make a couple of turns here and there, but i'm sure it'll be okay. I'm going to cut off some time from my walk at least.

Walking down the shortcut, I turned right, then left, then straight for a long while, then left again, then right, then left. Soon enough, I find myself lost in what is a maze of different ways to turn.

"Damn." I say to myself as I've turned into a dead end. There's a short brick wall blocking my way from continuing, but it's tall enough that I can't climb over it either.

I start to feel frustrated because what was supposed to be a short-cut has now turned into twenty minutes longer than it would've taken if I had just gone the normal way and dealt with the people.

Suddenly, I start to feel the hair at the nape of my neck standing. The tingling sensation of spiders crawled up my back and down my arms, covering my skin in goosebumps.

I get this sinking feeling in the pit of my stomach and start to feel this sense that I need to just get out of this area as quickly as possible.

This feeling screams to me that anywhere would be better than this spot right here right now. A feeling of fear washes over me, beginning to consume me more and more as the seconds pass. As if I just jumped head first into a pool, but instead of water, it's this petrifying feeling that insists on soaking every inch of me within it.

I turn around to try to quickly run a different direction and try to find my way back out, turning right and hoping to go back the way I came, and maybe even just going straight home after all of this, but, as I turned the corner I ran into something hard and fell back onto the ground instead.

My heart is pounding out of my chest, and my breath is now shallow and shaky. I don't know how I know this, but this is what I was afraid of. I can feel it in my gut that this is it.

Too afraid to even look up at first, I stay there frozen on the ground with my eyes locked on the shoes of what I now realize is a person. One of two people, to be exact.

"I shouldn't be here," I thought to myself as I felt every pain filled heartbeat trying to burst from my chest. Every part of my body screams within to get up and run, to get away from here, but my body feels stuck to the ground.

I start to hear laughing from what I now realize are two men who are standing in front of me. It breaks me from the trance I've been trapped in.

"Well, I wasn't expecting this at all today, but lucky us. I guess we have good timing, don't we, Benny? you were right about there being someone over here." the first man said.

looking up at them to examine what I'm dealing with, I see that the first man is roughly six feet tall, has broad shoulders, bulky and very muscular arms, looking as if he works out for hours upon hours every weekend.

He stood tall out of confidence as well and didn't seem too shy to this situation in the slightest. Covered in deep scars, tattoos that appeared to be very obviously gang related, his hair was shaved completely off, and his skin was just one step up from pale.

The second man let out a mischievous laugh, as if to agree, that this is, in fact, something they must have been waiting for.

"I told you, Ricky, I knew I heard someone over here." Benny replied. Benny was shorter than Ricky by a few inches and more thin, too, but still very muscular. His hair was shaved on the sides but longer on top, and he only seemed to have a couple scars on his face, which in comparison were hardly noticeable, though, he looked like he was still healing from getting hit in the face recently, and his skin looked as if he spends a lot of time in the sun.

I try to stand up and run the other direction, but as I turn to run, Ricky grabs my arm and pulls me back towards him aggressively.

My breath gets caught in my throat, causing me to let out a loud gasp. My body tenses up, as the feeling of panic hits me. "I'm so scared. I'm beyond scared, I'm terrified. what do I do? Scream, I have to scream." I think to myself as tears start to fill my eyes.

My book slips out of my hands and falls into a nearby puddle that was created by a leaking pipe higher up on the building, causing mud filled water to splash up at the three of us and cause a temporary distraction.

I start to scream as loud as I possibly can, but Ricky covers my mouth almost as soon as any sound could escape my lungs.

The police in this city never seem to help anyone, but I just pray that someone heard me and will help, anyone at all.

He shoves me hard up against the brick wall beside us. The impact immediately knocked the breath out of me for a moment.

He then pulls out a small pocket knife from the pocket of his pants and holds it close to my neck.

"If you try to scream again, if you try to run again, you don't want to find out what's going to happen. You do as I say, got it?" Ricky says as he brings the knife closer to my neck and puts pressure on it so that it presses into my skin with his other hand still tightly covering my mouth.

I can feel the sharp blade scratching and scraping away at my skin little by little with every movement either of us makes.

Benny laughs again and says, "This is going to be fun, i've been waiting for this type of thing to happen since I joined you guys."

I nod to Ricky, agreeing that I heard him and got the message. Tears were now streaming down my face. I am completely panicking, feeling desperate to get away, but I'm nowhere near strong enough to take on one of these guys, let alone two.

Not to mention what they'd do if I did manage to do anything to them or if they caught me again if I managed to get away in the first place.

Ricky demands that I hand him my wallet, so I reach into my pocket and hand it to him without hesitation.

Once he takes it from me, he puts it in his pocket and then holds me tightly up against the wall and begins to kiss my neck.

Every kiss feels like acid eating away at my skin. His hands pull my body closer to his, so tightly that I can barely wiggle or even attempt to pull away at all.

He grabs a handful of my hair to gain more control, as if to show me that there's nothing I can do but follow his lead.

Benny stands ready nearby by holding his own knife, and I can only assume he's waiting for the word to say it's his turn or something.

I closed my eyes, realizing the full reality of the situation I'm in, feeling like there's absolutely nothing I can do to get out of this situation by myself. I'm completely stuck here with no way out. I feel so helpless, still almost frozen out of fear.

Ricky began to touch and kiss other places on my body and I decide to just keep my eyes closed, wincing with every touch, just hoping to escape in my mind to any where else I can imagine. "Anywhere but here." I begged in my mind.

All of sudden, I feel his grip quickly release from my body and I open my eyes to see a random guy who was now throwing punches at the other two and knocked their knives out of their hands.

CHAPTER 2

This man looks to be a couple inches past six feet tall, with short dark hair. His features are very masculine and strong. His skin is a bit on the paler side, and his face is clean shaven.

part of the fight seems like a blur due to my utter shock, but I quickly come back to reality a few moments later to see Benny grabbing this guy from behind, his arms locking around the guys chest as Ricky punches the guy in the face a couple times and then tries to land a punch to his stomach, but then the guy uses Benny's hold as an opportunity to bring both legs up to kick Ricky in the chest, causing Ricky to fall back.

He then leans forward, flipping Benny over his shoulder, causing him to land hard onto the ground and knock the air out of him.

Ricky then tries to take advantage of the moment and rush the the dark haired guy as he starts standing back up straight, grabbing him by the throat and throwing him against the wall, but the dark haired guy gets a solid punch to Ricky's face and brings up one leg to kick him away, gaining a little distance between them, and then grabs Ricky's arm and throws him hard into the wall.

A loud crack comes from his direction, and he falls to the ground for a second, completely dazed.

The two men eventually land a few more punches to the dark haired guy and He lands a few more hits to the two of them before they finally call it quits and run away as fast as they can, realizing that they couldn't quite keep up and were out matched.

Once they were gone, the dark-haired man fell to his knees, leaning forward so he could hold up his own weight on his arms for a minute and try to catch his breath.

I was still glued to my spot, sitting on the ground, stunned. I'm not sure what I'm supposed to do at the moment or how I ended up sitting on the ground in the first place.

I'm still petrified from what had just happened and now shocked that some random guy came to my rescue.

He's breathing heavy from the hard throws he landed on them, knuckles swollen, lip and cheek bleeding from them getting the few hard hits they got on him.

He stands up, still catching his breath, and walks over to me. He then leans down in front of me and extends his hand, showing pure concern and worry for me.

"Are you okay?" he asks as he helps me to my feet. I still have tears falling from my eyes at this point without even realizing it was happening, as I'm trying to fully comprehend the reality of everything that just happened.

I wipe away my tears and say, "I'm okay now, I guess, all things considered. Thank you for helping me."

His genuine look of concern quickly changes to a look of relief. it was almost like hearing in my own voice, that i'm okay, was more relieving than seeing for himself that I wasn't too badly hurt physically.

"Good. I'm really relieved to hear that. Why on earth were you going down this alley alone anyway?"

He began to say, sounding genuinely confused as he tried to keep his voice steady from worry over the thought,

"Haven't you watched any movies of all the bad things that tend to happen in an alley? They weren't just randomly made up. They're based on real-life things that actually happen."

He said, still not understanding why I would risk it alone when really anything could happen, and he was beginning to over explain.

His face twisted into a mixture of showing fear, worry, and concern, thinking of what he just stopped from happening.

My heart stops for a moment, unsure of what to say, not at all expecting this stranger to be so worried for my safety, and not quite sure how to reply.

"I-I just, I was trying to take a shortcut to get to the park and got lost. I didn't think anything like that would actually happen in real life."

I mumbled out as I was still trembling from the stress of everything and the roller coaster of emotions I had experienced in such a short time.

He sighed, guilt written on his face for not waiting to say something like that and not meaning to sound so insensitive to it all.

"I'm really sorry, I know you couldn't have known that those guys would be here or find you here or what their intentions were going to be, or that anyone else at all would be here to begin with for that matter. it just scared me is all, I know it scared you too. I was really worried and thought I was too late... I know im over explaining and should probably just shut up... please, will you let me walk you home?"

He asked as he reached his arm out to softly grab me around the upper part of my back to lead me.

"Yes," I whispered as I let him lead. I feel this warmth and comfort slowly flood across me as I stand up next to him.

I feel safe, despite the dangerous situation that occurred only just a few moments ago, and despite the fact that he's still a complete stranger.

neither of us say anything for a while. It's mostly this painfully awkward silence that lurks between the two of us. About halfway to my apartment, I can't take the silence anymore.

"My name is Hayven." I say as I try to force a smile.

He glances at me as I'm speaking and smirks as he says, "My name is Damien."

"It's nice to meet you, Damien," I reply.

Despite this awkward silence, I feel strangely comfortable around him, like I've known him my whole life even though we just met.

"It's nice to meet you too," he mumbled as he looked away.

The silence continued once again, but this time, it wasn't quite as awkward. I feel content at least knowing his name. This mysterious man who saved me from two awful men who had nothing but the worst intentions toward me.

For the first time in a long time, really, in this moment, I simply feel content and not quite so lonely.

We finally get to my front door, and I pull my keys out from my pocket and unlock the door.

Before I can turn the knob on the door, he pulls a pen out from his pocket and reaches out to gently grab my hand.

He starts to write a number across my wrist, "This is my phone number. If you ever need help with anything, or even just want to talk, please call me."

He said hesitantly and then quickly turned and rushed away, turning down the hall before I could hardly even react.

"Thank you!" I try to say in a hurry, in hopes that he would hear me before he was too far out of sight or ear shot. I hope he could feel how truly grateful I was that he saved me.

I turn the door knob and push open my front door, walking into the warmth and safety of my own home. Feeling relief wash over me as I lock the door behind me.

It's still the middle of the day, but todays events just drained me. I feel like I could sleep for weeks or months even.

I grabbed my phone and put in Damien's number before I could forget to do it and then sit on my couch and let out a big sigh of relief.

I was still scared, scarred, and traumatized over the fact that something like that could happen, or almost happen thanks to Damien stepping in.

With all things considered, I feel lucky and so thankful that things didn't turn out worse. I don't know how bad it truly would've ended up being, but thanks to him, I didn't have to find out.

I made sure my doors and windows were all locked once again, and I headed to my room to lay in my bed. It was hot, but the comfort of being home out weighed the heat for the time being.

As I was drifting off to sleep, I realized I never told Damien the directions to my apartment.

CHAPTER 3

I contemplate whether or not I should text him or call him even. Whether I should ask how he knew where I lived, or something else entirely, but I almost feel as though I don't have the right to question him after he saved me. I know I do, but I'm also not sure if I want to know the answer, honestly.

I sit here with my eyes locked on my phone for a few minutes, wondering if I should call him at all.

"Am I just being paranoid? Did I tell him and just forget due to the stress or trauma of what happened? Am I just being crazy?" I thought to myself.

I shook my head almost as if to rid myself of those thoughts entirely.

I brought his number up in a message to text him.

Me: Hey, it's Hayven. Thank you again so much for saving me. You have no idea just how grateful I am for what you did for me.

Him: You don't need to thank me. I'm just glad I got there when I did. Please, stay safe.

Me: I am definitely never taking any shortcuts ever again, that's for sure, so don't worry. um, can I ask you a question?

Him: Anything you can do to stay safe, and absolutely, go ahead, I'm all ears.

Me: Um, well, how exactly did you know where I live? I don't remember telling you the directions or anything. It's like you just somehow already knew. Please don't lie to me. Just be honest.

Him: I can explain, please let me meet you somewhere in person and I will explain everything. I promise I won't lie to you.

I was right. He knew where I lived without me ever telling him. Now I'm so confused. Maybe I shouldn't meet with him, but I have to know how he knew, I have to know who this guy is.

Me: Okay... meet me at Juvany's Restaurant tonight at 5pm.

Him: Okay, I will be there... I promise I will explain.

My heart is racing again. I can once again feel every painful beat pounding in my chest.

Maybe this is a horrible idea to be here right now, but if he meant to do any kind of harm to me, then why would he save me? Wouldn't he have done something by now? He already had at least one chance that I know of for sure.

I ask one of the servers if I can sit in a booth closest to the entrance. It's a good spot because if anything does happen, I can run, or people can hear me if I yell, but its also a more private spot because unless people sit right next to you then the rest of the restaurant cant hear much of casual conversation since all the speakers that play music constantly surround the rest of them.

"I hope that this isn't a horrible mistake." I think to myself as I lean my head down into my hands, feeling pulled down by the weight of everything.

Damien walks through the entrance just as I look up, and he notices me right away. He looks like he's nervous.

He's putting up a good poker face with it all, but I can just tell some how that he's feeling nervous.

"I know that this looks bad," he says as he slides into the booth across from me. "But please, hear me out. I'm going to explain everything I can." He continued.

"You're right. It looks really bad, but okay, I'm here. I'm listening, " I said as I started to hold my breath, bracing for the impact of the words he's going to say.

I almost expect him to say he's some crazy stalker, or he saw me walking into my apartment one day, and just for some reason, I stood out in his mind. well, maybe the second one is really more of a hope, that it's really just all a coincidence.

"Okay. well, this might be a lot of information to absorb, so let me start off by telling you, I knew your dad." He said, rushing out the last four words, as if it pained him to let those words creep past his lips.

"You knew my dad? are you some kind of scientist or something too? Did you work with him?" I asked equally, eager and confused.

He paused for a moment, trying to piece together the right words to explain everything and then continued on to say,

"Work together? Yes, kind of. Scientist? No. I was more like a volunteer who helped him with some experiments."

There was an awkward silence now surrounding our little table. Even the music seemed to be silent for a moment.

The waitress walked up and asked if we were ready to order. "Just a cup of coffee, please." I replied. Damien nodded in agreement, "Yeah, same for me, please."

Those guys took off with my wallet, so I don't have much cash on me, but a warm coffee quite possibly be all I can tolerate right now aways honestly.

The silence surrounded us again as she walked away to grab some already made plates of food for some other customers.

"Did you... did you work with him around the time he died?" I quietly asked, my voice almost a whisper.

He looked downward, away from my direction, like he was afraid to make eye contact with me. He bit the inside of his cheeks and just nodded yes.

My mind was filled with so many questions now, and every answer seemed to fill me with more and more questions that needed an answer, too.

I was practically on the edge of my seat, looking at his face, studying every emotion that crossed it.

"Do you know how he died?" I asked, hopeful, wishing for closure. Though secretly in my heart, I knew it would also be an answer that would bring more questions.

He leaned forward, elbows on the table, and sighed. Shoulders seem to hold so much weight as he leans his head down for a moment. He looks back up at me and sympathetically says, "I can't tell you."

I felt my heart stop for a moment. "What do you mean you can't tell me?" I asked, annoyed.

He crossed his arms and almost seemed to show me the same annoyed attitude that I was now putting off while also seeming afraid that the next sentence could be the one that chases me off.

He replied, "I promised your dad, okay? I promised that I'd never tell you. I promised you that I wouldn't lie, so i'm telling you the truth, that I can't tell you because I promised your dad I wouldn't tell you."

I quietly sat for a minute, feeling defeated by those words. I was angry, confused by why my dad wouldn't want him to tell me, but I understood why he wouldn't tell me, and he seemed sincere about it all. It's because he promised my dad he wouldn't, but of course, once again, I'm filled with more questions with every answer.

I tried to calm myself, though it was hard to hold back the tears that so desperately wanted to escape my eyes. Tears of frustration, tears of confusion, and tears from feeling overwhelmed.

"Fine.. I understand why you can't tell me that, for now at least... but tell me how exactly you knew where I live. It's not the same house that I lived in with dad, and I don't remember him ever bringing anyone he worked with to our house in the first place." I said.

He paused for a moment. "It was your dads last dying wish that I look out for you and protect you, so I promised him that I would. I wasn't even going to meet you in person ever,

I was just going to keep my distance and leave you alone to live your life. Leave you to just move on in life and never know that I exist,

but then you went walking alone down that alley and wound up in an extremely dangerous situation that I just couldn't ignore.

I had to help you, I needed to make sure you were safe, and then when I saw what was happening, I had no choice but to intervene. I had to help you." Once again, sounding filled with worry at the thought of what could've happened if he hadn't been there.

I was a bit stunned by his answer. "My dad trusted this guy enough to ask him to look out for me and protect me?" I thought to myself.

The waitress interrupted my thoughts as she brought us both our coffees.

"Honestly, I have so many questions that I think it would take forever to go over them all, but why did you give me your phone number and why did you meet with me and explain all of this if you never wanted to meet me or talk to me in the first place?

Why did you even promise my dad something like that? It's not like it's your responsibility or anything." I asked as I cupped my hands around my warm drink, now feeling exhausted with all this information filling my head and the vast new amount of unanswered questions now nagging at me.

"It's not that I didn't want to. it's just... it was safer and better if you had never had to meet me. If you never knew I even existed, but I had to help you, I couldn't just let something bad like that happen, and then you put together that I knew where you lived because I was so focused on getting you home safe that I forgot to ask the directions, so, it just seemed like I couldn't keep it from you anymore anyways and I feel like you deserve to know something at least...

Now, as for making the promise and why, well, your dad helped me through more than you can ever imagine. He saved me more times than I can count.

He was my friend, and even more so than that, he was like family to me. I respected him more than words can ever come close to explaining. I don't know why he asked me to protect you and watch over you, but he did...

so I promised him I would try my hardest to keep you safe, and I don't plan on letting him down." He explained.

I pulled a five dollar bill out of my pocket and sat it on the table as I quickly stood up and started walking outside. "I need some air." I told him as I turned to walk out.

He quickly jumped up too and followed, stopping right beside me and said,

"I know that this is a lot to take in, and I'm sorry that I can't tell you everything. I hope that i've at least proven that your safe around me, and that I would never do anything to harm you in any way and I hope that you'll let me walk you home again, since its starting to get dark."

I stood there with my arms crossed over my chest, listening to him speak. I feel confused, overwhelmed, and even farther from closure with my dad than before. I'm really not sure what to think of it all, but I do feel safe around him.

I nodded yes, and without looking at him, I turned in the direction to walk home, and he quietly followed along close beside me.

"Thank you for meeting with me, answering my questions, walking me home, and again, for saving me today." I told him as I kept my eyes straight ahead.

"You don't have to thank me." He replied. I couldn't quite read the emotions that accompanied the tone of his voice.

There was silence for most of the walk home. When we reached my door, I turned to him and asked, "Are you going to be able to get home, okay? It's already really dark outside."

He chuckled and nodded, "Yeah, I will be fine. I'm more concerned about you getting home safely anyway than I am for myself.
"

I hesitantly headed inside and locked the door behind me. It's been an extremely long day, and I'm ready to go to sleep, but first, I just want to take a shower and relax.

After my shower, I went to grab a quick drink of water, and I saw a piece of paper folded up right past my front door on the floor. It looks like it was ripped off a newspaper or something. I unfolded it and saw writing that read,

"Please don't worry about paying for anything when you're with me

-Damien"

And just below the writing was two five-dollar bills. It was almost ridiculous that he would take the time to do that, and to pay me double what I paid for our coffees today on top of it, but at the same time, I thought it was sweet. I sat the money and note on my counter and went to bed to finally sleep after this seemingly endless day.

It was much cooler tonight than this morning, so I passed out almost as soon as I closed my eyes.

CHAPTER 4

The next few days were pretty quiet overall. I went to work like usual, texted Damien a couple of times, and then went home. It was pretty much the same as before, except I had someone to talk to now.

I used to have a best friend, whom I cared very much about, to talk to every day. Her name was Sierra.

A little over a year ago, there was an accident, and sadly, she didn't make it. She fell off the roof of her apartment complex and died two days later while she was still in the hospital trying to be saved.

They ruled it as a suicide, but I knew her, and she would have never even thought of doing something like that. She was truly the happiest person I knew, and even if she was secretly unhappy or something that whole time, she would've never done that without at least leaving a note for me and her family. If there's anything I know, it's that.

She cared so deeply for her family, and we had been best friends since kindergarten. We were practically inseparable.

It was another strange death I've had the displeasure of not getting full closure from. I miss her.

Recently, I applied for, and thankfully, I was hired on the spot for a new job that pays more than my last job. it's at a local mom and pop cafe. I'm starting as a waitress and working up to be assistant manager.

Everything is going great, and there's this really handsome guy who comes in a lot. His name is Elix. He's always so nice to me, and he's very good-looking. Tall, dark, and handsome type.

"So, Hayven. I know we haven't known each other long, but I want to change that. I feel like I have to get to know you better. What do you say I take you on a date sometime?" he said after he finished drinking his last sip of coffee.

I was a little surprise that he would be so straightforward and that he would ask me out at all, really.

I smiled and gestured towards the coffee to silently ask if he would like some more, and he nodded yes.

As I poured him more coffee, I smiled and asked, "Would you like to take me out sometime?"

He grabbed a napkin and started writing his number down on it and then slid it across the countertop. "Any time, any place." He replied.

I took the napkin and put it in my pocket and said,

"I think you're very handsome and very nice, but I'm not sure if it'd be very professional if I started dating a regular customer during my first month of working." I said.

He nodded to let me know that he understood and wasn't upset with my answer.

The next few weeks seem to just fly by, and we've texted a few times, but he hasn't brought it up again.

Damien and I have hung out a few times since the day he told me about how he promised my dad that he would protect me and everything.

Just like, stopping to have coffee together, hanging out at the park I always go to, just simple things, and then he usually walks me back home. We've gotten a lot closer, too, really quickly.

I guess it's kind of easier to get close to someone who you immediately felt like you had already known for forever and who saved you from some disgusting guys in a gang. Kind of cuts out the initial awkwardness and small talk. Both of us knowing my dad was also a big ice breaker.

While I was sitting on my couch watching tv, my phone started to ring.

"it's Damien." I said out loud to myself.

"Hello?" I said after accepting the call.

"Hey, can you come to my house today? I found a letter from your dad in some stuff he left behind with me. I think you'd like to read it, it's written to you. You don't have work tonight, right?" Damien said on the other side of the phone.

"Oh, okay yea I will get ready right now, and then I can come over. I'm off for a couple days, the owners decided to shut down for a couple of days to get some new equipment set up and get some new menus put out. Wait, what's your address? some of us aren't stalkers," I replied, ending in a laugh.

He mockingly laughed back to me and then said, "I will just stop by your house and walk with you. I have to run a couple of quick errands not far from you, so it's not a problem."

"Okay, see you soon then. Bye." I replied.

"Yep, see you soon. Bye." he ended as we both hung up the phone.

I quickly got ready and got all my stuff together.

"keys, wallet, phone." I whisper to myself as I double-check all my pockets to make sure I have everything.

I hear a knock come from the door. "Well, finally you get -" I start to say as I open the door and realize that it wasn't Damien standing there. It was Elix. "Uh, sorry, I thought you were my friend. How did you know where I lived?" I continue.

"Well, I seen you dropped your bracelet when you were getting off work a couple days ago and it looks like it might be expensive so I wanted to return it to you, but you weren't at work yesterday and I seen that the café was going to be closed for a few days so I asked the other girl that works with you if she knew your address so I could return it. I hope that's okay." He said.

"Oh! Yes, I've been looking for that bracelet every where, I thought it was lost forever. Yes, please go ahead and come in for a minute. Thank you so much!" I excitedly said as I jumped for joy that I had it back.

I wasn't sure where I had lost it and thought I might've dropped it on the road walking somewhere. It was a bracelet from my best friend for my 15th birthday with both of our birth stones on it.

He steps inside and stands off to the side out of my way after he hands me the bracelet.

I step over to my counter, which is right by the front door, and start to put in on, clasping it together with my wrist on the countertop so that it's easier.

"I don't know how I can thank you. Honestly, this bracelet means so much to me." I told him.

"Well this is in no way an obligation or saying you owe me, you are completely free to answer honestly, but I was hoping that this would also put me in your good graces and that maybe you would let me finally take you on that date?" he said with a hopeful tone.

"Hmm. Okay, yea, I will let you take me on a date sometime. Thank you again so much." I said with a smile. "I actually have to go somewhere right now, but text me later, okay?" I continued as I started to grab my purse.

"Okay, yea, no problem, sounds good! I will talk to you later then." He said as he began to walk out the front door and down the back hall.

As he was walking away, Damien showed up and saw him walking from my apartment.

"Who was that guy?" Damien asked curiously, pointing back at him.

"Um. That's a guy who comes into the place where I work a lot. I lost my bracelet and he just returned it to me. His name is Elix." I answered.

"Uh-huh. Right, okay. Be careful around him. I get a weird feeling from him." He said.

"Yea, of course. I will be careful. He's really nice, though. He's asked me to go on a date with him some time and I told him yes." I replied happily.

Damien looked at me for a moment without saying anything, then softly jutted his head to the side as if to say let's go, and he started to walk away. So I shut and locked my door and hurried to follow closely behind him.

When we got to Damien's house, I wasn't expecting to see this big nice house with a yard and everything of its own. I was a bit in awe of how beautiful it was.

"Are you rich or something!?" I blurt out.

"Not rich, but I do have a pretty decent job." He says as he walks up to the door and holds it open for me.

It was a beautiful and very spacious house. The air was cool when I walked in, and it felt so nice.

All the furniture looked new, almost like it was never used. There was even a big fireplace off to the side of the living room. It's like the house of my dreams.

Damien told me as soon as we stepped inside, "I don't care where you go in my house or what you do, just please don't go in the room I have to go in to right now so I can get your letter, thats the only room that is off limits here."

I nodded in agreement, and then he proceeded to walk into a room just down the hall and came back a minute later and handed the letter over to me.

"To my sunshine,

There are so many things I wish I could tell you. There are so many things that you don't know, and I pray you'll never have to know.

My darling sunshine, please be careful in this world without me. I suspect that my time is coming soon. There is evil in this world. It surrounds you even when you don't know it, because you are a light in this world.

Those who are light in this world tend to attract the most extreme darkness. Never stop being light in this dark world, but please stay safe when I'm gone.

I have someone that I'm going to ask to watch out for you and keep you safe. I know he will say yes. I know he will keep you safe, and don't feel worried about him, I trust him entirely.

He is like you, a light in a world that is so chaotic and dark. You both are such amazing people inside, even if neither of you see it for yourselves.

I did my best to keep you safe up until this point. Now, I will trust in him to keep you safe. I believe he is capable of doing so, as well as far more. I hope you learn to trust in him as much as I do.

Always with love, ~Dad~"

I sat down on the ground and started to cry. I could hear his voice in every word he wrote. "I miss him so much." I say through tears.

Damien just sat down next to me and quietly put his arm around me, and we both just sat right there on the floor together.

"Me too." He quietly whispered as he put one hand up on my head, holding me near him, comforting me.

After a few minutes, I was able to pull myself back together, and we both stood up.

Normally, Damien would joke over everything he possibly could think a joke up for, but this time, he just stayed quiet.

"I'm going to go make us some tea." He said as he started to walk off in a direction I was obviously unfamiliar with.

The door for the room he didn't want me to go in to was cracked open. I don't want to go against his wishes, but he has some of my dads stuff in there, and I really want answers.

I stared at the door for a moment, then snapped back to reality. "I'm not going to go against what Damien wants. He must have a good reason why he doesn't want me to go in there." I thought to myself.

I walked over to the couch and sat down, just looking around at the room and all of the furniture and decorations.

Soon, Damien came out with the tea and sat down near me. "Hey, can I ask you a question?" I asked.

"Sure." He replied. I wondered what the best way to word it would be for a moment and then continued,

"Well, what's so important in that room? Why can't I go in there, and what would you do if I did?"

He sat forward closer to me and looked me in my eyes as he gently grabbed my forearms and said,

"Please, Hayven, do not go in there ever. There are certain things that it's just better if you don't know anything about, okay? and I'm asking you to please, please not try to dig or go into that room ever."

I hesitantly nodded and leaned away from him to grab my tea. The rest of the night was pretty peaceful, although his words lingered in my mind.

We played some games together on our phones, we talked, hung out, watched tv. It was a really nice night.

I always feel so comfortable and at peace when I'm with Damien, almost as if the rest of the world doesn't exist. As if were the only people who ever existed to begin with, besides my dad, of course. it just feels so effortlessly comforting.

I ended up falling asleep on the couch and woke up a few hours after I said I had planned on going home. I had a blanket over me, and Damien wasn't sitting next to me anymore.

"Damien? Where'd you go? Why didn't you wake me up?" I said through a groggy voice.

He yelled from the kitchen, "You're awake finally? Sorry, I was hungry, so I got something to eat. Are you hungry? I just figured you needed the sleep. You were snoring loud enough to wake up all of my neighbors." He laughed.

I made a face to myself, mocking him. "I do not snore," I replied.

"If you say so, snore-asaurus rex," he said, laughing louder at his own joke.

I let him have his fun and decided not to say anything back. His laugh is contagious, and I find his humor funny, but I wasn't going to let him know that I thought it was funny.That, and I was too tired to put up a fight with him, so I just stayed silent.

I turned on the tv, and Damien brought out some snacks. A few minutes into the show we were watching, we heard,

"Breaking news, an apartment building on north main street has been completely engulfed in flames. The police aren't giving out all the information they have at the moment.

All they've let on thus far is that it does look like someone intentionally set the fire using some flammable chemicals and a fire starter of some kind. As far as they've told us, they've only found three injured, and no deceased.

They can't confirm just yet, but they said they'll keep us updated as soon as they find out more. Seems like it just might've been everyone's lucky day after all."

The video came up on the screen panned over to the building as the news anchor continued to talk about the story.

An apartment building, my apartment building, was engulfed in flames.

"That's my apartment!" I yelled out loud as I moved to the edge of the couch in shock.

They continue on to talk about how the entrance had seemed to be set on fire, and it possibly traveled inwards and up from there.

Everything I own was in that apartment. Everything I had from my dad, from my best friend, everything that I worked so hard for. It's all gone. all I can do is sit here in disbelief, almost unable to even cry until I get up to run outside for fresh air.

I tried my best to hold it in, attempting to not let a single tear fall. Damien rushes out behind me and softly asks, "Are you alright, Hayven?" sounding shocked himself, and not completely sure what to do in this situation.

Him asking me if I'm alright was the beginning to the end, I had no control over my emotions anymore and couldn't help but to just start sobbing.

"Why do bad things always have to happen to me?" I ask him, my voice cracks from crying, knowing there's no way he would know the answer to that anyways, "is the world punishing me or something?" I continue to ask.

Damien silently walked over to me with no hesitation in his steps and wrapped both of his arms tightly around me, and I collapsed into him entirely, crying into his chest as he held me tighter

After a minute of letting me just practically lose my mind, he quietly whispers,

"I don't know why bad things happen. I don't know why they keep happening. You're not being punished. Just like in the letter from your dad, he used to tell me that people who are light, who are good, attract the worst things.

Everything bad and evil can't stand to see that there's someone like that out there, and it will try to break them, but its important to continue being the light in the world, because light is contagious and brings as many good things as bad, as long as we can get through those bad things. The light in us is exactly what saves us and what saves others."

I calmed down from sobbing to my tears just dripping down my face as I listened to him speak. I was silent and stayed put, held tightly to him.

"You can stay here with me, I know it might be weird, but I have the space, and I don't mind. I will even stay gone most of the time if it makes you feel more comfortable. Even if it's just until you can get a new place, just please stay here." He continued.

I paused for a moment and looked up at him, surprised, "Damien, I can't intrude in your home like that. It's not your fault that this happened, and it's my responsibility to figure things out." I said, feeling guilty at the thought of him feeling like he has to let me stay with him even if he doesn't want me to.

"Hayven, you dont have to do everything alone. You can count on me now more than ever. It would be nice to have company here anyways and just because it isn't my fault or if you see it as only your responsibility doesn't mean I can't offer. I promised your dad that I would help keep you safe and take care of you. I really wouldn't mind if you stayed with me."

I wasn't sure what to say back to that at first, so I just nodded, and then a few seconds later, I replied, "I guess I don't have much of a choice either way. Thank you so much. For everything. You don't have to stay away at all. Please just act like you normally would. I dont know how I could possibly ever repay you for everything you've already done for me. I'm sorry for being such a burden on you."

He grabbed my face and, with one hand on each side of my face and made me face upward to look at him again, and in a very serious and stern yet soft and gentle tone, he said,

"Don't ever ever say that again. You never have been, You aren't now, and you never will be a burden to me. Ever."

He then dropped his hands from my face and gently grabbed my arm to lead me to one of the other rooms I hadn't been in yet.

it was a guest room with a big bed and a dresser and a few other decorations and furniture. He pulled me over towards the bed and said,

"Get some sleep. I think you really need it after today, and it's getting late anyway. If you need me or need anything at all, my room is two doors to the left, and the bathroom is one room over to the right. I will see you in the morning, everything is going to be okay."

He gently pulled on my arm to guide me to lay down. He's right, I do need to get some sleep. I don't want to think right now, I don't want to feel right now, I just want to sleep it all away.

the next morning, Damien took me to get some things that I would need since I'm staying with him now and lost all of my stuff in the fire.

I tried to pay for them myself, but he would just grab my hand and say, "Nope, not happening."

What I appreciated most about it is that he never said it in a way that was controlling or mean or like he pitied me.

He said in a way that's more like, i'm not taking no for an answer because I genuinely do care about you and I have the money to help so i'm going to because I want to.

He genuinely wants to make sure i'm taken care of like he promised my dad. I know that if I really put up a fight he would let me pay but I get the sense that it helps him feel like he is keeping his promise more, so I dont dare say a single word. If he didn't want to, then he wouldn't.

CHAPTER 5

It's been about a month now since I lost my apartment. I still feel depressed over it all, and I don't fully understand what happened.

They discovered a little while later that it was not only for sure a fire that someone had intentionally set, but that there was another area that the building caught fire at the same time as the entrances to the building.

The strangest part is that it was on the same floor and hallway that my apartment was on. It's hard to just chalk it up to being nothing but a weird coincidence.

Everything else has seemed to calm down a lot. Damien has kept his distance some besides when I ask him to hang out. I've been back to work for a couple of weeks now, and Elix is still there every day to tell me that he's ready whenever I am to go on our date.

I think i'm going to finally tell him that we should go out this weekend. With Damien hardly ever around, being in this big house by myself just starts to feel lonely after a while. I'm not used to it at all.

My apartment was so much smaller, so being alone felt fine, but this house is easily at least four times bigger than my apartment was, if not more.

So I pulled my phone out and texted Elix to tell him that I would be happy to go out tonight around 6 if that works for him, too.

He replied almost right away, saying he would love to. We agreed to go to the movies and grab some dinner somewhere after.

I start to get ready, do my makeup really nice, straighten my hair, and I'm thinking a pair of cute jeans and a black off the shoulder top would be great for tonight. Comfortable but cute and date worthy.

Damien walked through the front door as I was heading to the kitchen, "Hey... um." he said as he started looking around like he lost something.

"Hey, what are you doing?" I asked, almost concerned for his state of mental health at this point.

"Where did the normal girl who lives here go? the one who drools on her pillow and snores so loud that I have to tell the neighbors sorry the next morning." he continued as he kept looking around for a moment.

I let out a sigh and rolled my eyes as I said, "Ha!" some what sarcastically as I turned to continue walking to the kitchen and pulled a cup out of the cupboard to get a glass water.

Damien chuckled to himself for his joke and then said, "Okay, but for real, why are you all dressed up? do you have plans or something?"

I slightly nod yes as I take my first drink of water and set the cup back down, not yet looking in his direction.

"I'm going on a date with that guy Elix that I told you about. The one you saw walked down the hall that first day I ever came to your house."

Damien was quiet for a minute, so I looked over at him, and he was just staring at me. I'm not quite sure what that look was, but it caught me off guard.

"What?" I ask with slight agitation in my voice due to the uncomfortable feeling of being unsure what his look meant.

He looked away and resumed putting down the things he was holding as he said, "Nothing. I hope it's fun. You deserve it. Just be safe."

his tone was softer, as if he almost wanted to tell me not to go for one reason or another.

I looked at him for a moment and then smiled, "Thank you." he smiled back at me and then turned away.

"Call me or text me if you need me or anything." he said. I nodded at him with a smile and told him that we were going to see a movie and get some food after, and then I would be coming back home.

"home," I thought to myself. what a strange thing to say. I've so simply accepted this place as my home, but it's not really my home. In reality, i'm living with this mysterious and strange guy if you really think about it, in his home, and there's a whole other side with him and my dad that I don't even know anything about.

We said our see you laters, and I walked to the movie theater to meet up with Elix.

He was waiting outside the front doors for me already when I walked up.

I waved to him with a smile as I continued to walk towards him. He opened the door for me and followed close behind and then we both bought a small drink and some popcorn and he let me decide what to watch so I decided that we would watch this thriller type documentary movie about fantasy creatures like big foot, werewolves, and vampires.

It talked about the myths, the realities, and some crazy events that had happened before and shows everything as a possible truth to them existing.

When they were talking about the vampires, they interviewed this woman who was a doctor.

Her identity was hidden, and they used a fake name and a voice changer for her so no one would ever know who she really was.

"You see, some vampires are good, though many are, to put it simply, pure evil. There's a change in their DNA that causes most of them to be prone to frequent violent acts, and they almost act like animals that can't help but give into their natural desires and urges.

Most seek anything pleasurable, such as sex, drugs, blood, and killing. All these things are pleasurable in the sense that they release chemicals in the brain that are connected to pleasure, and something in them finds more pleasure in getting these things in the most cruel ways possible.

Most have evolved to hide themselves much better, but those desires are still there. They all struggle with the craving of blood, but there are ways to suppress the urges and cravings for the blood.

I've donated blood many times to a few good ones that I know, just enough to keep them going and not feeling the need to hurt anyone. I have had some very bad experiences with a few of them in the past, but I keep what I do to a small circle. If they are good, it helps us all in the end, really."

she spoke so fluidly, as if she really knew her stuff on vampires. As if it were actually real or something. The man then asked her to tell everyone some of the myths and some of the facts about vampires, and she nodded.

"Of course, of course. Okay, so the whole garlic thing, myth. The mirror thing is myth. The wooden stake to the heart is only partially true. It's not just wood that will kill them, it's anything straight to the heart. Every where else on their bodies can eventually heal itself fairly easily, though there are still other ways they can die or be killed as well, something straight to the heart is the quickest and easiest way by far.

Their bodies aren't actually ice cold. If anything, their natural body temperatures are often times only about one to three degrees lower than the average human.

They don't live forever. They age like normal aside from their bodies being able to function better than the average person does with age. They age like a human who ages gracefully.

They do get hurt if they go out into the sun, but it's not like in the movies where they burst into flames or start burning and melting or that kind of thing. Instead, what it does is cause them extreme pain that goes on until their heart gives out because their bodies can't tolerate the pain any longer.

I've heard it described as feeling like every bone in their body is breaking at the same time, but even more excruciating. It sounds truly awful if you ask me.

They are faster and stronger than most humans but not so much so that they could lift a car or run a hundred miles in a second or something like that, and they don't need as much sleep either but they do need to sleep, and they need go eat human food but they will still die if they consume blood often enough.

Needing permission before entering someone else's home is also a big myth. There is a lot that is actually dramatized a lot more than the reality of it, and there are a lot of misunderstandings about vampires.

Many of them are like humans in the way that they still feel and have dreams and just want to be happy, but overall, when they become vampires, their natural self is massively heightened.

So those who in their hearts were really caring, then that would be heightened. If they had evil in their hearts, then that would be heightened, and so on and so on."

The man transitioned from the interview to explain a few stories of vampires, some legends, some newspaper articles, and things like that, he continued on to say,

"Yes, I know that it all just sounds like someone had a dream and woke up to tell the tale, but it's so much more than that.

According to our secret sources, in the year 2013, there was a group of scientists who had secretly begun testing many torturous experiments on vampires.

It wasn't known until much later that the government had actually funded this program and provided the vampires.

They had taken normal people and turned them into vampires against their will so they could do research on them and perform many gruesome and torturous tests and experiments.

The project was created so they could learn more about pre-existing vampires that are descendants from similar projects from as early as the 1500s, when vampires were first created and it was called 'The Vamperial Disease', and it went on for about five years before they could no longer continue.

Most of the vampires had died while being experimented on. Fifty vampires in total was cut down to 3 and it is said that one of the scientists who worked there was actually at fault for why they shut down the program, because he couldn't handle seeing them go through the immense suffering anymore.

That same scientist was eventually hunted down for unknown reasons by some of the same few vampires that he saved, and he was brutally and mercilessly murdered, or so we suspect.

We have found records that the scientist had at least one living relative, a daughter who was just a teen at the time of his death, but there were no mentioning of her name or anything to lead to her since she was a minor at the time, so we couldn't interview her.

For all we know, perhaps she was eventually hunted down as well, just like her father."

This last scene left me in complete shock. The similarity is that a scientist with only one living relative, which was his teenage daughter who was murdered for unknown reasons.

"It can't be a coincidence, can it?" I thought to myself. I finished the rest of the movie, deep in thought, as I carefully listened to everything they spoke about on the topic of vampires, and then told Elix,

"I'm sorry, I've had a great time with you, but some thing has come up and I have to head back home. I would love to do this again sometime, though!"

He said he understood and told me he would be waiting to hear from me on the next time and day that we would get to go on a date.

I quickly left, feeling almost suffocated by this feeling of needing to know. I don't want to go against Damien because he has done so much for me, but I need to know. I can't take it anymore.

So I walked home as fast as I could, and once I reached the front door, I slowly opened it, looking around as I quietly walked in to see if Damien was anywhere in sight.

The lights were all off. I shut the door behind me and in a slightly louder than normal voice say,

"Damien, are you here?" it was already 8 at this point, so he might have gone to sleep early. There was no answer, so I sat all of my stuff down and quickly tip toed to the door of the room that i'm not allowed to go into.

I looked down to make sure there was no light coming from under the door. It was as dark as the rest of the house. Very quietly, I began to turn the door knob and opened the creaky door slowly.

The guilt inside of me was overwhelming, but somehow, the feeling of needing to know overpowered that feeling just a bit more.

For years, I've been left without answers, and now more than ever, I just need to find out what's going on.

As I tip toed in and quietly shut the door behind me, I took a good look around. The room was smaller, like an office room.

There was a desk with a small laptop off to the side and an opened box full of papers to the right side of the desk. There were a few shelves, filled with boxes and books and a few other random things, and a small freezer to the right side of the room, and on one of the shelves near by the freezer, there was a few medicine bottles.

although the choice for what was in the room is a bit odd, nothing strikes me as this big secret or anything yet.

I walk over to the box that's sitting on the desk. It's filled with newspaper articles and quite a few other professionally typed up papers that look like they would be put in a file.

I shuffled through the newspaper articles real quick and came across one that was talking about my dads death.

It didn't mention anything that I didn't already know, so I shuffled through a few more papers and came across a file that was filled with papers.

They were labeled things like "Sun treatment," "better life experiment," and so on. On top of the file was a "Patient/Volunteer info" sheet, so I picked it up and started to read it,

"Name: Damien Romaro. Birthdate: 2000. Species: Vampire. Hair Color: Black Eye Color: Green Subject #5 of Program Recovery."

CHAPTER 6

I was shocked and couldn't even begin to process that information. "This has to be a joke, right?" I thought to myself.

I continued to dig in the box and scan through paper after paper that talked about Damien taking part in some kind of vampire experiment or vampire testing something or other, and found another file.

As I picked it up, a few pictures fell out. One was of Damien and my dad from about four years ago, I can tell because the hair cut that my dad has in the photo.

Damien doesn't look much younger. He looks almost the same, other than this being taken about four years ago.

The second photo was a picture of some room filled with small cells in it.

The third one was my dad, on the ground of his lab, lifeless, bleeding from his neck as well as other part of his body.

It's from the day he was murdered but I've seen photos that the police took, and they don't look the same as this.

I threw the photos back into the box and began to tremble as reality was starting to set in.

Is Damien really a vampire? That just sounds so ridiculous to even consider. My dad was a scientist. Could it be that my dad was one of the scientists who saved those vampires, if that actually even happened? Could it be that Damien was one of the ones that my dad would have saved? Is Damien the one who killed my dad?

I put the rest of the papers back in the box and walked over to the freezer and opened the door up to see viles and bags full of something red so I quickly picked one of the glass vials up to check it out.

Realizing it was blood, I yelped and jumped back, accidentally dropping the glass vial, which caused the glass to break with a loud crash and splattered blood all over me.

I tried to pick up the glass pieces quickly, but I cut my hand on accident. It was a bit of a deep cut.

My heart was pounding so hard that I honestly thought it might explode and I started to feel nauseous, from all the information i've discovered tonight, from cutting my hand, from someone elses blood splattering all over me, and the stress of it all wrapped into one.

I should have never come in here, I can feel a knot forming in my throat. Was trusting Damien a bad idea after all?

Have I just been blinded by the hope that I wouldn't have to be alone anymore?

In hopes that maybe some piece of my dad could still be lingering around even if it's within another person?

Was this all some cruel game that's going to end in me becoming his meal one night or something?

The door swung open behind me, hitting the wall as Damien held it open.

With my heart beating so hard out of fear, I looked over at him standing there.

He looked panicked and I could see that his breathing was very unsteady.

I stared at him for a moment. Tears started streaming down my face as I stood there petrified.

Now that I know, what is he going to do? What does he think I know?

"Hayven, what all did you go through?" he started to say as I stood there silent, "what did you see?" he steps in the room closer towards me.

I try to lie, though I know it's pointless, "I didn't see anything except what's in the fridge, I just..." I couldn't even think of a full lie that would make sense with me covered in blood.

I can tell that Damien knows I've obviously seen a few things I shouldn't have in here.

I take off as fast as I can and try to run around him to get out the door but he's faster that me anyways and manages to close the door in one swift move with me right inside the room still with him, his arm now trapping me between his body and the door itself.

I stay facing the door with my hurt hand held to my chest, trembling. Tears are still painting my face.

"Hayven... please tell me what all you read and seen. Is your hand okay? please don't be afraid of me. I'm so sorry." he said to me almost in whisper.

I couldn't find the words to say, so I stayed silent.

"Do you know?" he asked as we still stood in our same positions.

I slowly turn to face him, but I can't keep eye contact, so I look away. I'm still scared of what he might say or do, but is it really him that i'm scared of, or is it just everything I dont know, and the way vampires are shown in stories?

"That you're a vampire?" I ask, the words sounding foreign as they creeped past my lips.

It looked as if his heart sank, and with that, so did mine.

"Yes, I read about how you did tests with my dad, and I seen the picture of you and my dad from four years ago, and..."

I paused, looking over at the freezer as I reached my hand up near my face to look at the deep cut on my palm, feeling sick to my stomach once again.

He glanced over to see where I was looking and then looked back at me and looked down at my hurt hand.

"Are you scared of me now?" he said with sadness in his voice. I look up at him now, my gaze meeting his as I ask, "Did you kill my dad?"

I could see that my question hurt him. He dropped his arm off of the door, still standing only inches from my body.

I reach behind my body to try to open the door and flee, but he threw his hands on either side of me again, stopping me from leaving.

"Hayven... no." he said with sadness filling his every word, "I would never, ever hurt your dad. He saved my life more than once. He was almost like a father to me. It was two other vampires that he had accidentally saved.

They found out that we were working on some medicines and cures for different things that only vampires suffer from, and your dad was working hard to find those for me and others who he felt were good enough.

I could never hurt him, or you, for that matter. I would never ever hurt you, please believe me. I really did promise your dad that I would protect you, and I meant it. Haven't I shown you that I will protect you and keep you safe?"

I felt a slight bit of relief fall over me as a flashback of everything he's done for me quickly crosses my mind.

"Can I really trust you? I want you to tell me everything, no more keeping it from me." I said to him as I looked him in the eyes now.

Damien quickly moves his arms off the door to wrap around me to hug me tightly. I gasp with my breath catching in my throat as the suddenness of it startles me.

He didn't say anything for a moment, but I know he could feel my heart pounding.

"Yes, I will tell you everything." he said as he slowly released from the tight hug he held me in. "Please trust me." he says as he hesitantly reaches for the door knob and opens the door.

I can tell he suspects that i'm just going to run, and to be honest, i'm not entirely sure that I shouldn't.

He grabs a small box off one of the shelves in the room, and then we walk over to the living room and sit on the couch on opposite sides from one another.

He pulls out some stuff from a small first aid kit and gently grabs my hurt hand and starts to bandage it up.

"I promise I will tell you everything, whatever you want to know," he starts and then pauses with a sigh, "but please tell me, why tonight of all nights? You've been here for a while now, and any one of those nights you could've decided to go in there, so why tonight? I thought you were supposed to be out with that guy, Elix."

I didn't expect him to remember Elix's name. Not that it matters at the moment. I guess that's not something that should even cross my mind right now, but it does for some reason.

I couldn't bring myself to look at him so I sat as far away on the couch as I could, legs facing away, one hand still with him as he bandages my hurt palm and the other hand now in my lap, as I look toward the ground in the opposite direction of him.

"when we went to the movies, we decided to watch this documentary type movie about all this fantasy stuff like, big foot, and werewolves, and vampires and there were these parts when they were talking about vampires, and everything they were talking about all just seemed too similar to my dads life and all these weird coincidences and I just couldn't take not knowing the truth anymore. it was driving me crazy!" I replied as I spun my body around to look at him.

I wasn't expecting to catch his gaze. His eyes were dead locked onto me, completely focused on what I was saying.

I started to remember the guilt I felt when I first entered the room. I felt bad that I went against his trust in me, but at the same time, I just could not stand not knowing anymore.

It's selfish, I know, but I felt like it was eating away at me, and the cure for that feeling seemed like it was right in front of me.

I avoided making direct eye contact again, but he continued to look at me. I couldn't tell if it was sadness, understanding, betrayal, or all of the above.

"I'm sorry, I really didn't want to go behind your back, I just couldn't take it anymore. Why didn't you tell me about... you?" I said.

a bit of frustration and guilt was written on his face now as he said, "Because, Hayven, it's not that simple. There's a few different reasons why I didn't tell you.

It's not safe to even know that secret. It puts the people who know and those around them in danger. It's almost like a magnet that you're given that just attracts that world and the chaos and drama that all comes with it.

I can't tell you how many times I wanted to tell you, but I couldn't, and... that's not a secret that you can so easily trust to people. Even people that you think can trust with your life, they turn on you, and the few that maybe believe you and trust you could end up dead.

More often than not, though, if they don't write you off as a crazy person first, they get scared of you... I mean, look at you tonight, after you found out... you tried to run from me.

I was afraid to tell you, I've made the mistake of telling people in the past, and when you seen for yourself, I just couldn't let you go until I at least explained. I want you to be safe, and I don't want you to be afraid of me. I would never ever hurt you, and I never want to lie to you. "

I looked at him and asked, "But... isn't that kind of what you did, is lie? hiding it is almost -"

Damien cut me off, and he quickly moved closer to me to say, "I didn't have a choice, Hayven! I wanted to tell you so many times about everything, all of it from beginning to end.

It killed me to keep any of it from you. That's partially why I have kept my distance from the house. I wanted to keep you safe.

No matter how much I wanted to tell you, not telling you was safer, until now, and I was afraid that if I didn't stay gone a lot, that I wouldn't be able to keep it from you. Please, you have to understand why I didn't tell you. why I did everything."

I didn't reply for a moment. I just sat there thinking. " I think I do understand," I thought to myself, "he had the best of intentions with everything he did.

Does that mean I shouldn't be scared? he has had plenty of chances to hurt me, and instead, all he's done is try to help me".

Without looking at him, I say, "I understand," and then continued on to say, "I trust you, and you can trust me. I just need a little time to get used to everything."

his whole body seemed to relax and un-tense itself, as if an unbearable weight had been lifted off of his shoulders.

"Do you want me to tell you more tonight then?" he asked. I nodded,

"Yes, I do. please tell me everything from the beginning. Not just about my dad, but with you too." I replied.

He nodded with a somewhat pained look on his face. "Okay. It actually all starts around the same time. I was about thirteen years old, and I didn't have any family. They had all died when I was younger, and I grew up jumping back and forth between different foster homes.

I had a few lifelong friends, and I had known them for as far back as I can remember, but other than them, I didn't have anyone.

One day, I was headed to school, I was studying different sciences on my own, preparing for learning with the help of a science teacher, but on my way there, this van pulled up close behind me.

I didn't think anything of it at the time, I was just focused on some stuff we had been studying together that I was excited to get back into that day. I was excited to learn it, but it was difficult, so I was trying to understand it. I was studying it more on the way.

Before I knew it, a couple of different men jumped out of the van and injected me with something that made me pass out within seconds. Everything was really foggy and unclear for a while.

All I really remember is being in a lot of pain, and there being a lot of people around me. The next thing I really remember is waking up about two weeks later, and the people started to tell me that they had turned me into a vampire.

I could feel something was different, and I was still in a lot of pain from whatever it is they did during that time.

They explained that because there was no one who would miss me, that's why they chose me.

I had no family, the foster families I lived with were only keeping me for the money, and they said that my friends would forget about me soon enough.

They told me I was nothing and that now my life had purpose if nothing else, and that was to help them study what they referred to as 'disgusting beings.' They made it seem as though they did me a favor, in a way.

Then they said that now that I was one of them though, my life was almost even more meaningless than before at that same time, that I was now one of those disgusting beings and I was going to serve my purpose by being researched in a lab for the rest of my life.

They expected me to die sooner rather than later. I was sent to the lab a few days later, and that's where I met your dad. He was forced to be a part of the program because people threatened that he would lose everything if he didn't.

The other scientists were cruel to no end. They forcefully did experiments and tests on me and the other now vampires with no concern or care in the world for if they killed us, and sometimes they would just simply do things for the sake of seeing us suffer. I saw them take quite a few body bags out of there.

We weren't allowed to talk to each other or anything, so I didn't know them but it was a terrifying experience to watch all these people who were once normal just like me, die from what the scientists were doing.

Your dad is the reason I made it as long as I did and why i'm alive today. He would sneak me food, sneak me blood, and help in any ways that he could.

It had to be a secret, and even just him talking to me in a kind voice the way he did, helped more than I think he ever truly knew. He told me that one day he would get me out.

He didn't believe the lies the government told him about vampires all being awful and disgusting creatures, and that he knew I was good. That I was worth so much more, and that I deserved so much more. I couldn't see it at the time, and I still don't, but those words helped me fight to stay alive.

Finally, one day, your dad set up a staged accidental fire that damaged the controls that kept us all locked inside cells.

They normally kept us all drugged so that we would stand no chance of fighting back at all, but your dad did what he could to hide that he wasn't giving me all of the drugs that he was supposed to by giving himself some. He wasn't sure that he would make it out, or that I would, and he wasn't expecting the other two to make it out, he told me that he didn't trust them, but that this was his only chance and we all made it out before the fire consumed the rest of the lab.

They were forced to shut down and ruled it as an accident. It turned out that a few of the other scientists were doing other illegal and unauthorized experiments so they kept everything they might've known a secret and then your dad was free to leave and no one even knew that I, or the other two vampires even were alive.

Your dad promised me that from that point on, he would only do good, no matter the risk. He promised that he would try his best to make up for what I went through and what he was unwillingly apart of.

So, for a long while, we both worked on some experiments for the benefit of good vampires. Like we discovered that a certain medicine allows us to walk in the sun without being in any pain, and we accidentally came across a drug type combination that can be used for terrible things, like convincing people to do whatever we want.

We discovered a few different things that could do a lot of good, but also a lot of bad if it was left to the wrong people.

Those same discoveries are what lead to your dads death. I wasn't around to see everything they did, or I would've done anything in my power to stop it.

I showed up when it was already done and over with, and I regret that I didn't show up even ten minutes sooner every single day that i'm alive and he's not.

He helped me through more than I can even fully explain. I lost what few people I had after telling them that i'm a vampire, either through death or them thinking I've lost my mind or just becoming terrified of me.

Your dad was the only one who was always there for me. He was patient and kind. He was the only one who ever told me that I was good and worth something. Worth anything really.

He told me stories about you all the time. His sunshine, and how you made the world a better place. How even on your worst days, you would smile because you couldn't help but radiate light and happiness into the world.

I wish I could've saved him, but by the time I got there, it was already too late.

Some of what you hear about vampires from movies and books is true, but a lot of it only holds some truth.

Our blood contains a lot more antibodies than the normal human and mixed with a few medications it can be a very powerful healing medicine, but he was only minutes from dying, and there was no way to know if the medicine would work or if we would've wasted the last moments we had together.

In those moments, he asked me to watch over you and protect you. He asked me to promise him that I would never tell you about this life, the truth about his death, the existence of vampires, anything like that unless I felt it was necessary to protect you.

We talked a lot in those moments about a lot of things, and i'm happy to say that he was happy in his last moments. He knew you would be safe and okay, and although it was only a couple of minutes, it felt like we had talked for hours. We talked about the fact that the main thing we both would regret is that you couldn't have talked to him to say goodbye. I'm so sorry that you didn't get to say goodbye to him.

He also told me who was to blame. It was the two vampires that he saved from the lab. The two other vampires that escaped with us. I tried so hard to find them and get revenge for you and your dad, but it seems like they vanished just like I did."

Damien stopped talking for a moment as if to let me absorb the massive amount of information that I've just received.

Tears began pouring down my face and seemed out of my control once again.

I glanced over at Damien, and his eyes still never left their gaze on me. It was as if he was examining my every emotion, my every reaction, my every movement.

He had a sad look on his face, and I got the sense that he felt bad that I was upset and wasn't sure how to make it better or how to help.

I pulled my legs up on the couch against my chest as I held myself close. There's so much that I didn't know about my dad, and there's even more that I didn't and still don't know about this man that i'm living with.

I'm feeling such a mixture of emotions, and all of its being over run by the feeling of being overwhelmed.

Damien slowly began to reach his hand over to comfort me but hesitated as he said, "Do you really still trust me? are you still scared of me at all?" he sounded worried, almost afraid of what my answer would be.

I wiped my tears from my face and turned back to face him. "No, i'm not afraid of you. You've already proven that I can trust you with my safety, and I should've never doubted you, i'm sorry. My dad is right about you."

Damien didn't even say a word before leaping over to me and embracing me so tightly I could hardly breathe.

The force of his impact made us both fall backward on the couch, his body next to mine. We both laughed as we fell, and his face was hidden beside mine as I reached around him to hug him back. I felt like we both really just needed it.

He let go of me, and I could see that his eyes had tears in them that he was fighting to hold back. I thought it'd be best that I didn't mention it, though.

"I do have one more question for now," I started to say as we got back in our original spots, now no feeling of distance between us.

"Do you still crave blood? or vampires in general, I supposed. Did you and my dad ever discover a cure for the craving?" I continued.

"No. I wish I could say we did. Vampires in general, even me. I crave blood. I try to manage it with the blood that's donated to me, but it only helps so much. That is the unfortunate curse of being a vampire, but if you're wondering if i'm capable of controlling myself when something happens like how you've cut your hand, then yes, as long as I do what needs done to manage everything." he replied.

In reality, I had so many more questions. Had he ever killed anyone, has me being in the house been difficult for his craving of blood, so on and so on, but I felt like neither of us could handle any more tonight.

"Thank you for being honest with me. Honesty is really important to me, and I know it wasn't easy to talk about that stuff." I told him.

he nodded in agreement with me and said, "Well, being left in the dark all this time all alone couldn't have been easy either."

He stood up off the couch and extended his hand to help me up, and I accepted the offer.

We both decided it was time that we get some sleep, so cleaned up the glass and blood splatter in the little office room and we said our good nights and went our separate ways.

I walked to the bathroom and decided to shower so I could wash up and get all the blood off of me, and then I went to my room and lay down on my bed.

Before closing my eyes, I decided to check my phone and see that I have a text from Elix.

"Hey Hayven, can we go on a date tomorrow? There's this really cool place that just opened, and I would love to take you." his message said.

I don't want to lead him on. He seems so sweet and like a really cool guy, and he doesn't deserve to be constantly turned down again and again.

I like him, but i'm just not in a good place in my life to be thinking about him as any more than a friend.

"Hey Elix, i'm so sorry that I keep having to turn you down. To be honest, I just have so much going on right now, and I just can't add other things to it. I think you're really cute and cool and sweet. It's completely my fault. I hope you can understand."

I waited a few minutes, and there was no reply. After ten minutes had passed with no reply, I decided to put my phone down and roll over for bed.

My mind was racing with all these thoughts in my head, and my heart was too, but before I knew it, I had fallen asleep.

CHAPTER 7

The next day, I woke up as the sun was rising. Damien knocked on my door and slowly began to open it.

"I brought you some coffee, I hope it's not too early." he said. I started to sit up in bed, still feeling so tired, and said, "Did you know I was awake?"

he laughed and said, "Yeah. I heard you moving around in here. I also figured you could use the coffee. I couldn't sleep last night and thought that you might've had trouble sleeping, too."

I chose not to reply to the last part of what he said, and instead, I thanked him for the coffee.

Damien sat on the end of my bed as we drank our coffees together. I checked my phone to see if Elix ever replied. "No new messages," it read as I tried to refresh my texts.

"What wrong?" Damien asked curiously. I shook my head and did my best to hide my true emotions of feeling guilty and anxious.

"You're off today, right?" Damien continued to say to change the subject, sensing that I didn't want to talk about it. I nodded my head yes and waited for him to continue.

"Can we maybe hang out today? Maybe go do something fun to just get away for an hour or two?" he continued.

"That actually sounds really great, I would love to." I smiled, and he smiled back. We could both really use a fun time together after what happened last night.

We finished our coffees and he left me alone for a while. We decided that we wanted to go somewhere later in the day since we we're both tired still and just wanted to hang out around the house and be lazy for the day.

So the day had passed, and we both relaxed some on the couch watching tv most of the day, and then we finally went to get ready.

I tossed on a tank top with some jeans and tennis shoes and pulled my hair up into a ponytail, and quickly did some light makeup.

I'm feeling really excited and happy that we're going to hang out and just go do something fun.

It's been a while, and I want to forget the hard stuff for a bit and just have a good time. Damien makes me laugh a lot, and last night there wasn't a lot of laughing, the opposite of laughing, really.

Which makes me feel sad and uneasy to begin with, and then this stuff with Elix on top of it all.

So, today, I just want it to be a day that I don't have to think about my dad or vampires or any of the other horrors and sadness in mine or Damien lives.

We both finished getting ready and decided that we wanted to go to this carnival that's in town for the weekend.

It's going to be pretty busy, but neither of us mind much tonight. We get on ride after ride, go through mazes and buildings with mirrors at every turn.

It is so much fun, and I can almost forget about everything else, besides the occasional time here and there that reminds me that Damien is a vampire.

We stopped to play this game where you knocked down pins with a ball, and Damien said he was going to try to win something.

I watched him as his arm stretched back to throw the three different balls. The way he smiled at me when he missed the first two, the way he smiled when he knocked them all down on the last try and won a small teddy bear.

"I really like to see him smile," I thought to myself. "Here," Damien said, breaking me from my thoughts as he tossed the little teddy bear to me.

"Don't you want to keep your most treasured possession?" I joked and started to laugh. He glared at me for a moment and then playfully stuck his tongue out at me.

"I'm just kidding, thank you, this will be a nice keep sake to remember the day that we wanted to forget everything", I said as I got up from my seat and began to walk with him.

"To remember the day that we wanted to forget everything, huh?" he said with a chuckle. I nodded very confidently.

"Let's go get some food. Actually, do you even like food, or do you need it at all?" I asked.

"Well, it doesn't really do anything to fix my hunger if that's what you mean, but I do kind of need it, and I like it, yes.

I enjoy eating normal food and still have to eat to keep myself going, its just that I have to also have to have blood otherwise it wouldnt matter what food I ate or how much, it would never be enough to keep me alive." he answered to me in a whisper.

"Okay, then were going to get some food", I happily demanded as I grabbed his arm to pull him along side me, trying not to focus too much on all the details of what he just told me.

We ordered some chili cheese fries from a nearby food truck and walked to a park bench that was a little bit away from all the loud people and sounds from all of the rides.

It was already dark out with only the full moon providing light alongside the carnival lights. There was no one else around, and it felt so peaceful and nice. The soft cool breeze glided across my skin. We were sitting there just talking and laughing until Damien suddenly looked very panicked, like he had heard or seen something that frightened or startled him.

Before I could even react, we were both grabbed from behind. Neither one of us could do or say anything before we were injected with something, causing us both to pass out within seconds.

I remember looking at Damien as the darkness caved in on me from all corners of my vision. He was reaching out to me, and then he collapsed with me only mere seconds behind him.

I began to dream of the things my dad and Damien must have gone through, imagining the worst and the best moments. Picturing all the pain Damien must have already endured.

In the dream, I could feel myself running, but I wasn't moving. All I wanted to do was see if Damien was okay.

My dream transitioned to a replay of the look on Damien face as we were drugged. The look of worry, fear, and the desperate motion of him reaching out to me, but me being too far for him to grasp. So close, but just barely out of reach.

I came to for a moment, all I could see were street lights passing above me. I was in a car. "Where's Damien?" I thought to myself as I attempted to sit up as fast as I could and look around.

I felt the sharp sting of someone injecting me with more of whatever drug it is that they're using. I let out a sharp yelp from the pain of it, and the darkness caved in on me once again.

This time, I didn't dream. Instead, everything was lost to my mind for what seemed like years.

Finally I started to come to again. My head is pounding, and I feel like I had slept a million years but was still somehow exhausted.

There was a bump on my head from where I must have hit my head after passing out. My vision is so blurry that I can hardly make out what's around me.

As I look up, I can see that someone is across the room. It takes me a moment, but I finally recognize that it's Damien who is on the other side of the room from me.

My hands were tied in front of me, and I was leaning against a cold concrete wall. The room was mostly dark and very cold in general.

It looked like we were in some kind of basement room or something similar. I started to look around and saw a door across the room. There doesn't seem to be a door knob on the inside, though.

"Damien," I whispered as loudly as I could without talking at a normal tone, "Are you okay?" I still feel so groggy, and all of this feels almost like another drug induced dream.

He wasn't tied up, but he looked exhausted, and I could see he had quite a few marks on him. Bruises and cuts covered all of his exposed skin, including his face. His cheek had a dark bruise near his eye, and his lip was bleeding.

"I'm... okay." he struggled out. "They drugged us, and they gave me a bigger dose to keep me from being able to fight them back or stop them." he continued.

He took a moment to catch his breath. Even talking seemed like a lot for him. "They didn't give me enough at first, so I came to and tried to fight off two of the guys. That's how I ended up getting these," he said as he pointed to his face. "Are you okay? Do you feel okay?" he asked.

"My head is killing me, and I feel so exhausted. Moving or even talking takes so much energy, but Im okay." I answered.

We both stayed quiet for a moment, taking in our current situation and looking around the room. I'm so relieved to know that he is okay at least, bruised up and a few cuts, maybe, but he's okay.

I almost don't even care about the fact that we're in some dark and cold room after being drugged and kidnapped, just knowing he's okay and that he's here with me makes me feel better. More calm than if he wasn't here, and if I didn't know he was alive and okay. If you really call this situation okay that is.

The noise of a latch on the outside of the door being undone loudly echoed through the room. Adrenaline rushed through my body, and I jumped to my feet, almost falling due to my body still feeling so weak.

I couldn't get my hands untied myself, and Damien couldn't do much of anything at all at the moment, not that it would make much difference if he did untie me.

I saw him shift his body to sitting up more, as much as he could, as he let out a deep huff from struggling to gather the strength.

The only light in the room came from under a dying light above us. It was very dull but enough to see.

A man walked through the door, and someone shut the door behind him. The light began to illuminate his face, and I could finally see who it was. "Elix!?" I gasped.

He laughed, "Yes! That's the exact expression I pictured you would make. The betrayal and confusion written all over your face. It's so satisfying. I tried so hard to get you to trust me and to get you completely alone, but every time, you would turn me down.

Finally I got you to go on a date with me, and you wanted to watch that stupid documentary that told you about your moron of a father that made you have to desperately leave our date and make me lose my chance to get you alone with me.

Had I known that movie was about that I would've suggested a different one, so that's my bad I suppose, but then, after you texted me last night to tell me all that stuff about it not being a good time and all that, I realized that my original plan wasn't working and that we had to switch it up", He explained.

"You're the only moron here," Damien retorted through gritted teeth.

"What did you say to me!?" Elix said as he moved to pull Damien to his feet and grab his throat, pinning him up against the wall.

"You were just a pet for that disgusting coward father of hers. Hardly even worth keeping alive." He released his grip from Damiens neck, and Damien coughed as he just barely caught his balance, grabbing his throat as if he hoped that it would help the burning pain that remained.

Elix began slowly walking over towards me. "Dont you dare touch her," Damien demanded.

I felt as if I was almost stuck in place. unsure of where I would run to if I could get that chance even.

Elix gently ran his fingertips from my cheekbone down to my chin and then reached his hand over and began to play with my hair.

"Such a pretty face, sunshine." He whispered tauntingly.

I winced at the sound of those words coming out his mouth and then looked at him wide-eyed. "Why would you call me that?" I asked, surprised.

He chuckled. "Your father was one of the scientists who took my brother and tortured him. When my brother escaped, after your father started that fire, he found me and turned me into a vampire too, and we laid low for a very long time.

Eventually we ended up running into one of the other guys who escaped in the fire and he told us all about your dad, and that piece of shit over there, and how they were doing experiments on their own. Ones that would make it easier for us to live a normal life and do whatever we want.

We all wanted to get revenge on him for being a part of those torturous experiments, for taking my brother away from me for so long, and because it would just be fun.

So after we heard that his research could help us live like normal humans do too, and how that other guy knew where he lived and did his research and all that, we decided that it was time to go ahead and take our revenge. So we broke into the lab he worked in and caught him by surprise."

He paused to laugh once again and then, in a menacing voice, continued, "Oh, we sure enjoyed every second of torturing him, just like they did to my brother.

After a long night of getting our revenge, we decided that it was time to find his paperwork that he willingly told us about, and we were able to take a lot of it.

Thanks to him I can walk in the sun, but while we were searching, your father some how got ahold of a syringe with something poisonous to vampires and when my brother got near him again, he was caught off guard and was injected with that poison. He didn't make it...

We didn't know that he had a daughter at first, but you were mentioned a few times in his work and the files that we took, and eventually, I figured out who sunshine was.

It was bitter sweet finding out that the scientist had a daughter. So many more ways I could've tortured him if we knew he had a daughter at the time, but now that I have you, it's going to feel so great when I get to watch the life fade from your eyes, and what's going to be even better is it's going to be him who kills you."

he ended pointing at Damien as a smile stretched across his now rather creepy face.

He quickly grabbed my arms tightly as he leaned his head down into me and bit my neck. His teeth sink into me with a sharp sting.

I didn't even have a chance to fully realize what he was doing until the pain hit me. I let out a sharp scream as I tried to break free, but it was useless.

Blood started to stream down my chest and onto my shirt. Damien attempted to run over to stop him, but his balance was a bit off, and almost as soon as he started,

Elix stopped and brushed his hand up against my blood soaked skin, catching the blood as it streamed out of my body, and then turned to flick his hand towards Damien, causing the blood on his hand to splatter all over Damiens face.

Then he rushed out of the now open door, locking the door once again behind him, leaving me standing there with my blood soaked skin and clothes, and Damien with my blood now all over his face, looking stunned and panicked.

CHAPTER 8

I feel sick at the thought of it. Before I could even process everything, suddenly Damien was in front of me, face to face, with his eyes fixated on the blood.

He looked as though he was a starving animal that just got it's first chance to eat in days. Has it been days? At least a day or two I think.

His right hand reached around me, gripping the back of my neck. His strong hand was tensed, but he was barely holding onto me.

His left forearm heavily leaned on the wall that was behind me, and his whole body seemed so weighted down, as if he was using every last bit of energy he had left to stop himself.

His head leaned down toward my neck, and I could feel his warm breath on my skin as he stood there, no more than an inch away from his whole body pressing against mine.

I was too scared to move and held in a breath as I braced myself for what seemed likely to happen at any second now.

Damien may be weaker than he normally is, but his strength still far surpasses mine.

"Damien," I managed to say, my voice cracking from holding back tears and then suddenly breaking through as I reached my hands up to touch his chest.

Something wet drips onto my shoulder, and then Damien heavily pulls himself away from me and leans on the wall a couple of feet away from me.

He had one arm against the wall, and his head was leaning on the back of his forearm with his other hand covering his face.

He breathed deep harsh breaths for a minute and then spoke in a hushed and sad tone, "I'm so sorry, Hayven... I'm so weak right now, I haven't drank any blood in at least 2 days now, and I lost control of myself for a minute..."

The bleeding has seemed to slow down a lot, but I was still covered in blood, and so is he. I can't even imagine how hard this is for him right now. It's hard for both of us right now, obviously, with everything that's going on.

"Are you okay?" he continued.

"I'm okay." I answered, "Could you, maybe untie me?" I asked as I took a step towards him.

He dropped his arm down from the wall and took in a long, deep breath, preparing to look my direction again. He turned and kept his eyes looking down, only focusing on the rope around my wrists.

The muscles in his neck and jaw tensed as he clenched his teeth together.

He untied my hands and then turned around to look away again. It hurt that he couldn't even look at me, although I understand why.

"Would you... be able to gain enough strength back to try and get us out of here if I let you drink some of my blood?" I asked hesitantly.

Damien spun around to look at me with widened eyes and furiously breathed out in a deep toned whisper,

"Dont you ever offer for me to drink your blood, ever!" he took a couple steps back toward me and grabbed my shoulders as he continued,

"if you ever offer that to me again, I might not be able to say no, and I will not be able to control myself. I would kill you and hate myself more than I already do for the rest of my life."

Damien reached his hands up to hold my face and looked at me in the eyes with a new look filled with sadness,

"and how could I..." he started and trailed off as he turned around and forced himself to walk back to the other side of the room and sat down.

I'm scared, and Damien is too, I think. He's trying to hide it, but who wouldn't be at least a little scared in our situation.

we both sat there quietly for a long time. It felt like hours, but in this room, there's no way to tell how much time had really passed.

There's no clocks, no windows, nothing at all to tell us how long we've been here, though we're both pretty sure we've been here a couple of days overall at least.

We heard the door unlock from the outside again, and Elix walks in, looking at Damien as he shuts the door behind him,

"I didn't expect you to be able to hold yourself back. I thought for sure you were going to taste that sweet, sweet blood of hers and not be able to stop, and the look of betrayal would be plastered on her face as she takes her very last breath" he taunted and then continued,

"but you clearly didn't. So I started thinking. I thought to myself, how would this guy, who is also a vampire, and a weak one at that, who has been deprived of blood for 2 days, be able to stop himself from drinking her dry.

I mean, I know that you've been watching over her, but could it possible be that..." he paused for a moment and then continued again,

"You haven't told her why, have you? I mean, the real reason as to why you take care of her and watch over her, the real reason you were able to stop yourself from giving in and ripping her to pieces?"

Damien glared at him as he spoke.

"I know the reason he watches over me. He promised my dad that he would!" I yell to him from across the room, annoyed at the sound of him talking so much.

Elix looked at me, smirked, and then looked at Damien again and said, "But that's not the real reason, is it?" He asked, ending with a questioning hum. A smirk appeared on his lips once again.

"This is very, very interesting if you ask me," he added.

Damien's face told me that he wanted to rip this guys head off.

"Shut the hell up," Damien demanded in a low growl.

Elix began to laugh menacingly, out of pure amusement, "Oh, that's great. I just keep getting luckier and luckier. This makes thing's even better and more interesting than I had originally thought they'd be. This is going to be so much more fun than I ever imagined. It's definitely worth the wait."

He said through a smile that showed just how much he was enjoying all of this.

My heart started beating faster, and I began to feel more anxious than I already was.

"What's he talking about, Damien? What is it that I don't know?" I stuttered out confused.

Elix looked as though he was getting the biggest sick thrill out of this entire situation.

Damien wouldn't look at me. He shook his head, and with an irritated gesture with his hand, he answered frustrated, "Nothing."

Elix chuckled and asked, "So I'm wrong then?"

Damien replied, warning with rage, filling his voice, "If you don't shut the hell up, I swear."

"Yeah, that's what I thought." Elix said confidently. As he turned to walk back out of the room, with the door opening up for him once again, he smirks at me and says,

"He's hiding something from you, and it's some pretty big news if you ask me. Ask him about it."

Damien yelled back to him, "Just shut your damn mouth already!"

Elix laughed hysterically as he shut and locked the door back as he left the room finally, showing us even more that he enjoyed toying with us.

"Damien? Please, is there something that you're not telling me?" I asked as I took a few steps towards him, narrowing the distance between us and limiting the chance for him to look somewhere else.

I didn't want to let Elix get to me, but I couldn't help it when he was able to poke at the one thing that triggers the worst in me, secrets and lies.

"No, Hayven, that guy is... He's just trying to start crap between us, okay? There's nothing." he replied.

I paused for a moment, feeling sadness overwhelm me. He's lying, even though he said he would never lie to me.

I could feel my shoulders drop from the heavy weight of the disappointment I was feeling as it sunk in. "Dont... dont lie to me, Damien. You said you would tell me everything. You told me that you wouldn't lie to me." I said as I walked directly in front of him now and made eye contact with him.

"Hayven... don't. Don't make me say it..." he quietly pleaded while still not looking at me.

"Damien! Please just tell me, I can't stand any more secrets and lies, and if I'm going to end up dying in this place, then I at least just want to know the whole truth, please!" I begged.

He didn't say anything back and still refused to look at me. An overwhelming feeling of rage washed over me, and tears began to streak down my face once again.

I started to push on him in frustration, which didn't do much to him since i'm so weak right now anyways and I yelled,

"i'm tired of secrets! i'm tired of lies! I just want you to be honest with me! why can't anyone just ever be honest with me!?"

He grabbed my hands and tried to stop me from pushing on him and I fought back, trying to pull away from him because I was so angry that I didn't want him to touch me, which eventually caused us both to trip, with him landing on top of me. He took that chance to pin my arms down until I calmed down.

"I'm in love with you. There, are you happy? I am helplessly and madly in love with you, and I hate myself for it." he confessed with a forced calmness. He was now looking me straight in the eyes, and he still held my arms down in case I would start freaking out again.

"You're... you're what?" I asked in a shocked and much calmer tone, now calming down and beginning to process what he just said.

He started to let go of my arms and get off of me, sitting on the ground right beside me. I sat up, looking straight into his eyes.

"I said I'm in love with you. That's the big secret." he answered.

"You're in love with me? why would you... hate yourself for that?" I ask, confused.

"Because I wasn't supposed to fall in love with you, Hayven. I was supposed to just be someone who watched over you and made sure you were safe and taken care of from afar, but I selfishly fell in love with you. As if it's okay for someone like me to love someone like you." he answered, frustrated.

"What do you mean?" I ask, confused again.

"In case you haven't noticed, i'm kind of a monster, and you're like this angel that was sent here straight from heaven or something.

I fell in love with you way before we even met. There was this one day, you saw this cute little cat, and you stopped to pet it for a minute.

You shared some food you had with him, and you had this absolutely beautiful and genuinely happy smile on your face.

Despite everything that you had been through, you still smiled like nothing bad had ever happened to you, in life, like nothing bad at all could ever happen.

I admired that and it was the most beautiful thing I have ever seen. You are the most beautiful person I have ever seen.

I never smiled anymore at that point until you became a part of my life. Before you, I couldn't find a reason to be happy, and I didn't care what happened to anyone else.

Your dad was the last person I cared about, and just like everyone, he died because everyone around me dies.

I never wanted to fall in love with you, I never wanted you to have to meet me. I wanted you to be able to live a perfectly normal life and eventually meet some normal human man and fall in love.

I don't deserve someone as amazing, beautiful, and smart as you. I don't deserve someone who has a heart like yours. I haven't done anything in my life to deserve it. I didn't even mean to fall in love with you. It just happened.

One day I was just trying to keep my promise to your dad, then the next thing I knew, I fell for you hard and had to fight this burning need in my chest to actually meet you.

Before that, all I was, was just some orphaned kid who no one gave a shit about. There was nothing special about me, destined for nothing great.

I was taken in the first place because no one would miss me, and I was turned into a monster who has to drink blood to survive, who almost lost control and drank your blood, the person who I claim to love and promised to protect and keep safe, all because i've gone a couple days without drinking any.

When I told what few friends I had that I was turned into a vampire and what happened to me, most of them left and wanted nothing to do with me, either because they thought I lost my mind, or from being absolutely terrified of me. The rest of the few that were left of them ended up dying.

I'm nothing but this damaged, lonely, awful monster and you're like some kind of perfect angel that lights up everything and everyone around her with happiness, as if happiness is some kind of contagious disease that you have.

You're someone who almost everyone seems to love instantly. How selfish could I be to fall in love with you and want to meet you in person. You deserve so much more than all of this." he gestured around the room, pointing out the situation we're currently in.

His eyes were holding back tears, his expression filled with deep and heavy pain.

I didn't even know where to begin with everything I wanted to tell him, but words didn't even feel appropriate in that moment.

After looking at him silently for a moment, I quickly reached my arms over and wrapped them tightly around his neck before he could react.

Soon, his arms reached around my body and held me tight, as if my hug gave him life when he so desperately needed it most.

I pulled my head back some to whisper in his ear. My heart fluttered in my chest as I whisper out, "It's my choice. It's my choice whether or not to love you back and be a part of this life with you.

No matter what you think, I get to decide and choose that for myself, not you, just because you dont think you're worthy of me or something.

Whether you like it or not, everything you've thought about me is what i've thought about you.

I wasn't aware of how you felt before, but I think i'm in love with you too."

Damien pulled back from the hug to look at my face. His expression reading relief, confusion, surprise, and sadness all at the same time.

"You're in love with me too? why?" he asked.

"Because how could I not fall in love with someone like you? That day that you saved me, I didn't see some monster. I saw a man who came to my rescue like a true modern-day hero, and as we walked to my apartment, the way you smiled at me, it was something I thought about for weeks.

You let me stay in your home when my home was burned down, not because you had some kind of ulterior motives, but because you actually cared and wanted to make sure I was safe.

Ever since you came into my life, you've been there for me through every difficult thing I, or we, have gone through.

You've been so understanding, patient, caring, and sweet to me. Not to mention you make me laugh all the time, and you're crazy smart, considerate, and thoughtful.

I dont see you as some orphaned monster who no one would miss because I would miss you. I never want to go back to a time where I dont know you, Damien.

Your heart is amazing, and i've never been happier than during the time that i've known you. How could I not fall in love with someone like you?" I replied to him.

He looked shocked to hear that I genuinely thought so highly of him, just like he thinks of me. He gently grabbed both sides of my face.

"i'm sorry, I can't wait any longer to do this." he said as he leaned forward to give me a long and passionate kiss.

I grabbed both of his hands that were framing my face. My heart raced in my chest as I kissed him back.

"Nows my queue to enter," we heard from outside the door. The lock clicked, and the door flung open to Elix standing there with another man.

"Perfectly timed to ruin your precious moment together and ruin that first kiss that he just couldn't wait for any longer." he mocked.

"This is hendrick, the other vampire that your father helped torture but then accidentally set free." he continued.

Damien and I quickly stood up, and Damien stepped in front of me, ready to do what he could to protect me if need be.

"Oh, that's not going to help you anymore than before." He held up syringes full of whatever medicine it was that knocked us out before and continued,

"Now that I know you both are in love with each other, what better torture than to separate you and torture you separately so you can hear each other scream but you cant do anything to help and you wont know whats happening to each other. Like I said before, this is going to be fun."

They both then quickly rushed in, Hendrick ran around Damien and grabbed me and pushed the syringe into my arm as I tried to fight him off, and everything quickly started to fade but I could hear what they were saying still.

Elix had rushed towards Damien, and they fought for a minute before Damien was defeated and injected with some of the medicine as well.

"I'm only giving enough for you to feel too weak to do anything. So you get to watch as we take her somewhere else and know that there's nothing you can do to stop us. Just think of everything we are going to do, and there's nothing you can do about it," Elix said with a laugh at the end, clearly enjoying torturing us in any way he could.

I heard Damien fall to the ground and begged in a defeated tone, "No, please dont hurt her. Don't take her away from me."

I was still barely conscious as Hendrick held my lifeless like body in his arms to carry me away and managed to whisper out, "Damien." Before the drug finely took full effect, and I passed out completely.

CHAPTER 9

I woke up in another dark room. No windows, big door that locks from the outside just like the last room, everything in general looking very similar to the last room I was in with Damien, except, Damien was no where in sight.

I was tied to a chair, up against the opposite wall from the door, and I could hear noises coming from somewhere else.

It sounded like people were fighting and running into things. I felt panicked as I couldn't help but to worry that it might be Damien and whatever is happening to him.

What are they going to do before they kill me? did they hurt him? Is that who i'm hearing from the other room? I hear the door unlock and hendrick walks in.

"What happened to Damien?" I asked, unable to hide how worried I am.

"Oh, such sweet, sweet revenge. You know, when they took me to turn me into a vampire for the program that your father took part in, they killed my girlfriend. They staged it to look like I had killed her and fled from the crime scene.

Never did I think that I'd get my revenge on that scientist and then later on the pathetic human sympathizer vampire who worked with him, through that same scientists daughter." He finished with a laugh.

"But I didn't do anything to you, and neither did Damien! My dad was only apart of that program because he was forced to be!" I yelled out.

"But someone has to pay! He could've said no, but he didn't! He could've set that fire to save us sooner and save all of us, but instead, he stood by and almost let us all die!" he retorted.

"What is this going to help if you hurt me?" I asked desperately, hoping I could change his mind.

"It's simple really, hurting you is going to make me feel better", he said with a smirk, "I already hunted down and killed most of the scientists, and drank every last ounce of blood they had in their bodies while they were still alive and conscious. After I tortured and killed their families in front of their eyes, of course.

It made me feel better to know that they were dead and that they all died an excruciatingly painful death, mentally and physically.

I hate you disgusting humans. The only good one was my girlfriend, and she's long gone." he continued.

"But what would she say if she was alive now?" I asked.

"You dont get to talk about her!" he replied loudly, disgusted that I'd talk about her at all.

"Besides, it doesn't matter what she would've said. She's gone, and it's pointless to even consider." he continued in a calmer tone.

He pulled a knife out from his pocket and walked over to me, cutting the rope on one side of the chair, releasing my left arm and then grabbed my left wrist tightly and held my arm out as he began to slowly cut me from my shoulder, down to my wrist.

I screamed from the excuciating pain and begged him to stop. Blood started to stream down my arm and drip onto the floor off of my fingertips.

He treated himself to a taste of the blood off of my arm. Every touch burned, causing me to cry out once again.

I had already lost a lot of blood the last time, and I haven't eaten anything either the entire time we've been held here. I feel weak and faint.

My body aching from the combination of stress, dehydration, and starvation. Not to mention the side effects of the drugs they've been injecting me with.

I have a vague memory of being taken to the bathroom at least and allowed to drink a small amount of water after they drugged me again, but the water wasn't even close to enough. It was just enough to postpone me dying from dehydration. They didn't want me to die due to any other cause besides whatever they chose to do to me.

"I think I'm going to die here," I thought to myself.

He put the knife to my throat and whispered in my ear, "Maybe I should just end it now. nothing would make me happier than watching the life fade from your eyes as your blood spews from your body."

I tried to keep my breathing steady and dare not say a word at this moment.

"Then again, it would be fun to watch you hear your little boyfriend in pain while there's nothing you can do. Just as I can imagine Elix is enjoying every second of that P.O.S. hearing you scream out in pain, while there's nothing he can do." he continued.

"Damien has already been through so much in his life. I haven't even gone through a fraction of the pain he's had to suffer through, and now he's back into a situation where he's going to suffer because of me. My body will give out long before his will. This is all my fault," I thought.

"Or maybe it would be fun to turn you into a vampire too. You probably have lost enough blood, all I would need to do now is make you drink enough of my blood, then i'd get to watch you go through the excruciating process of your body turning into a vampire.

Then you would have to suffer through the cravings, and the unbearable pain that the sun causes, every awful thing that comes with being a vampire, and we could take you to the edge of death over and over again just to let your body recover soon enough after if we wanted to." he chuckled out.

I was too tired to say anything back, so I just continued to stay silent.

"Hmm, well, this isn't going to be as much fun if you dont fight back in some way or another. Maybe I should give you a little more incentive by going to visit your little boyfriend," he said in a serious tone as he stood up and walked towards the door.

"No! no! just get your revenge on me and let him go! I'm the real one you want anyway, right? Because my dad was a part of that program? Just kill me and let him go." I demanded angrily.

He now stood a few feet in front of the door. He turned around with a satisfied smile on his face, and in a voice that lacked any emotion other than pleasure, he said,

"That's more like it. I'm glad to see you do still have some fight left in you. I guess that means I can keep going." he had started to take a couple of steps towards me as he neared the end of his sentence.

The door behind him suddenly flung open, hitting the wall beside it with a loud bang and before Hendrick could even react, Damien had him pinned against the wall, with his left forearm to his neck and his right hand drove a knife into his chest where his heart would be.

Hendrick had a look of shock written all over his face. Blood poured from the wound, his skin began to look extremely pale, and he was unconscious in seconds.

Damien pulled away from him, keeping the knife in his hand and letting Hendricks now lifeless body fall to the ground with a loud thud. Damien was completely emotionless as he watched the life fade from Hendricks.

He continued to look down at his body for a moment, and then he made his way over to me. His eyes seemed to lack any empathy or sympathy for the now dead man, and his fangs appeared more visible, or perhaps i'm just now noticing them more. They're not that noticeable in general just by looking at him.

Most people would just think that his canine teeth are sharper than most peoples. No one would even question it, but they're a bit longer than most peoples also.

His face was covered in blood, as well as his clothes and hands. He almost looked like a different person entirely. He looked terrifying instead of gentle, but I felt relieved that he was safe. Relieved that he was here with me. I'm not even going to dare ask what happened or what he did to Elix.

He's also covered in more marks again that show he was fighting. Cuts, bruises, blood, dried blood, swelling.

he cut the rest of the ropes that had kept me tied to the chair and ripped apart of his shirt to wrap up my arm, not saying a single word.

I was extremely weak, but adrenaline allowed me enough strength to get up and run with Damien out the door.

There was a long hallway with a couple of doors on each side. We decided to go right, and we ran as fast as we could until we reached the end and saw a set of stairs going up.

We were both hesitant, already having gone through so much, we can't take any more surprises right now.

"Come on, let's go." Damien finally whispers to me. Slowly, we made our way up the stairs into what seemed to look like a regular persons home.

We finally had sight of what looked like a door that led outside of the house and I could see a few sets of keys hanging on a hook just beside the door and grabbed one that I recognized being for a car of some kind, and then we ran outside as fast we could move.

I went first, and Damien was right behind me. All of a sudden, Damien let out a gut-wrenching scream in agony.

I turned around to see that he was on the ground, grasping his body anywhere he could, visibly in excruciating pain.

"The sun," he yelled out in between the screams in pain. I couldn't help him hold his weight entirely, so I ran to the nearest car I could reach that was parked in the driveway about 20 feet from us and tried the key.

"It worked, thank god," I thought to myself. I quickly unlocked all the rest of the doors and ran to Damien's side to try to help him the best I can right now to get into the back seat, onto the floor so the seats and everything could hopefully help shield as much sun as possible.

It was early morning at this point, and there wasn't a single cloud in the sky. I didn't have any strength left, but I didn't have a choice, I helped him in, shut the door, and then went to the drivers side and hopped in.

I started the car and floored it in any direction I could go away from this place. There was a dirt road with trees all around, like were in some kind of forest.

"Had we not gotten out of there ourselves, no one is around for miles, so no one would've heard our screams and would've never suspected a thing." I thought to myself.

Damien's spot on the floor seemed to be shielding enough of the sun for him to get a break. I still heard him groan in pain from time to time, but most of the ride was quiet.

We reached a main road and turned left to head towards the nearby town. Soon enough, the area began to look familiar, and I started to recognize the direction we needed to take to get home.

"Seeing as we stole this car, though, I don't think that it's wise to drive all the way home in it. Who knows who it belongs to really" I thought to myself, "but how can we get past the sun?"

When we were right down the road from home, I pulled over and started to look around to see what was in the car that we could maybe use.

I popped the trunk open and got out to look. "A blanket, perfect!" I said out loud to myself.

I grabbed it and began to unfold it and hold it up to prepare to shield Damien from the sun. Slowly opening the back door, I held the blanket out over him.

He cautiously started to climb out of the car with what little strength he could manage as he covered his skin with it.

"Are you okay? Will that work to get us home?" I asked.

He nodded yes and didn't say a word. We stumbled our way home and locked the doors and windows as soon as we got there.

Once everything was checked and locked, we both sat on the couch, and the adrenaline quickly left our systems as we passed out from the exhaustion.

CHAPTER 10

I could feel my body aching excruciatingly, so sore and in pain. Moving my body at all felt more like torture.

My eyes were still closed as I felt the soft blanket covering me. I could smell the familiar and comforting scent of Damien and the way his house smelled. The way his couch smelled of sweet flowers beneath me.

I heard the sound of a glass cup being sat on the table, along with a plate and some other things. I forced myself to open my eyes and saw that Damien brought me water, some medicine, and he made some breakfast for me.

I'm not sure how long I was asleep for, but it definitely couldn't be the same day that we made it home.

Damien didn't say a word as he moved over to me and allowed me to use as little strength as possible by pulling me up into a sitting position.

He pulled the table over to me as he kept one arm tightly around my back to my other side.

"Damie--" I began to say but was cut off,

"No, we can talk after you eat, you need to eat something and drink some water, and I got you some medicine that should help with any pain you have." Damien said sternly.

I found my strength some and was able to reach out and grab the medicine and water and swallow it. Then I reached over to the fork that was sitting on the plate and started to eat.

Things felt strange between me and Damien. After everything we just went through, I guess I can't expect it to all be exactly the same, but I dont like this uncomfortable feeling in the air. My chest felt hallow as we sat there in silence.

After I finished eating, Damien slowly let go of me. To make sure that I could hold myself up, and then he picked up all the dishes and took them to the sink. He was gone for what seemed like forever.

I could feel that the medicine was starting to kick in, and my pain started to feel almost non-existent.

"Damien," I spoke out. I could hear him washing dishes, but he didn't offer any reply. "We don't have to talk if you don't want to, but please don't ignore me or avoid me..." I continued, realizing what he's doing.

I heard the sound of him stopping for a moment as the water still ran. Then he shut it off and walked back over to the couch and sat beside me, staring off somewhere else, anywhere else to avoid looking at me.

We sat there for a god awful amount of time again in silence until he said, "If you're wondering... the reason I couldn't go in the sun is because for days, I wasn't able to take any of the medicine that helped fix that."

I could tell that's not what was on his mind, but I decided to just go with it because just him talking gave me some relief.

"Yes, that makes sense. Are you okay now? Are there any longer lasting effects from that?" I asked, both to keep him talking and because I genuinely wanted to know.

"You're sore for a while, but compared to the actual pain of it, it's nothing, and we heal faster than humans anyways, so it's fine, I'm fine." he answered.

"I was so happy that you were okay. When I saw you walk through that door, I was so relieved. I thought that they might've hurt you really badly," I said.

He scowled as he thought back to it all. "Can I ask you... did you do what I think you did?" I asked.

"I killed him, as well as a couple others, yes." He answered and then continued. "I heard you screaming, and I could hear how much pain you were in. I didn't know what they were doing. All I knew was that I had to get to you.

So, when Elix turned around to gloat on the sound of you screaming, I grabbed around his head and twisted hard, breaking his neck.

Then I grabbed the knife he was carrying, and then two other guys came in when they heard the noises and tried to attack me, so I fought them and stabbed them in the heart.

I left the room and followed the voices I could hear, and it was only a couple of doors down from where I was. I could hear what he was saying to you and waited for the right moment to come in and kill him, too.

I know... you must really think I'm a monster now... I bet you're scared of me again and just trying to hide it... I was covered in blood and looked like one, so how could you not think of me as a monster?" he still avoided looking at me as he finished explaining.

"Ah, okay, I get it now," I thought to myself, "He's worried that I will see him differently because of what he had to do to save us. He's worried that I will reject him now and want nothing to do with him.

After everything he's been through in his life, and then everything that happened when we were at that place. He's scared I'm going to turn and run the first chance I get."

He was leaning back on the couch, visibly trying to prepare for, what to him seems like the inevitable, so I leaned over and layed on his chest, and I wrapped my arm across his body.

I felt his body tighten from the surprise of me laying on him and the stress that filled him from everything that was racing through his mind.

"No. you saved me. Again. I see a man who will do whatever it takes to keep me safe. I don't see a monster, and i'm not afraid of you." I said as I cuddled my head deeper into him.

I could feel the relief wash over him with my words, even though it didn't take it completely away.

He didn't say a word as he turned his body more towards me and wrapped his arms around me. It was so comfortable and safe feeling just laying on him, with his arms embracing me.

Soon enough, I began to fall back asleep. A few hours later, I woke up. I was still laying on him, and he was fast asleep.

He didn't move the whole time. He just stayed there as I slept on him until he fell asleep, too. It was dark outside now, and I still felt tired, so I covered up Damien and walked to my room to sleep. I didn't want to wake him up in case he hadn't gotten much sleep.

The next 2 weeks were pretty calm and quiet. I began to heal up, Damien was already better. We slowly started to get back to normal and began to laugh again.

My work called me and told me that my next shift would be my last shift, I tried to tell them that I got into a car crash,

but I didn't have a doctors note to confirm and I couldn't exactly explain that I was kidnapped by vampires who had something against my scientist father who worked with vampires and was in a secret program against his will for the government to do awful tests and experiments on those vampires,

and the vampire who my dad asked to protect me, killed a few of the other vampires and was able to save me, and now were home and healing, so they told me that since I've been missing work, they're giving me my notice that they're firing me and my next shift, which is tonight, will be my last one and then I'm officially fired.

I got ready, and Damien walked me to work. We were both on guard the entire time, worried to relax for even a moment because of what happened the last time we were out together.

I worked like normal, and nothing crazy happened. The same customers, besides Elix. The same routine.

"Hayven? Is that you?" a man said from the end of the counter.

Confusion washed over my face, not recognizing the man at first.

"It's me, Jeremiah. We were in the same classes in 6th and 7th grade. We went to the same school. I was kind of a jerk to you?" he said, trying to help spark a memory of him.

"Oh yeah, that's right. I remember you now." I replied as I remembered how he used to be so rude to me and how much I disliked him when we were in class together.

"Yeah, yeah, i'm sorry. I was such a jerk to you. There's no excuse for how I acted, and I apologize." he said.

I was a bit caught off guard with his apology, but I always respected a nice, genuine apology and honesty.

"Yeah, I definitely didn't like you then, but hey, dont worry about it. It was a long time ago." I replied.

"No, no, please, can I try to make it up to you? Let me meet you somewhere later, or some time, and I can explain why I acted that way, and just let me treat you to a nice meal or dessert or something. please? I won't take no for an answer, " he joked, genuinely seeming to want to make it up to me.

I was very hesitant to accept his invitation because of recent events.

"Please, let me take you out for an apology dinner to try to make up for it all. I know it won't make up for it, but I think about how I acted toward you a lot, and I just would really like to say that I'm sorry. I never thought I'd run into you, but here of all places, it must be fate. This is my first time ever coming here." he insisted.

I have known him since elementary school, so what harm could it do to accept really? My shift was nearing its end, and Damien walked through the door, ready to walk back home with me.

"Okay, yeah. I guess I can meet up with you this saturday out front here, and you pick the place. around 6?" I asked.

"Okay, sounds great! thank you, I will meet you then, saturday at 6 pm out in front of this place to meet for a friendly apology dinner." he confirmed.

He paid for his meal and left. I took off my apron and started putting everything away to get ready to leave. "Who was that?" Damien asked curiously.

"That was this guy I went to school with pretty much my entire school life and was in the same class in 6th and 7th grade. He used to bully me a lot, and he recognized me here when he was eating and asked if he could apologize to me for everything by taking me to get a nice meal or dessert or something." I replied.

"You've known him for a long time? What did you say?" he asked.

"Yes, I never liked him, but only because he was mean to me when we were growing up. He didn't bother me much in high school, and I told him yeah, that saturaday at 6. He can take me out to a friendly dinner as an apology. He said he thinks about how he treated me a lot, and he just wants to apologize." I replied.

"Okay, well, just be safe. You have a much better heart than me, that's for sure." he laughed out towards the end.

"Hey, best case scenario, I make a new friend, and we start over and forget the past. Worst case scenario, I get a little annoyed, but I get a free meal and dessert, right? So win-win situation if you ask me." I chuckled.

"Well, I definitely wouldn't say that's the worst-case scenario, but I get what you mean." he laughed back.

I cringed at the of what the worse case scenarios really could be. Flashing back to our recent experiences that left us both traumatized.

I did feel a little weary about going anywhere with him, even as an apology, because he used to be so mean to me and i'm not feeling too trusting towards people since the whole Incident with Elix.

As we walked home together, we talked about how work was, what kinds of things Jeramiah used to do and say, and a bunch of random topics that made us laugh.

I looked up at the sky and noticed the stars were shining extra bright because the moon hadn't come up yet.

I suddenly felt Damiens hand start to intertwine our fingers and hold my hand. I felt flutters in the pit of my stomach and started to feel nervous surprisingly.

"So... I've been afraid to say or do anything since we got back home and everything... but when I told you that I love you, did you really mean it when you said you love me too?

I understand if you say you didn't mean it or if you only said it because of where we were or something. I won't blame you if you tell me you didn't mean it or anything. I dont want to make you feel uncomfortable or anything..." Damien said as he soaked up every second of holding my hand, as if he truly expected it to be the last time he would ever get to.

I stopped walking and turned to face him and say, "Of course I meant it. I meant every word. I'm in love with you, Damien.

No matter how much you think I shouldn't be or couldn't possibly be, i'm in love with you, and that's not going to change."

he smiled both times I said that i'm in love with him.

"Did you mean it when you said you love me? and everything you said," I asked back.

"Yes, more than anything I've ever said in my entire life. I love you more than I can even put into words." He admitted.

For a moment, I felt my heart stop. I so badly want to feel his lips passionately kissing mine again, but i'm too nervous to say anything and dont want to push him if he's not ready.

So we walked the rest of the way home, just holding hands and occasionally talking.

When we got home, I told him I was tired and that I was going to go ahead and get ready for bed and go to sleep, and we went our separate ways for the night.

CHAPTER 11

My birthday is next weekend. I'm going to be 20. I wonder if Damien knows it's coming up or if I should bring it up to him.

I got out of bed and started to get dressed and ready for the day. Damien said he wanted to go look at cars today so we don't have to walk everywhere anymore and asked if I wanted to go with him.

Getting out of the house sounds nice, so I said yes. He never really felt like he had a need to get a car before, but now he's been thinking it might be easier to just drive places instead of walking everywhere.

I walked out of my room wearing a sun dress and tennis shoes and left my hair loosely hanging down to the middle of my back.

"I know we're going to look at cars, but does it matter what if I wear this?" I asked him, unsure if I should wear pants instead of something else.

He looked at me, eyes quickly scanning me up and down, and then he sweetly smiled as he looked back at his laptop on the coffee table.

"No that's fine. You look very beautiful." he said as he looked back over at me, still smiling and looking me up and down once again.

I felt my face getting really hot, and I could tell I was starting to blush. Damien started to laugh and say, "Are you blushing?" he stood up and walked over towards me and continued on to say, "Does it make you blush when I say you look beautiful? what about if I said you look cute?"

I tried to laugh it off and walk past him as I felt the butterflies in my stomach growing worse and worse with every step he took towards me.

He gently grabbed my arm and pulled me back to him, and wrapped his arms around me.

"I never thought I would see you blush over anything," he said, almost giggling.

I leaned back away from him while he was still hugging me to tease him back, but stopped as I saw he was gazing back down at me.

We lovingly stared back at each other for a moment, and then he let go of me and told me to grab a sweater in case it starts getting cold later, since fall has officially started, and then we left to look at cars.

Thankfully, the first dealership we went to we found a nice car that wasn't too expensive and decided to celebrate the new car by going to get lunch from a restaurant down the road.

While we were sitting at our table eating food and talking, I heard my name being called, and we both turned to see Jeramiah at a nearby table.

He didn't have food at his table yet, so it looked like he had just arrived there and just so happened to notice me.

He invited himself over and scooted in next to Damien. "Hey, I wasn't expecting to run into you here!" Jeramiah said with excitement radiating off of him.

"Well, I've never been here before. We just decided to stop for lunch." I replied. Damien looked to be pouting at the other side of the booth.

"Oh, is this your boyfriend?" Jeramiah asked. I paused for a moment looking over a Damien, not really sure what to answer, because we've confessed that we were in love with each other but never actually made it official by asking to be boyfriend and girlfriend.

Damien looked over at me, waiting to see what I would say. "Um, well, we haven't officially asked each other yet, but yea, he basically kind of is."

Jeramiah just nodded acknowledging my answer and said, "Well hey, I know you're birthday is coming up soon, instead of taking you to an apology dinner I was wondering if you would want to go to a party at my house tonight instead? Free alcohol, celebrate your birthday early. Your boyfriend can come too, of course."

I looked at Damien to see if he would want to go, but his response didn't give me much to work with because he just went back to eating.

"You know my birthday is coming up? Uh, sure. You know what, why not? Yeah, that sounds like fun." I replied to him.

He started to write down the address and time as he said "Okay great, yeah, see you there then."

He finally went back to his table, and I asked Damien if he was okay with going.

"Honestly, it sounds like it could be fun. If it's what you want to do, then it's fine by me." he replied to me as we both continued to eat our food and enjoy our nice day together.

A few hours later, we started to get ready for the party. I put on a black lacy dress with some black matching high heels and decided to redo my makeup and add some eyeshadow and liquid eyeliner to the tops of my eyelids. I walked out of my room to meet Damien and asked if I looked okay.

He suddenly pretended to jump as if he was startled suddenly, "How do you always look so beautiful?" he asked with his hand on his chest, as though to say his heart had stopped beating for a moment.

I was caught off guard by his startled jump but then couldn't help but smile as I said thank you.

His dark hair had grown out a few inches since the day we first met, it was now to a length that he will have to run his hand through his hair to push it out of his face some.

I looked at him and just admired the way it suited him. With the shape of his face and the way his dark hair paired with his lighter toned soft skin.

He decided to also get dressed up some in a white button-up shirt with the sleeves rolled up on his forearms just below his elbows and a black vest over the top of it with some dark jeans

"You look really handsome too." I said to him as I walked over to him to softly wrap my arm around his. To be honest, he didn't just look handsome. He looked incredibly attractive.

I could stare at him all night and be content with not doing anything else. "Are we ready to go then?" I continued on to ask.

His perfect smile slowly rose across his face, sending butterflies straight to my stomach.

I could almost believe my heart had stopped in that moment had I not been able to feel it start to race. I wondered if in those moments, he could feel it when I was too close or even hear it, as I heard it in my own ears like drums playing on loudly.

He nodded yes and tightened his hold on my arm, and we headed off. We had high hopes for the night being fun. Perhaps it was more so that we needed it to be.

We made it to the address Jeremiah gave me. It wasn't too far from Damien's house, and since we were planning on drinking, we decided to just walk over. It was a big vacation house right next to a lake with its own pier.

Walking in, we saw a hallway filled with decorative lights that hung from the ceiling heading down a hallway and people crowded around inside the house.

I've never been much of a party person, but once in a while, it's nice to dress up and get out, just forgetting the rest of the world for a little while. Plus, this will be my first time going to anything like this with Damien.

"I don't think I've ever seen you drink." I say to him. "Hmm. That's right, you haven't, huh?" He said, realizing as he thought back and then continued,

"I dont drink very often anymore. There was a long period of time where that was pretty much the only thing I did, but that's an extremely long story for a later time, though."

He had a very intense and sad look to his face as he told me that. "I want to hear everything he's been through. I want to know his whole past. Any and every detail that I can." I thought to myself as

I watched his expression change back to happy and smiling once again.

I desire to know him better than anyone ever has. I desire to show him that not everyone will leave and that someone can love him despite all the reasons he may believe that he is unlovable or unworthy of love.

Jeremiah walked through a small group of people that were near the front entrance and held his arms out, beginning to speak in a welcoming and excited tone.

"Hey, you guys made it!" He walked over to me, and to my surprise, he gave me a hug. The kind of hug you give a long time close friend who you havnt seen in a while.

"Let's go get you guys something to drink." He said as he put his hand on the upper part of my back between my shoulder blades so he could guide me.

Damien followed close to me on the opposite side, and we were led to a long table in what looked to be a large living room area with couches and speakers that played upbeat music.

The table had multiple different types of alcohol placed neatly around a few trays of snacks and candy.

Jeremiah poured us both a couple of shots of vodka, which we both shot back quickly. Then we grabbed a couple cups and filled them with beer, and decided to go sit on an open couch together.

We all began to talk about different topics, the party, what Jeremiah does for work, how I'm no longer working at the place he first seen me and invited me out to apologize, and mostly just random things to keep the conversation going.

I went to take another drink and realized I had finished it all. "Oh, I'm all out." I said as I held my cup to the side to show them, laughing slightly over the embarrassment of trying to drink from an empty cup. "Me too." Damien replied with a soft chuckle. "Me three," Jeremiah said.

He looked over to Damien and asked, "Hey bud, would you mind getting us all another drink?"

Damien scratched his forehead with raised eyebrows for a moment without saying anything and then stood up and said, "Yeah. Sure. No problem."

He took a few steps and then turned back to look at me for a second, seeming hesitant to leave. I wasn't sure why, but I just smiled sweetly at him.

The table wasn't too far from where we were sitting but it was loud and the room was filled with people dancing.

Once Damien was out of sight, Jeremiah looked over to me and said, "Sorry, I hope the host asking the guest to get me and his girlfriend a drink wasn't too rude of me.

I just wanted a moment with just you. I wanted to tell you that I am truly and sincerely sorry for always being such a jerk to you.

The truth is that I had the biggest crush on you all growing up and when we were in the same classes I got an even bigger crush on you and thought that being mean to you was a good way to show you how much I liked you for whatever reason.

Anyways, that's ancient history, of course. You look fantastic tonight, by the way!" I was shocked to hear that he had a crush on me.

I scooted over on the couch to put a little distance between us and replied, "Oh. Thank you. Yeah, I definitely can't say that I would've ever guessed that."

My voice was somewhat monotone as I thought back to how mean he was, though I tried to hide my real expression and instead just kept a slight smile on my face.

He scooted closer to me again, putting an arm around my shoulder this time, and then he said, "Yeah, I hope you can forgive me. I would love it if we could be friends."

I tried to scoot over a little more without straight pushing his arm off of me.

"Yeah. I can forgive you." I'm not a big fan of guys that I dont know very well just tossing their arm over my shoulder or touching me at all, really.

Damien came walking back over holding three cups in his hands and with an almost smug smile written across his face he squeezed into the small space between me and Jeremiah causing Jeremiah to have to scoot over to compensate for the space Damien was now taking up.

He handed us both our drinks as he said, "a drink for you, and a drink for you. So what'd I miss?" He wrapped his arm around me and gently pulled me closer to him.

"Not much, man. Was just telling your girlfriend here that I hoped she could forgive me for how I treated her when we were kids. Then you came back with our drinks." Jeremiah answered as he started to chug his drink.

After that, we all stayed quiet for a while until we got to feeling really good, and then we spent the rest of the party dancing and just having fun. Jeremiah went off on his own for a while and then met up with us a little while later right before we were about to leave.

CHAPTER 12

"Hey, are you guys heading out?" Jeramiah asked.

I smiled and said, "Yes, but thank you for inviting us. We had a lot of fun."

"Damn. So soon? It's only been a couple of hours since you got here." Jeremiah said with a fake laugh.

"Yeah, we're both just starting to get kind of tired, so we just thought that must be our queue to go ahead and end party time." I replied.

"Well, here, take my phone number, and please let me know when you make it home safe, Hayven. Is he going to walk you home?"

Jeremiah asked as he gestured towards Damien and then pulled a paper out of his pocket with his number already written on it and grabbed my wrist to place the paper softly in my hand.

I laughed, realizing he probably didn't know that Damien and I had been living together since my last place burnt down. It would've been a lot to explain, so I just simply said,

"Yes. He's walking me home." "Okay good. Well, it was great seeing you, I hope we do this again soon!" Jeremiah said as he leaned in to hug me.

Then he pulled away from me, and he looked towards Damien and reached his hand out to do that hug guys do where they grab each other hand and pull each in to pat each other on the back.

Jeremiah started whispering something in Damien's ear that I couldn't hear and then pulled away with a big smile on his face as he waved to us and started heading back to his party.

"What'd he say?" I asked with a chuckle as we started walking out the front door. Damien reached down for my hand to hold it tightly in his.

"Oh. Um, nothing. He was just drunk." He answered with a shrug and a soft smile that faded quickly.

I didn't think too much of it at the time, and we just continued on our way home.

About halfway home, my pace started to slow down quite a bit because my feet began hurting a little too much from wearing heels all night and walking so much.

"Do you mind if I sit down for a minute?" I asked.

Damien laughed. "Did the party wear you out?" He asked in reply.

I smirked admittedly and answered, "Maybe a little bit. Wearing heels all night and all this walking is kind of killing my feet."

Damiens' face went serious for a moment, and then he smirked. "Well, why didn't you say something to me sooner?" He asked, and then before I could reply he started undoing the ankle strap on my heels, pulled them off my feet, held them both by the straps in one hand and then turned around to kneel down.

"Hop on, I will carry you the rest of the way." He said, using his empty hand to gesture towards his back.

"Oh no, I couldn't make you do that, Damien. I--" I denied and was suddenly stopped mid sentence by him starting to say something,

"You're not making me do anything. Your feet hurt, we're walking home. It's been a long night. Let me help you. Just hop on and let me carry you, okay?" Damien insisted.

"Okay," I said hesitantly, feeling guilty at the thought of him carrying me the rest of the way.

I leaned down and wrapped my arms down past his neck, holding his collarbone and chest area, and placed my legs on both sides of him where he could easily pick me up.

With one swift move, he picked me up and bounced me up to a higher spot to readjust so that he could carry me easier.

"See, not a problem at all." He said. I could hear him smile through his voice as he spoke. We started to walk again, or should I say, Damien started to walk again as he carried me.

We were both silent for what seemed like a really long time since we were both ready to just be home. Damien suddenly broke the silence by saying,

"You know, I realized something today. More so, you made me realize something today.."

"What did I make you realize?" I asked, perplexed and suddenly feeling a little nervous.

"Dont worry, it's nothing bad. At least, I hope it's nothing you would consider to be bad..." he started and paused for a moment as I listened.

I could feel his body tense up a bit, and then he continued, sounding almost nervous himself now,

"Well, It didn't occur to me until today, but after we confessed how we feel about each other, I never actually asked if you would be my girlfriend.

Today, when that guy asked you if I was your boyfriend, I honestly didn't know what you were going to say.

Part of me was almost scared you were going to say no because technically, I never did actually ask you, I just kind of assumed, and I know that must have also been a bit confusing and difficult question for you to answer at the time, because I never asked you out right.

So it got me thinking that I just never asked, and I should have so, Hayven. Will you be my girlfriend?"

I giggled because of how sweet and unexpected it was. He thought so deeply about this topic it seems.

I guess in a way, I kind of assumed the same thing. Since we had confessed our love to each other then it kind of just automatically made us a couple,

I mean between that and us living together, despite the reason why we started living together in the first place, but when Jeremiah asked me that question, I had also realized that we never actually made it official.

I was worried to say yes because if he didnt see us that way just yet then I didn't want to force him into being a couple if it wasnt a step he was ready to take, but I didnt want to say no and make it seem like everything we had said and gone through had meant nothing.

We had already made it to the front porch of the house before I could answer, so he gently let me down and then turned to face me as he waited for me to answer. He scanned my face with his eyes.

"Of course I will be your girlfriend," I began to say as I grinned from ear to ear, "I'm not upset with you at all, I -"

before I could finish my last sentence, in one quick motion, Damien placed both hands on my face. His thumbs lightly touching my cheeks and the rest of his hand gently placed to where his fingers rested in my hair that layed just behind my ear and near the nape of my neck, and he leaned down towards my face and kissed me so passionately that I felt like I could hardly catch my breath.

As though he was desperate to feel my lips against his own once again. In the suddenness of it all, I found myself gently pressed up against the wall, with one of my hands softly touching his arm and one hand placed on his chest as I deeply kissed him back.

In that moment, I could feel his heart beating as fast as mine. His lips were soft and gentle with every movement, yet forceful enough that he made his touch known.

He tasted like the vodka and soda from the party and smelled like cologne. I felt like I couldn't get enough of him, and I hoped this moment would never end.

Damiens POV:

I scanned every inch of her face as I waited to hear her answer.

The moonlight was just bright enough to illuminate every beautiful feature, lighting up her whole face.

I felt scared that her answer would be no. That maybe I already messed things up by not asking her sooner.

That guy pointed out that I never asked her to be my girlfriend, and I immediately felt like I had messed up. Then suddenly, I started to feel jealous.

The way he would slyly put his arm around her or touch her whenever he got the chance to. The way he looked at her.

I never wanted anyone to be able to touch her or look at her like that ever again, knowing she isn't officially taken by me.

It's not that guys looking at her bothered me at all, necessarily, or even a friendly hug, for that matter.

She's beautiful. It's truly as if she's an angel that had come down to bless the earth with her presence, and everyone around her is lucky to have had the chance to see her, to talk to her.

Her voice is soothing and comforting, her touch soft and magnetizing, she's kind and loving and caring, shes just this absolutely beautiful, intelligent, pure hearted, angel who lights up anyone and everyone around her just by, being. Just by existing.

But it was the fact that I loved her, and I didn't get to know that she was completely mine in those moments, and it was all my fault.

I dont believe I deserve her anyway, with everything I've been through. All the things I've done. She deserves better than just some monster that knew her dad.

Like she said before, though, it's her choice, and I never want to take any of her choices from her. Whether that choice is to love me or not, I will respect it. Even if one day she decides she hates me and never wants to see me again, then I will respect it.

As long as she's safe and happy. Although, I can't bear the thought of losing her. I can't bear the thought of someone else getting to hold her, getting to kiss her, getting to touch her, and getting to be loved by her.

I didn't think she had a thing for that guy by any means, but he knew it was bothering me that in that moment, we weren't officially a couple. That it was merely just an assumption that we were a couple.

Then, with what he whispered to me when we were leaving, I hope it really was just because he was drunk. I didn't want to tell her if that's all that it was, a drunken mentioning that he didn't actually mean, but I won't forget what he said.

"Of course I will be your girlfriend," she said with a smile beautifully painted across her face. I can't believe it. I almost expected her to say no, as if there was absolutely no way she would ever really say yes to that.

So many times now that I've wanted to kiss her again, it's been so long and it has been almost painful not giving in and kissing her, but I dont want her to feel smothered by my love for her.

To feel like it's all too much or anything, so I had to wait to make sure it was what she wanted, too, and not just what I desired.

My heart stopped as those words left her lips and then desperately started to beat again twice as fast, trying to remind me that I'm alive and this is real.

I could barely breathe. I could barely hear what she was saying anymore because the sound of my heart pounding in my chest was echoing so loud up to my ears.

"I'm not upset with you at all," she continued. "Thank god she's not upset with me. She said yes, if this is a dream, I never want to wake up. If this is a dream, I have to kiss her at least one last time before it ends." I thought to myself.

Before I knew it, my hands were holding her face, and I was kissing her deeply and intensely.

Her body pressed against the wall soon enough and kissing me back. Her hands were softly touching my arm and chest. I could hardly breathe.

Every time our lips met and with every touch, I was desperate to show her how much I had wanted to feel her touch and feel her lips kissing mine again.

Desperate to show her how much I cared about her. Kissing her somehow also felt like I was catching my breath once again after not being able to breathe for so long.

Like I had been suffocating this whole time and was close to going unconscious from the lack of air, but then she brought me back again and made me feel like suffocating was nothing but a distant memory, if it ever really existed at all.

I dont know how I lived even a second before without her here, without knowing what this feels like, and I never want to go back to the days when she was just a distant face that I fell in love with but could never do anything about.

She smelled like sweet vanilla from her perfume and tasted like candy from the lipstick she was wearing.

With every kiss and every touch, I felt myself becoming more and more addicted to the feeling, to the way she smelled, to the way she tasted, to her.

Hayvens POV:

Damien slowly and heavily pulled his face a few inches away from mine as he placed his hands on the wall on either side of me to support the weight of his body leaning forward towards me.

Both of us breathing heavier than before, trying to catch our breaths now.

He held his head down, facing to the side away from me for a moment. He licked his lips and pulled one hand off the wall as he leaned up more to wipe his face,

getting any lipstick off his mouth and then reaching his hand to my face to wipe around my lips for me in the spots that lipstick remained and had smeared on my face at all.

"As badly, and I mean this with everything in me, as badly as I want to keep kissing you, were both still very drunk from the party and I dont want to do anything that either of us regrets doing when were not drunk anymore."

He said as he dropped his other hand off the wall and then lovingly held one side of my face once again, caressing my cheek with his thumb.

I nodded in agreement, still feeling like I was catching my breath. My heart was still racing, and butterflies filled my stomach, like they were all simultaneously doing back flips.

He grabbed my hand, leading me into the house, and then we went our separate ways to get ready for bed.

Going our separate ways felt almost like how nails on a chalkboard sounds. Everything in me wanted me to stay with him.

I took off my makeup and changed into pajama bottom shorts and a t-shirt and went to lay in bed to sleep.

The longer I layed there, the more my skin felt like it was crawling. So after an hour of trying to sleep and being unsuccessful, I decided to get up and get some water.

I walked into the kitchen to see Damien sitting at the island counter drinking something too.

"Guessing you couldn't sleep either?" I asked with a slight chuckle. He smirked up at me and said, "Yeah, you can say that." He finished his drink and got up to walk back to bed and told me goodnight before heading back to his bedroom.

I sat down to drink my water and still couldn't shake the feeling of my skin crawling.

When I was done, I started to walk back to my room but stopped just a few feet outside my door in the hallway.

It felt like I was being pulled to the Damiens' room, and I just couldn't shake the feeling anymore.

So I knocked on his door and in a somewhat groggy deep voice I heard him say to come in.

He was in bed laying down, lights all shut off. He lifted his head up to look at me as I walked up to the side of his bed. I tried to bring myself to ask if I could just simply sleep in his bed with him, but every time I tried to form the words, they refused to escape past my lips.

Damien let out a little sleepy chuckle as he scooted back some in his bed and held up the blanket, welcoming me to lay next to him.

I climbed in bed with him, facing the outer part of the bed, and I cuddled up close to him.

He wrapped his arm across my stomach, holding me close and layed his head down, leaning against my back. "Good night, my Angel," I heard him whisper.

My heart fluttered. I smiled and replied, "Good night." Then we both slowly began drifting off to sleep finally. Just simply laying together.

The next morning, I woke up with the golden sunlight barely creeping through the curtains. I was facing Damien, and he was facing me.

I didn't want to move in case he was a light sleeper, so I just layed there admiring his face. The shape of his lips, his soft, pale toned skin, his long dark eyelashes. Watching as his chest rose and fell with every breath.

Suddenly, I felt almost scared that this would come to an end. Leaving me left alone in the end.

Somehow, that seems to almost always be the end of every story for me. My mom, my dad, my best friend, and then my crappy ex boyfriends, not that I regret not being with them anymore, but for one reason or another it seems like I always end up alone.

Damien opened his eyes and startled me. It embarrassed me actually because I was staring at him while he was sleeping, which I can imagine might be pretty creepy.

Especially since this was the first night we've ever slept in the same bed. We've slept together on the couch, but I dont really count that.

I laughed out of reaction to feeling embarrassed and shy and started to roll over to get out of the bed quickly but just as my body left the bed, Damien reached his arm around my hips and pulled me back into the bed.

Pulling me halfway under him, where his face was just above mine. He didn't say a word, but his gaze was locked on my face, looking back and forth into my eyes, down to my lips and back to my eyes again.

I felt my face getting hot. He started to bring his face closer to mine, slowly leaning in for a kiss. Both of us close our eyes as our lips connect.

It wasn't a hot and heavy, passionate kiss like last night. Instead, it was a gentle and sweet kiss that ended soon after it started.

I could feel him smiling through the kiss, which made me smile in return. After a moment, he pulled his face back away from mine and smiled as he sweetly said, "Good morning."

"Good morning," I replied back. He pulled my hand up and played with my fingers in his for a moment and then reached over and lightly tapped my nose as he said, "told you that you snore."

And then he jumped up out of bed, almost giggling like a child would. I rolled my eyes and started laughing as I sat up in the bed and started to stand up, not actually replying to his comment.

We both went our separate ways to get ready, feeling content and happy.

CHAPTER 13

A few hours later, there was a knock on the door. Damien was in the other room, and I was in the kitchen, so I decided to just answer since I was closer anyway.

A man I had never seen before stood there. He had dark blonde hair and grey eyes, about as tall as Damien, and had very broad shoulders that fit well with the natural looking muscles on his arms and chest.

"Uh. Hi there." He said, sounding a little confused.

I smiled at him and said, "Hi. Can I help you with something

"Oh, I can think of a lot of things you could help me with, but uh, is Damien here?" He asked as he looked me up and down.

I felt a bit annoyed at his comment but decided to just ignore it.

"Yeah, he's here. Go ahead and come in, and I will get him." I said to him as I gestured towards a specific area for him to wait.

He stepped in, and I shut the door, but before I could go get Damien, he walked around the corner about to ask who was at the door.

His face changed from looking calm to annoyed at the sight of this man.

"What do you want, Daniel?" He asked in a slightly irritated tone as he dropped his arms down to his sides.

The guy smiled and said, "Nice to see you too, Damien. Always a joyous occasion for the both of us."

Damien rubbed his forehead and sighed, "Can you ever just tell me what you're here for and just leave?" He said as he started walking towards the coffee table to set down a pen and a couple of books he was holding.

"No, of course not. That wouldn't be any fun now, would it?" Daniel said with a chuckle and then continued, "So is this girl your girlfriend or something?" He pointed back towards me.

"Yes, she is my girlfriend. Why?" Damien answered.

"Oh, no reason," Daniel started to say and then looked over at me to look me up and down again, "I'm just really impressed, that's all. Didn't think you had it in you to get a girl like that."

I rolled my eyes and decided to go sit down on the couch.

"For one, her name is Hayven. Stop talking about her like she's not here. For two, what do you want Daniel?" Damien said as he sat halfway on the arm of the couch facing his direction.

"Okay, okay. My bad. You're right. I apologize, Hayven." He said as he looked over to me and then looked back at Damien with a slightly more serious look, "but, I'm not sure if it's a topic you want brought up here, if you catch my drift."

"She knows pretty much everything, so just tell me." Damien replied, seeming both appreciative of him, not just bringing it up in case I didn't know and wanting him to just leave already.

"Okay. Well, Cindi asked me to come over here and tell you that some of the other people she was sending supplies to started to kill and drink from humans instead of drinking what they needed to get by from the supplies so she had to cut them off.

Now they're pissed off and running around trying to kill everyone she still sends supplies to, plus anyone they care about, and she's going to have to go into hiding for a while.

She also wanted me to bring over some extra containers full for you to help you get by until things get figured out." Daniel explained.

Damien got a worried expression on his face and muttered, "Oh, okay." He paused for a moment and then continued on to ask, "Did you bring them here with you?"

Daniel casually put his hands in his pockets, and with a grin plastered on his face, he answered, "Nope! I'm not your errand boy. Plus, it looks like you have an endless supply right there on the couch, so maybe I will just keep them for myself. Unless you want to trade that is."

In what seemed like the blink of an eye, Damien had shoved Daniel up to the wall and had him pinned with a hand full of his shirt in each hand.

"Listen here you little shit, I don't drink her blood and I never will and if you talk about her like that even one more time, I'm going tear your head off of your body and toss both sides of you into two separate oceans and let the fish eat what's left of you." Damien threatened as he continued to pin him against the wall and give him a death glare.

Daniel had a surprised look on his face and didn't say anything. As Damien let him go and turned around to come sit next to me, Daniel smirked smugly and said, "Jeez, touchy subjects, I guess."

He fixed his shirt and headed over to the door to open it. "Okay, fine. You've convinced me. I will bring it over later today. Just remember to be on high alert in case anything happens." He finished as he shut the door behind him.

"I'm sorry about all that, Hayven." Damien said, looking at me.

"Yeah, that was kind of a lot, but it's okay. Who is he exactly anyway?" I asked in reply.

"That would be Daniel. I've known him for a couple of years now. He works with the doctor who provides good vampires with blood so they don't have to hurt anyone to survive. He's like the extremely annoying little brother I never wanted.

To put it simply, before he became a vampire, he was a cocky, arrogant, spoiled brat who never knew when to shut up. Now, as a vampire, all that's been heightened. He means well, usually, but he likes to get under my skin any chance he can.

We've never gotten along, and we kind of can't stand each other, but we can't really avoid each other." Damien answered.

I nodded to let him know I was listening. "So, what's it mean for us exactly, that these other vampires are on a revenge mission trying to hunt everyone down?" I asked, sounding concerned.

"It means we have to be extra cautious and on guard. Very aware of our surroundings. I'm strong and trained in fighting, but I dont know if I could take on more than two of them for sure.

Those two men I saved you from that first day we met were just human so it wasnt too much of a challenge, but these guys being pissed off vampires, I dont know that I could even protect myself, let alone you.

So we just have to be careful. Hopefully, they won't even make it as far as coming after me, and if they do, they dont know about you as far as I know, so maybe we will just get lucky." Damien answered.

Later that night, we were getting ready for bed when there was a knock at the door.

We were both a little hesitant to answer it because we didn't know if it was Daniel or if it could be one of the other angry guys.

"Hey, it's just me! Can you let me in? It's cold out here!" We heard Daniel yell through the door.

Damien went and unlocked the door and opened it. Daniel pushed it the rest of the way open so he could come in and find some warmth, and Damien shut the door back behind him, locking It just in case.

Daniel quickly handed Damien two containers from pockets on the inside of his jacket, and Damien said thank you as he hid them behind his back and walked to the room he keeps them all in.

I dont think he wanted me to see the containers, even though I know about them. He hates the fact that he's a vampire and has to drink blood at all. I think it's one of the things that makes him feel most like a monster.

Me and Daniel both sat on opposite ends of the couch and stayed quiet, not speaking to each other. The atmosphere in the room felt awkward.

Damien came back quickly and sat in a nearby chair. "Thank you for bringing those over here. How many guys are there who are trying to hunt everyone down?" He asked.

Daniel leaned forward to rest his elbows on his knees. "As far as we know, theres four or five of them. We are not sure who exactly is working with who, but it's a small group.

They've already hunted down and killed at least five other people in the program, along with any family they had and even a few of their friends. Anyone they could find who was important to them." Daniel spoke, actually seeming more serious now than he was earlier.

Damien nodded and asked, "How are they finding everyone?"

"Well with some of the people, we know that at least one person in the group had been to their houses before and had some kind of previous contact so they already knew the addresses, but with the others were not quite sure.

There are ways to find the people within the program, and then from there it's not too hard to find their family and friends and such, if they're smart enough figure out the different ways to find the main person.

Such as tracking down the few times samples were sent through the mail." Daniel paused for a moment, looking uncomfortable and then continued,

"Speaking of which... I hate more than anything to ask this, but would it be possible if I could stay with you?"

"Absolutely not! No, nope, no way in hell." Damien replied.

"Hey man, it's not an ideal situation for me either. Trust me, but I dont really have anyone else to ask.

Cindi is in hiding, and that whole group of people already know where I live. Besides, I'm pretty sure they already broke into my house looking for me when I went back home to get your stuff." He said.

Damien sat back and paused for a moment, taking a deep breath and in a calm voice asked, "how do you know you didnt just lead them here to kill off two of us in one go?"

I sat there listening intensely to the conversation they were having.

"Why do you think it took me so long to get back here? I'm not trying to die and I'm also not trying lead them back here where you stupidly have a human girl as your girlfriend living with you, so I took a lot of back roads trying to stay unnoticed by anyone, and making sure nobody was following me.

Went a lot of places, stayed there for a while, and as far as I know, there was absolutely no one following me." Daniel said, sounding frustrated.

"Why is it stupid to have my girlfriend living with me, and why should I let you stay here?" Damien asked.

"It's stupid because times like these when there's a group of other vampires that are on the loose going crazy or something, your girlfriend is in extra Danger living with you vs living alone, some where away from all of this,

and if they do find out where you live and come after you, do you think they're just going to kill her off real fast?

or do you think they're going to enjoy their time with her and make it extra long and painful before killing her off and probably doing everything right in front of you,

and you should let me stay with you because as much as we don't get along and I dislike you and you dislike me, if the roles were reversed I would let you stay with me, that's why." Daniel replied, getting a little worked up.

Damien paused for a moment, as the words seemed to have resonated with him, and then he looked over to me and asked, "Is this something you would be comfortable with?"

and I nodded and said, "I mean, it's not ideal of course but if they've already been to his house and know where he lives to begin with, then I guess we can't really say no. It wouldn't be right, so I don't mind if he stays here."

Damien sighed deeply and thought for a moment and then looked over to Daniel and said,

"Okay, fine. You can stay here for a while, but only until this is all over, and while you're here you will be sleeping on the couch, and you have to promise me that if they do find us here then you take Hayven and get out of here."

I looked over at him, shocked, and said, "No. Hey, if they find us, then don't even worry about me. I can just go hide somewhere or something.

I don't want to be the burden that everyone worries about and makes you risk your lives over, just for you to be in as much danger as I am."

Daniel looked over to me and said, "They will be able to smell you. No matter where you hide, no matter where you go, your scent is in this house, and their senses are even more heightened than usual, since they are frequently consuming massive amounts of blood from people.

They will find you. I could smell you the second I walk into this house, and I only drink from my samples just as much as I'm sure Damien does. You're in danger being here." he stopped talking to me and looked over to Damien to say, "yes, I will promise you that I will do that if they find us. I'll get her, and we'll go, and I'll do my best to keep her safe."

Damien nodded and said, "Okay, then we have a deal. You can stay here for a while.

Until they either calm down and stop hunting everyone down or somebody takes them down instead.

Just whenever they stop and things go back to being more safe for the time being, but the day everything goes back to being somewhat safer, you're gone, okay? No more Casa de Damien after that for you, got it?" Daniel paused for a second.

"Yeah, I got it. Trust me, I don't want to be here any longer than I have to be."

And with that being said, Damien went and grabbed him a blanket and a pillow from the hallway closet, and we went our separate ways for the night.

In this moment, I didn't feel that I had much of a choice or very many options other than to just accept any help or protection I was offered.

I guess they might be kind of right. That I might be in slightly more danger compared to them just being killed off quickly.

They may have to worry about being killed in general from these people but for me there's a high chance that it would be a much more drawn-out and torturous situation before they would even end up killing me.

Which also means that Damien has more to worry about as well, since he has to worry about me.

We all decided to go to bed, and I locked my door just in case since I'm not very familiar with Daniel.

Damien and I we're worried about moving too fast since we've both been through so much that we decided that we're not going to sleep in the same bed on a regular basis we're just going to sleep in our own beds, especially while Daniel is here, and every once in a while, maybe sleep in the same bed if the situation is like last night where we feel like we're almost magnetized.

Drawn to each other and can't escape the feeling.

Chapter 14

A week passes by with nothing out of the ordinary happening. Other than celebrating my birthday.

Every once in a while, Damien and Daniel argue, Damien threatens to kick Daniel out and leave him for the wolves but inevitably lets him back in.

It's almost amusing watching them together. Like watching two siblings who fight and argue all the time but you can see that at the end of the day, they do actually care about each other.

We all started to make it a habit to eat breakfast and dinner together in the living room, and it was nice. It started to feel like we all were creating this little family together that all of us lacked due to one reason or another.

In a weird way, it was comforting. We had really started to think that nothing was going to happen at this point, and Daniel was thinking of heading home in a day or two.

So we relaxed some, and Damien surprised me with a cake and said, "Happy birthday, Hayven!"

Daniel looked confused and asked, "Wait a second, it's your birthday today? Why didn't you tell me?"

I looked at him a little surprised, "Well, I didn't think much of it, to be honest. I didn't think we were going to get to do anything for it since we've all been so on guard lately."

Daniel got up and left the house without saying a word. "Why did he just leave like that?" I asked Damien.

"I'm not sure, honestly. Maybe he feels bad that he didn't know that today was your birthday. I wasn't trying to make him feel bad or anything." Damien replied, looking like he also felt guilty because he made Daniel feel guilty.

"Anyways, i'm sure he will be back in a little while. let's just enjoy a little alone time and eat some of this cake together." Damien said with a smile.

I nodded and said, "Yes, that sounds great. Let's save Daniel a special piece, though, too." Damien nodded.

He told me to wait there for a moment and then went to the kitchen. He walked back out with three plates, a knife, two forks, and a little box. He handed me the box and put everything else on the coffee table next to the couch.

"So, I actually got this before all this crazy stuff started happening. I remembered you looked just a little bit longer at it when we walked by it at the store once. So go ahead and open it." he said, sitting down next to me.

I opened the box to find a beautiful crystal opal necklace inside. I got a huge smile on my face and leaned forward to hug Damien tightly, "Thank you! I absolutely love it. It's so beautiful!" I said while still hugging him.

"Perfectly fit for you then, isn't it?" Damien asked rhetorically. I pulled away from him just enough to look at his face and said, "I love you, Damien."

He smiled and replied," I love you too, Hayven." As he leaned down and kissed my lips softly.

I turned around and asked, "Will you please help me put it on right now?" Damien chuckled and said, "Of course."

As he grabbed the necklace and helped me clasp the back together. I turned around, touching it lightly.

"It looks amazing on you." he said. We dished out a piece of cake for us both and put an extra piece on the third plate and put the rest away to have later. Then we put on a movie and just cuddled on the couch together.

A few hours later, Damien had decided to go to bed, so I kissed him good night.

I wasn't going to be able to sleep until Daniel got back, and I knew that he was okay, so I didn't bother even trying to go to sleep.

I stayed in the living room watching tv for a while, then changed into a comfortable t-shirt and leggings for bed, and then decided to snack on another small piece of cake in the kitchen.

I was beginning to feel exhausted at this point because it was going on 11pm. Normally, I'm passed out by 10 pm at the latest, and we all usually wake up pretty early.

Finally, I heard a key unlocking the front door, and I watched as it opened, peeking out from the kitchen just in case it wasn't Daniel.

Daniel walked in with a bag and noticed me peeking around the corner.

"Hey, you're still awake?" he asked me, looking a little surprised.

"Well, yeah. Of course I am. You stormed out of the house upset earlier and were gone a really long time. You didn't reply to any of mine or Damiens texts either, so I wasn't going to be able to sleep until I knew you were okay." I replied.

A look of surprise crossed his face for a moment, and then I walked over to the counter to finish my little piece of cake, and Daniel followed me in there and sat down next to me. He put the bag on the counter.

"We also saved you special piece of cake from when we cut it, just in case you wanted some." I said.

"Hey, um. I'm sorry for storming out on your birthday and making you have to stay up late and worry. I just, I felt so bad that I didn't even know it was your birthday today.

So I rushed out to go and try to find you a present. I didn't even realize either of you had texted me or anything until I was almost home and then figured I might as well not reply because you'd both be in bed by now."

he said, sounding even more guilty that he missed my birthday by being gone and then because I stayed up to make sure he was okay.

He grabbed the bag and pushed it over to me.

"You really got me a present?" I asked, confused, since I wasn't expecting anything in the slightest.

"Yes, absolutely. It's nothing much, but I didn't really know what kind of stuff you liked a lot anyways so I just got what I thought I'd like if I was a girl." he answered.

I laughed with a smile across my face and slowly reached into the bag. There was a small puppy stuffed animal, a couple of different types of candy, and a small scented candle. Three reciepts fell out with the candle, and he grabbed them quickly.

"Wait, how many stores did you go to?" I asked him.

"I think it was about seven. The first two I didn't see anything I thought you might like, the third one had stuffed animals so I got you that one, the fourth one had a couple candles but they all smelled horrible, the fifth one was specifically a candle store so I was able to find that one, the sixth one was closing before I could find what I was looking for, and the last one is where I got the candy." he said in a nonchalant way.

My eyes grew wide, and I replied, shocked, "You went to seven different stores just to find me a couple of presents? Why would you go to so many stores, Daniel? I didn't expect you to get me anything, I would've been happy with anything at all."

"Well, I dont really know how this whole birthday stuff or getting presents really works, and I think you're a really cool person, and I wanted to find you something special. You're my friend, so I didn't think going to a few different stores was that big of a deal." he replied.

I smiled at him and said, "It's just surprising that you went through all that effort just for me. Thank you, though. I love what you got me, and i'm very happy. You see me as your friend?"

he smiled back and said, "Yeah, you're quite possibly my best friend and my only friend. I don't think Damien really likes me very much still, and I don't have any friends aside from you two.

You're just always so nice to me, and don't treat me like some kind of weirdo or jerk or monster." I looked at him for a moment.

"Damien likes you, and he's your friend too. He just has a bit of a short fuse with you when you say certain things, but we're both happy to be your friend." I chuckled out.

Daniel smiled and thanked me for being honest and for being his friend, and I decided to finally go to bed now that I knew he was okay.

I sat my stuff down on top of my dresser and took off my necklace and layed it next to everything else so it wouldn't get broken while I was asleep.

The second I layed in bed and closed my eye, I fell straight asleep. That night, maybe around two hours later at most, I woke up to a loud noise coming from somewhere in the house.

It was almost completely dark in my room, the only light coming in through my window from the moon shining down. Even with the moonlight, though, it was hard to see anything.

More loud thuds and crashing noises began to erupt somewhere in the house that I couldn't quite pinpoint.

Suddenly, my door quickly opened up and then very quietly closed back behind someone who was silently tip toeing in.

My heart stopped, and I froze in fear for a moment, unable to see who it was and unsure what I should do. I was still so tired that I could barely comprehend everything that was happening.

The figure walked over to my bed fast and quiet and whispered, "Hayven, get out of bed, I think they're here, and we need to hide."

I recognized the voice, and my eyes started to adjust to the darkness with him being so close to me now, it's Daniel.

He grabbed my arm, pulling me out of bed and through my blanket back up on my bed, making it look like no one had slept in it tonight.

"Hurry, get under the bed and hide," Daniel whispered as he followed me underneath the bed to hide, too.

"What about Damien? What is all that noise?" I said as quietly as my voice would allow through the fear and worry of what might be happening.

"Damien will be okay, I think it's those guys. It sounded like they found a way in through Damien's room or somewhere on that side of the house, and It sounded like Damien was fighting them. I wasn't sure how much time I would have, so I just came straight in here to try to make sure you're safe."

The door to my bedroom swung open, and a light someone had turned on in the living room now flooded my bedroom.

We could see what looks like six separate sets of shoes plus Damien standing their bare foot.

"We can smell that someone human was or is here. It's almost like a fresh tray of cookies was just baked and filled the house with its scent. Where are they?" One of the men asked.

"I don't know what you're talking about. There's no one else here." Damien choked out.

My blanket hung down, helping cover our hiding spot. I could just barely peek out of the small gap between the bottom of the blanket and the floor, but I leaned my head down to try to get a better view of what was happening exactly.

Three of the men were holding Damien, one had a hand around his neck, and the other two held his arms as they all stood at my doorway.

All of their faces twisted to somehow look completely non-human. The man that was talking held what looked like a long silver dagger.

"This room smells the most like a human so far that we've been in, and there's no way it would smell like this if no one was here.

Someone is either here now or they were here within the past hour. If you keep lying to me, then I'm just going to shove this in your heart and find them without your help." The man said while chuckling.

"Okay, fine, someone was here a while ago, but it was just a delivery man who had the wrong address." Damien replied.

"Okay, fine, I guess we will just have to do this the hard way. I know you're still lying. Why would you risk your life to try to save the life of a delivery man who had the wrong address?

Answer, you wouldn't. It's just another lie. Not to mention, I can see items around the room that look like they belong to a girl.

I want to taste the sweet blood of whoever this smell belongs to, and you're wasting my time, so i'm just going to kill you and get it over with." The man said as he started to walk over towards Damien.

"No, okay, listen, man, you don't have to do this. I know you're upset and mad, but what's killing me going to fix?" Damien pleaded.

The man laughed meniacly, "Simple answer my soon to be dead friend. It probably won't fix anything, but it makes me feel better because if all of you are dead, then there will be no one around to stop us from doing what we want.

Killing all of your loved ones is just a fun bonus, so I'm going to shove this in your heart and watch you die with the look of pain and panic written on your face."

I can't take it anymore. This man is going to kill Damien, and I can't just sit back and let it happen so that I'm safe, if I even would end up being safe in the end anyway.

I rolled out from under the bed before Daniel could grab me and stood to my feet.

"No, don't kill him, please! I'm here, I'm right here. He was just trying to protect me. Please." I begged,

"If I let you drink my blood without fighting, will you let him go? You said you wanted to taste the blood that the scent belongs to. That's me. I won't fight you if you just let him go."

CHAPTER 15

All the men laughed as the one man with the dagger started to walk over to me.

Damien shouted, "No! No! If any one of you lays a single finger on her in any way, then I will kill you. Don't you dare touch her!"

They started to laugh more hysterically. The man walked behind me, brushing my hair to one side.

The man leaned down to my ear from behind me and said, "Okay. You seem fun, so maybe I will think about it. First, though, I need you to answer something honestly for me. Otherwise, I'm going to kill him right here, right now in front of you."

I nodded in agreement, and he continued.

"I noticed there was a blanket and pillow on the couch out there. Is there anyone else here? Answer truthfully." He smiled at me menacingly at me.

"No. There's no one else here. I fell asleep out there and had woken up just as I heard noises in the house, so I ran in here to hide.

That's why my bed is still made. I just forgot to grab the blanket and pillow and put them up." I said, sounding as convincing as I possibly could and trying not to hesitate in my words.

I couldn't give away that Daniel is here. All I can do is hope that they dont find out about him. Otherwise, they'll kill Damien.

"Fair enough. I believe you." He said in reply.

"Take him out there. Away from this room." He continued.

Damien started to kick and fight them.

"Don't touch her! Just leave her out of this! You're here for me, so just do what you're going to do and leave her alone!"

Damien shouted as he kicked one of the other guys in the face so hard that his head was thrown back into the wall, and he fell the ground unconscious.

The other four men had to drag him across the house in a direction that I couldn't see anymore.

The man with the dagger pulled me to sit in front of him at the bottom of my bed. He was significantly taller than me, so the angle worked out for him to be able to lean down to my neck.

"Remember, if you don't fight me, then I will think about letting him live. If you do fight me, though, then I will do what I want anyway and kill you both."

He said as he brushed a few remaining strands of hair to the other side of my neck. I was wearing a t-shirt, so he had to pull it down away from my neck, and then he leaned down and pierced my skin with his teeth as he started to drink my blood.

I couldn't help but let out a whimpered cry from the pain that was made even more excruciating because he was so aggressive.

It was as if he never knew what the word "gentle" even was. He held his arm across my upper chest to keep me steady, and blood started to pour past his lips, soaking my shirt and dripping down to my elbow.

It began to puddle on the floor by my feet. I could still hear Damien on the other side of the house trying to fight the remaining four men who were keeping him away from here,

and I could feel myself slowly starting to get faint. Darkness is beginning to fade inward from my peripheral vision.

I felt his face pull back away from me, and then his body went limp with a crack noise, and I had no strength, so I began to fall forward, but Daniel caught me.

"It's going to be okay Hayven, it's going to be okay." He began repeating over and over, almost to reassure himself as he picked me up and laid me in my bed.

He grabbed the dagger that fell out of the main guys hand and stabbed him in the heart and then stabbed the other unconscious guy in the heart.

He suddenly noticed that my blood was completely covering his hand. He stared at it for a moment and didn't realize that I was still conscious and watching what he was doing.

He tasted the blood from his hand as if he couldn't control himself. It looked as if his thirst had just been quenched after a month without water.

He pulled his hand away from his mouth, looking pained and wiping the blood on his pants, and then he ran out with the dagger to help Damien. I could hear the fight that ensued.

Daniel's pov.

"Damn it." I thought to myself. She's going to get herself killed, offering herself like that. She rolled out before I even had the chance to grab her.

I can't believe she didn't give me up to them, even with the threat of killing Damien. Damiens is going to kill me for sure, though.

I watched and listened as they took Damien away, the thud of the body that hit the floor, and I watched as the main guy walked over to the bed and Hayven followed, sitting what looked to be right in front of him.

I could see her legs tense up as he bit her and could tell he was rough with drinking her blood, making it even more painful for her than it should've been.

I hear her crying, her letting out pained whimpers that she's trying to keep quiet.

She may be risking her life, but she's buying everyone a little more time to figure out a way out of this.

I wish I could reach out and touch her leg, just to let her know that I'm here and that I'm trying to figure out what to do to help, but I didnt want to give my hiding spot away before I could think of what to do.

Ever since I started staying here, she's the only one who looks at me like I'm really still a person.

Even Damien hates himself being a vampire so much that I think he projects that on every other one, too, whether they're good or bad.

So I feel like if I can only save one, it has to be Hayven, but if I dont at least try to save Damien then I don't think I could forgive myself and I know that she could never forgive me either.

I was jolted out of my thoughts by the smell of her blood getting stronger as it started to puddle on the floor. It smelled so sweet, and I found myself starting to crave it. It's almost like a drug.

I suddenly got the idea that while he's distracted, I can sneak out from under the bed and snap his neck.

I slowly crawled out from underneath the bed, and as quietly and quickly as I could, I reached my hand around his head, pulled him away from Hayven, and twisted it as hard as I could.

Hayven looked like she couldn't support the weight of her own body anymore due to the amount of blood shes lost.

It looks like he was just going to keep drinking until there was nothing left to drink.

I managed to catch her before she fell on the ground and looked at her face, and at all the blood, I started to worry.

"It's going to be okay Hayven, its going to be okay." I started to repeat out loud, trying to reassure her, but really, trying to reassure myself.

It looked like she was only seconds from passing out, so I doubt it would even matter what I say at this point.

I used my hand to put pressure on her neck to help the bleeding stop for a moment, and then I felt the anger swell up inside of me.

I turned around to pick up the dagger off the ground and used it to stab both the guy whose neck I snapped and the guy that was unconscious on the floor in the heart.

They were too far gone to be saved, and I wasn't going to risk our lives anymore by letting them stay alive.

All of a sudden, my hand felt cold and wet, so I lifted it up to my face to look at why it felt that way. "It's her blood." I thought to myself.

At that second, I could barely remember how it got covered in her blood to begin with.

The scent of it, once again hitting me, but this time even harder. I couldn't fight the craving anymore, I had to taste it now, or I felt like I might just explode.

So I licked it off my fingers, and I quickly started to feel as if I was high from it. Like a drug I've craved for so long, and finally, after all this time, I was able to get my fix.

I almost wanted to go straight over to Hayven and try it straight from her veins, but I knew that if I did, she would die. Either because she's lost too much blood already, or because I dont think I'd be able to stop.

I snapped back into reality and quickly ran out of the room to find Damien. They had him in another room on the opposite end of the house from Hayvens room. Looked to be just another extra bedroom but not much furniture was in this one.

Damien was fighting two of them while the two other men tried to grab him and hold him.

He really wanted to get away from them, but I dont think it was because he feared for his own life.

No, I think it was because he feared for Hayvens' life. He would really rather die himself than let her die.

I was able to sneak behind the two who were trying to hold him and dagger them both.

Then Damien grabbed one of the last two men, and I grabbed the other, and we both snapped their necks almost simultaneously.

This isn't the first time we have worked together like this. Cindi has sent us on jobs together in the past, which is how we met in the first place.

Damien took the dagger from me and stabbed them both in the heart.

"There, now they can't hurt anyone else ever again." He said sternly.

I nodded to agree with him, beginning to feel a little guilty about tasting his girlfriends blood.

"Is Hayven okay, Daniel?" He asked, "She's okay for now. She lost a lot of blood, and I think she's unconscious now, but she's alive. A little of your special medicines will help her in no time, I'm sure," I answered.

We both ran back to the other room where she was at, and Damien ran straight to her side.

Damien's pov.

I would give my life to make sure she's safe. My life has become significantly better with her in it, and I would die happy knowing that for this short while, I got to love her and know what it's like to be loved back by her.

Everything that we've been through together, getting to actually know her, I felt like that made me content enough with life that if I were to die right now, it would be okay, but I couldnt die not knowing if she was safe, not knowing if she would make it out of all of this.

I tried my hardest to lie and tell them that there was no one else here, but they easily figured out I was lying.

Thank god when we opened her door, she wasn't in bed. Daniel was gone too, so hopefully, I was able to buy them enough time and make enough noise to alert them so they could both get out.

When the man with the dagger started to walk over to me, telling me he would just kill me, I didn't know what else to do except try to reason with him.

Suddenly, I see her roll out from under the bed, and my heart stops.

"No, no, she was safe. They didn't know she was there. Why would she come out?" I asked myself.

I was scared now, wondering what was going to possibly happen.

"If I let you drink my blood without fighting, will you let him go?..." she asked.

"No, Hayven, no!" I screamed in my head. I felt frozen for a minute. She doesn't realize the risk she's really taking.

Aside from the fact that she could die, or they'd still kill me after killing her and countless other things, she doesn't know that certain blood types can become addictive to certain vampires.

Like a drug, it's part of what drives us crazy. Cindi is able to take our blood to see which blood type is like a drug to us, which blood type is more likely to make us sick, and which blood type works for us.

For me, type A positive, type AB positive, type O positive, and type B negative are ones that I can drink without a problem.

Type A negative, AB negative, and B positive would make me possibly get sick like if I ate some bad food, and type O negative would be like a drug to me.

O negative is one of the most common addictive drug like blood types for most vampires. That's one thing me and her dad had studied and experimented with when he was alive.

Everyone is different, so for some, just smelling their addictive blood type can cause them to crave it and even start having withdrawals and seeing hallucinations from not drinking it.

For others, sometimes they can even drink it multiple times before they suddenly notice they're completely addicted to it and can't stop.

We called it the sunshine test, named after the nickname Hayvens dad called her because she has the most addictive blood type, Type O negative.

That's why I wouldn't take her blood even when we were being held captive by those other psycho vampires hell bent on getting back at her dad through us, because I wouldn't have been able to stop.

Every vampire that gets even a taste of her blood, risks them getting addicted and either killing her, or draining her until shes just barely away from death but can stay alive and heal so that they can drain her over and over again.

I snapped back to reality as the man with the dagger started walking over to her and touched her hair.

"No! No! If any one of you lays a single hand on her in any way, then I will kill you. Dont you dare touch her!" I shouted.

I couldn't get out of the grip of the three men that held me, and it infuriated me that they all laughed at what I said.

When he told them to take me away, I lost control of my own body and kicked the guy in front of me, causing his head to slam into the wall, and then he fell to the floor unconscious.

I couldn't let them take me away, and I couldn't let Hayven get hurt, but four guys against one made it a little hard to fight.

I lost sight of her as they dragged me to the other side of the house. I hoped that Daniel would keep his promise to me and help her, since, at this moment, there was nothing I could do but keep fighting and hope that I would be able to get free from them to save her. So I keep fighting.

I smelled the strong scent of her blood filling the house and could only imagine what was happening in her room. I didn't hear her scream or even cry out in pain. I hope she's okay.

Hayven's pov:

I could barely stay conscious. It seemed like I was laying in the bed alone for what felt like decades, completely soaked from my own blood.

I wondered for a moment if I was going to die, and even worse than that, if I was going to die alone, just barely out of reach of the people I care about.

I tried to snap out of those thoughts and just layed there with my eyes closed.

I heard all the noises of fighting suddenly come to a hault, and then moments later, I heard Damien and Daniel run back into the room.

Damien came over to my side. He checked my pulse and made sure I was breathing.

"Damien." I used all my strength to cry out in a whisper. I wasn't sure if any noise had even actually escaped my lips until he rubbed his hand through my hair and said, "I'm here, Hayven, I'm here. I'm not going anywhere. You're safe now."

I could feel the tears I held back just flooding my face now. He picked me up and held my head close to his chest. I couldn't help but to worry about all the blood all over me and now getting all over Damien.

"Daniel, do you think that we can all maybe go stay at your house tonight?" Damien asked.

"Yes, absolutely. Grab whatever you need, and we can go over there right now. Here I will take her to the car. You just grab whatever you guys need."

Damien hesitated for a moment, and I didn't want to leave his side, but I didn't have the energy to say anything or even move.

He agreed and handed me over to Daniel. Daniel tried his best to gently adjust me in his arms and took me out to his car.

He was able to open the back door and halfway climb in with me in his arms so he could lay me down as gently as possible.

He leaned down to my ear and whispered, "I'm sorry I couldn't help you sooner, Hayven. I hate seeing you like this. I'm just, I'm so sorry for so many things."

He moved my hair out of my face and ran his hand across the side of my face as he started to climb back out and go to the driver's set.

A few minutes later, Damien opened up the trunk and set our stuff in there and then climbed in the passenger side seat.

We all drove in silence for a few minutes, and then Daniel struck up a conversation with Damien to try to ease the stress momentarily.

"I'm pretty sure she passed out. Im sure she will be alright, though." He said.

"I grabbed some medicines that should help her out a lot, I'm going to give them to her as soon as we get her settled somewhere in your house." Damien replied.

"I have a guest room that you both can stay in. It's nothing fancy, but it has a queen-size bed, a tv, and a little nightstand and dresser." Daniel said.

There was a momentary pause. "That we both can stay in?" Damien asked.

Daniel chuckled and replied, "Yes, you both can share a room, can't you? You're a couple, aren't you?"

Damien started to chuckle a bit too and said, "Well, yeah, of course. I guess I just hadn't thought about it."

Daniel laughed again at Damiens' response and asked, "Hey, I've been meaning to ask you this but didn't want to ask in front of Hayven. What ever happened to that girl you were completely obsessed with, and in love with that you said you wished things could be different?"

Damien started to laugh again, "You're kind of dense, aren't you? That was Hayven.

It's a long story but things just ended up working out and even though I wish she could have a different life than this, she says shes in love with me too and chose to stay apart of it all, so I'm just trying to keep my promise to her and her dad and keep her safe no matter what.

It's her choice, and I never want to take that away from her. She's already been through so much, in her life, since we met, so I'm just doing my best to give her everything she deserves.

Though I dont think i'm doing a very great job considering she almost died tonight," he ended sadly.

Daniel stayed quiet for a moment and said, "I'm happy things worked out to where you both became a couple.

She's a really amazing person as far as I've seen and you're a really great person too.

She's changed you into a much cooler person than you used to be. I think all things considered, you're doing the best you can."

Damien chuckled at the part of the sentence saying he's a cooler person now and said, "Yeah, man, you have no idea. I used to feel so numb.

I'd drink just to try to feel something, anything. I was alone, mad at what I am, broken from everything I've gone through and all the people I had lost.

At one point, I almost just didn't care if I was going to die. Heck, I almost wished something would happen to put me out of my misery.

My life started to veer back on track one day, when I went to check on her. Everything I saw her go through, losing her dad, losing her best friend, dating assholes, being all alone, I saw her go through it all.

I seen her cry so many times, but that day I went to check on her to make sure she was safe and okay and I seen her heading to the store, she didn't have much so she just barely scraped by every month, but this cat showed up and meowed at her, and the smile that crossed her face was so pure and genuine, like nothing bad had ever happened to her.

She just smiled like it was the easiest thing to do and leaned down to pet it and share some of her food with it.

That was the first day I started to fall in love with her, and that was the first day in so long that I didn't just feel numb. She made me feel again.

I was so sad for so long because staying away from her was just safer for her, but one day something really bad almost happened to her and I had no choice but to help her, and at that point, I didn't feel like I could pull myself away from her anymore.

I couldn't fight it anymore, and every day since then, just being with her has felt like a dream."

"I'm really happy for you, man." Daniel said through a smile.

They both stayed quiet for a couple minutes as the feeling of stress filled the car again, and then I felt the car pull in a driveway and turn off.

Damien went and grabbed our stuff and then came around to pick me up from the back seat and carry me inside.

Daniel held the door open and then led Damien to our room. He laid me down on the bed and started to get into one of the bags, pulling out a couple of different medicines.

He crushed them all and put them in a blue drink. "Hayven. Hayven," he said while trying to sit me up, "You need to drink this. It has medicine to help you."

I pulled my arm up to touch his. It felt like I was lifting a lead block. He helped me drink it and layed me back down and then left for a minute, coming back with a wet warm wash cloth and bowl filled with warm water.

"Hey, is it okay if I take off your shirt? so I can wipe off all the blood and put a clean, dry shirt on you," Damien asked.

"Yes." I whispered out. He shut the door and then gently pulled my shirt off, being careful not to hurt me.

I opened my eyes to see him. His face was covered in bruises, cuts, and different marks from fighting all those guys.

I wanted to hold him in my arms and just stay that way until we were both better, but I couldn't.

He very carefully wiped off all the blood and then bandaged my neck. Then he grabbed one of my shirts out of the bags and helped me put it on.

"Do you want me to sleep on the floor? I don't want to make you uncomfortable or anything." Damien asked.

I used all the strength I had in the moment and reached up to grab his shirt, pulling him towards me to try to let him know that I didn't want him to be anywhere but right next to me, so he climbed in bed next to me and started to run his fingers through my hair.

I felt him kiss my forehead as I finally allowed myself to drift off to sleep.

CHAPTER 16

The next morning, I woke up feeling extremely sore. My whole body ached, but it was much better than it was last night.

"I guess whatever it was that Damien gave me worked pretty well overall." I thought to myself.

I looked around me and saw that Damien wasn't in bed with me anymore.

Trying to sit up, I let out a pain filled groan but managed to still sit up through the pain.

Last night was mostly a blur after Daniel saved me. I remember most of the bigger things, I think.

What Daniel did after he saved me, him saying sorry in the car for something, them talking about me while we were driving, and Damien helping me change my shirt and get cleaned up and giving me that drink medicine.

I don't really remember anything besides that stuff, though, and even those things feel more like a dream than a memory.

If it wasn't for the fact that my body is so sore and were in someone else's house, I might wonder if everything last night actually happened.

I heard a soft knock at the door and heard Daniel on the other side asking if he could come in.

"Yeah, come in." I got out in a slightly strained voice.

He slowly opened the door and walked in with a small plate of food and a drink that looked similar to the one Damien had me drink last night.

"Damien left early this morning to start trying to clean up the house, and he asked if I would give you this medicine drink thing and help you with anything you needed while he's not here, so I told him of course and I wasn't sure what you would need but I thought a little food might be a good idea." He said as he walked over to the side of the bed.

He softly layed the plate on my lap and handed me the drink.

"Am I supposed to drink all of it?" I ask.

Daniel nodded yes but stayed quiet. I drank the medicine drink quickly, and my face showed slight disgust from the taste.

"I don't remember it tasting that bad last night. What's in it?" I asked Daniel.

He shrugged his shoulders and replied, "I'm assuming it's the same stuff he gave you last night. He didn't tell me which medicines he put in it in, though. He just asked if I would give it to you when you wake up. I didn't really question him about anything."

I nodded to show that I heard him. Damien is really good with medicines because that's what him and my dad focused on studying mostly.

I'm not sure what else they studied actually, but I know medicine was one of the bigger things.

Daniel sat there with me while I finished my food, and I thanked him for making it for me.

"Do you want to try to walk around some? Maybe get the medicine working faster and get you some sunlight of something?" He asked as he offered his hand.

I smiled and grabbed his hand, "Yeah, I think that might be nice." I replied.

He helped me get off the bed into a standing position. I could tell the medicine was already beginning to work.

Daniel slowly led me across his house to these beautiful glass double doors that led to his backyard.

He had a smaller yard that was filled with lots of flowers and fruit trees and rose bushes.

"I just enjoy them. It's nice sitting back here and feeling like I'm somewhere else for a little while," he said.

He sat down in a nice wooden patio chair. I smiled at what he said and went to sit down in the other patio chair and enjoy the sun.

Daniels pov:

I thought some sunshine might feel nice on her skin after the night we all had and figured my little garden would be a peaceful and safe spot that she could just relax in.

She got back up and walked over to the rose bushes and examined them closer, and then smiled.

There was something incredibly beautiful about her to me in that moment.

I mean, she's a beautiful girl already, by far one of the prettiest people I've ever seen, but the way she stood there, the way she smiled, in this moment of us both just being here, enjoying the peace, there's something even more beautiful about her.

Maybe it's like that story that Damien told me in the car last night. Even after everything that has happened, she still smiles and laughs.

It almost feels like the whole world gets brighter when she smiles or when she laughs.

It's infectious. Before you know it, you're smiling too or laughing along with her.

Out of nowhere, I began to feel extremely dizzy. I could feel my heart beating harder and could almost hear the blood in my body circulating. That scent that she puts off suddenly was the only thing that I could smell.

"Is it her I'm craving? Is it her blood I'm craving?" I thought to myself.

I knew that I was more likely to become addicted to type O negative blood, but I didn't know it would be just from smelling her blood or from one taste.

I didn't even know that was her blood type until I realized I wasn't able to stop myself from tasting it off of my blood-soaked hand.

Before I even realized it, I had gotten up and went to the chair she was now sitting in once again and was leaning over her.

She looked up at me with her beautiful face, seeming a little confused but also smiling because she wasn't sure what I was doing.

An overwhelming feeling washed over me, and in that moment, all I wanted to do was let myself fall into her.

My body felt like it weighed a ton. Just wanting to give in and kiss her. It was the kind of feeling that could be enough to drive someone insane if they didn't give in.

I closed my eyes for a moment, and when I opened my eyes, we were back to sitting just like we were.

"Was that... a dream? Did any of that really just happen, or did I imagine it?" I thought to myself.

I shook my head to try to snap myself out of my thoughts and stood up to walk back in the house, "I'm going to get us something to drink, I will be right back."

I said to her as I opened the doors and walked inside before she could respond. I felt like I needed to just get away from her. Maybe if I just step away for a minute, I can pull myself together.

Hayven's pov:

"Okay, that seemed a little weird," I thought to myself as Daniel rushed in the house, saying something about drinks.

I decided not to question it much more and try to just relax and enjoy the sun shining down on me.

Warming my skin. I already feel a lot better than I did last night. Of course, I'm going to be pretty sore for a few days, but whatever medicine Damien is giving me is definitely helping me.

I heard a door open and shut from the house and then heard Damien's voice saying something to Daniel, and then he walked in my direction.

He leaned down and kissed my cheek as he gently wrapped his arms around me from behind the chair.

"How are you feeling gorgeous?" He asked in a hushed tone, his breath tickling my ear.

I smiled and reached my hands up to touch his arm and hold one of his hands.

"I'm really sore, feeling very weak and a little tired, but I'm a lot better than I was last night thanks to whatever medicine you've been giving me."

He smiled and said, "That's great! Hopefully, you'll be all better within the next couple of days. "

Then he reached in his back pocket as he continued, "Oh, I grabbed this from the house. I didn't realize we left it, but I was sure you'd want it to keep you a little more entertained."

He pulled out my phone and handed it to me.

"Oh yeah, thank you." I said with a smile and pulled his hand to my lips to kiss it.

I checked my texts and seen a couple replies from ex co workers that I'm still friends with that I had missed and then a text from Jeremiah asking if we could grab some coffee together sometime this week to hang out as friends.

I wasn't quite sure what I should say to let everyone know I'm okay, so I just said I'm sorry and that my phone died after I lost it.

I texted Jeremiah and told him I could try to make plans with him to do that.

"You feel like you're getting a little cold. Do you want to come back inside?" Damien asked me once I finished replying to everyone's texts.

I nodded and replied, "Yeah, it is getting a bit chilly out here now."

He walked around to the front of the chair where I was sitting and started to put one arm around my back and the other arm underneath my legs to carry me.

I started to laugh and said, "Hey, I can walk now, you know."

He smiled back at me and said, "Well, as long as I'm here, you dont ever have to walk if you don't want to. I'd carry you anywhere you wanted me to." He ended in a chuckle.

He carried me over to a leather chair that was sitting in the living room area and sat me down carefully.

Daniel finally finished making us all some tea and brought it out to us and then sat on the main couch across from me.

"Hey man, do you care if we stay another night? I tried to clean up as much of it all as I could, but there's a lot I still need to get to." Damien asked as he sat next to Daniel.

"Yeah, of course. No problem." Daniel said as he took a drink of his tea.

For the next couple of days, we stayed over Daniel's house and then went back home.

Daniel mostly kept his distance for some reason unless I asked him for help with anything.

I also noticed he was even avoiding just looking at me. I wondered if it had to do with the other night but was too worried to bring it up to him.

After another couple of days, I still felt pretty weak and tired, but other than that, most of the soreness had gone away, and the wound itself was almost completely gone.

I'm healing faster than I thought I would be for sure.

Damien has been busy a lot trying to help Doctor Cindi with a couple of different things since we got back home.

I guess he used to work with her a lot when my dad was alive, and then he continued to do some jobs here and there for her.

He kissed me goodbye and told me he would be back in a little while, reminding me to call him if I needed anything.

It was starting to feel a bit lonely here again since he's been so busy and Daniel hasn't been around.

I went to stand up and walk to the kitchen to make something to eat, but suddenly someone knocked on the door.

I walked over and opened the door to see Daniel standing there.

"Daniel! What are you doing here?" I asked excitedly.

He walked in, not looking at me and not smiling.

"Is Damien here?" He asked, glancing around.

My excitement faded, and I started to feel sad instead.

"No, he just left a little while ago to go help Doctor Cindi."

I started to walk over to the kitchen, feeling a little upset and irritated.

"Oh. Do you know when he will be back?" He asked as he followed me.

"Not exactly. He just said he will be back in a little while. If it's important I'm sure you can call him."

I walked over to the sink to wash a couple of dishes that had been left from earlier in an attempt to not let him see that I was getting upset.

He sat at the counter and said, "Yeah. I just need to talk to him in person about a couple of things. By the way... how are you doing?"

I didn't turn around to look at him and just replied, "had better days, but I'm fine. I'm still a little weak and tired, and I still have a little healing to do, but I'm fine."

He stayed silent for a minute, and I could feel him staring at me.

"Can I ask you something?" I asked him as I finally turned around to look at him and leaned my lower back against the sink.

He nodded his head yes and quickly looked down, still not showing much emotion.

"Are you... are you mad at me? Did I do something?" I muttered out, trying not to let my voice crack or show that I was upset, but my voice cracked once anyways causing him to shoot his head up, now looking at my face wide-eyed.

"No, no, no. I'm not mad at you at all. I'm sorry I've been making you think that, or if I've made you feel bad, it's just... it's all a little hard to explain." He replied, looking down into his lap and playing with his fingers at the end of his sentence.

"Does it have anything to do with what happened after you saved me the other night?" I asked.

A worried look crossed his face for a moment before he asked, "What do you mean?"

I took a deep breath and uncrossed my arms, placing them behind me to support my body against the counter.

"Daniel, I saw it when you tasted my blood off of your hand, and I was awake to hear your apology in the car that night." I replied.

A look of shock and worry crossed his face, and he looked at me wide-eyed again. For a moment, he seemed speechless.

"You seen that? Why didn't you say anything? Does Damien know?" He poured out of him and continued to say,

"I'm so sorry, Hayven. I shouldn't have given in to the temptation, and I especially never should've tried yours.

I shouldn't have let that even be a thought in that moment when you were almost killed, and Damien was in the other room with four other guys trying to fight them off and not get killed. I -"

I walked over to him, sitting in the seat next to him, and lightly touched him arm as I cut him off to say, "Hey, hey. Enough. Calm down, okay? I forgive you."

I saw the tenseness in his shoulder leave, looking like his body just got ten times lighter.

"I didn't say anything because even though I wasn't comfortable with what you did, all things considered, I didn't really think it mattered. You saved me.

You helped save Damien. If it weren't for you, I might be dead right now. We all might've been dead now if it weren't for you, and no, I didn't tell Damien because, again, with all things considered, I didn't think it really mattered." I said, now feeling a little confused about why he is as upset as he is about everything.

"Have you heard of blood addictions?" He asked while looking back up at my face.

I shook my head and said, "No, what is that exactly?"

He shook his head, looking a little bit tense again. "You should ask Damien later. That's definitely more of his expertise, but definitely ask him about it." He muttered.

I nodded in reply and asked, "So, you're not mad at me, though? We're still friends?"

He smiled at me and said, "No, I'm not mad at you at all, and yes, we're most definitely still friends. It's a lot to explain, but I'm just going through something right now."

I looked at him in silence for a moment and then said, "Well, I'm always here for you."

I stood up and walked back over to the counter by the sink so I could grab two cups out of the cupboard and get us both some coffee.

Daniel's pov:

I felt relieved that she forgave me. I didn't know that she had even seen me do what I did, and I thought for sure that if she knew, she would hate me forever and want nothing to do with me ever again.

I don't think she knows the full extent of what she's actually forgiving me for though, since she doesn't know about blood addictions, but hopefully, it won't make much of a difference to her. I never want to do anything to hurt her.

Out of nowhere, I started to feel dizzy. It's been happening a lot lately, and I've been hallucinating a lot.

She's always in my hallucinations even when I'm alone, so it's hard to tell now if I'm hallucinating or not, because she is here with me this time.

I started to smell the scent she put off, craving her once again. So strongly that I can hardly hold myself away from her. I want to taste her blood again, I want to kiss her.

This craving pulls me in so many different directions, and I can hardly stand the feeling anymore.

It's beginning to drive me insane. Before I even realized what I'm doing I get up and walk over to where she's standing, with the lower part of her stomach lightly pressed against the counter top while she makes both of us some coffee.

My body felt like a ton lead bricks as I placed my hands on the countertop on both sides of her.

She jumped slightly, and air caught in her throat, making this quiet gasping noise, not realizing I was so close to her.

She turned her body around to face me as she leaned closer to the counter.

She's much shorter than me, so with her leaning back on the counter and me leaning against the counter top in front of her, my head comes down to be only inches from her face and neck.

I tried to not look in her direction because being this close to her, smelling her vanilla perfume, her rose scented shampoo, and her natural scent, plus this overwhelming feeling that has been taunting me for days now, over and over and over and over, is all temptation enough.

Looking at her feels like it would be the last straw, the one thing that would finally push me over the edge to give in, and I don't want to do that. Especially if all of this is real, and not just another hallucination.

"What are you doing, Daniel? Are you okay?" She whispered out.

Her breath tickled my skin as she whispered, "Hayven, damn it." I whispered.

I pulled my head back to look at her face. "God, she's beautiful." I thought to myself. I couldn't stop myself anymore.

"I cant take this anymore, I need to know what you taste like, I want to taste your blood again and I want to taste your lips as I feel what it's like to have them pressed against mine, what it feels like to hold you close to me. I can't take this feeling anymore. It's driving me insane." I said to her,

and before she could say anything, I wrapped one arm around her waist and placed my other hand on her face, and leaned in to kiss her.

I couldn't help but kiss her roughly and desperately, and she kissed me back.

I've never been closer to heaven than in this moment, standing here, kissing her like it's the only time I will ever get to.

"God, I think I'm in love with her," I thought to myself as my kissing became even more rough and desperate.

Part of me is begging that it is real life and the other part of me hoping it is all just another hallucination because I don't want Damien to be hurt. I truly can't tell anymore whether or not I'm hallucinating.

Before I knew it, I was sitting my head up off of the island counter where I was sitting before and see Hayven is still standing over at the counter by the sink finishing up the coffees she was making us both.

I felt my heart sink into my stomach, both from the realization that it was all a hallucination after all, making me feel sad and relieved at the same time.

I couldn't believe that I did what I did in the hallucination, but I should have known it wasn't real because Hayven would never kiss me back.

She cares about me, but she's in love with Damien and would never kiss me back.

I don't seem to have any control at all when those feelings start to overwhelm me.

"Um, hey Hayven, I'm so sorry, something just came up, and I have to leave right now. Can I rain check having coffee together? I will text you later, I swear, I'm sorry." I said as I got up, pretending to look at my phone.

I don't think staying here with her alone and sitting next to each other drinking coffee is a very good idea when I can't seem to tell what's a hallucination and what's real life anymore.

I think I'm going to have to come clean to Damien after all before I do something else stupid.

CHAPTER 17

A few hours later, I was woken up to a gentle body climbing onto the couch with me and cuddling up next to me.

I open my eyes to confirm who I think it is next to me, holding me close.

"Sorry, I didn't mean to wake you up." Damien chuckled shyly.

"Hey there. No, it's okay. I'm happy you're home. I missed you." I said as I smiled sincerely.

Damien smiled back at me as my words processed in his mind. "I missed you too. I'm sorry I was gone for so long today." He replied.

"what time is it?" I ask. Damien pulled his phone out of his pocket to check the clock.

"hmm. 8:20pm." He answered.

My eyes widened slightly in surprise, not realizing it was already so late.

"Oh it is getting kind of late. It's okay though, did you have a nice day working with Cindi?" I asked as we both simply layed on the couch holding each other close.

"Yeah, it was good. Pretty typical day. Nothing crazy happened, which was nice. Did you have a good day, beautiful?" he replied as he struggled to reach past me to put his phone on the table and fell back into cuddling me after using the extra effort to put his phone there.

I giggled at the unnecessary effort he exerted when he could've put his phone back in his pocket.

Damien smiled with his eyes still closed, laying his head on my chest, realizing what I was giggling about,

"What? It was uncomfortable in my pocket." He said.

I continued to giggle and said, "My day was good. I was looking at some colleges around here and thinking of getting my degree in something. I'm kind of tired of these jobs I've been doing and think it's time I figure out a career path. What do you think about that?"

he leaned up enough to look me in my eyes and said, "Well, if that's what you want to do then I think it's a great idea and I will support you with whatever you choose. What are you thinking of getting your degree in?"

I paused to think for a moment, "I'm not really sure yet, honestly. I'm still looking at my options, but I know I want to do something more than what i'm doing at these jobs I've been doing for so long."

Damien nodded his head and said, "I support you, we can take a trip to the colleges when you figure out what you would enjoy studying."

I smiled, feeling content with everything he had to say. His phone lit up and buzzed on the table suddenly.

He let out a deep sigh as he let his body go limp next to me, thinking about the wasted effort he exerted to put it there.

"Can you please hand me my phone?" he said with a defeated laugh. I grabbed it and handed it to him. Turning it on in front of me, it was a text from Daniel that read,

"Hey man, I really need to talk with you about something important. It has to be in person... so... yeah, please, if you could meet up with me tomorrow or something. Without Hayven.."

That reminded me, Daniel told me to ask Damien about blood addictions.

"Hey, um. What is a blood addiction?" I asked hesitatingly. Damien got a shocked look on his face, dropping his attention on his phone and returning it to me.

"What do you mean? Where did you hear about that?" he asked almost defensively.

I sat up and moved towards the opposite side of the couch, feeling like I asked a question I shouldn't have asked.

"I just heard about it. What is it?" I continued to ask.

Damien sat up, too, looking confused. He sighed, realizing he was going to have to explain it to me now that I've asked about it.

"it's, well, an addiction to blood. Every vampire has a specific blood type or even multiple that do one of three things, either cures your hunger and sustains you, makes you sick, or is like a drug that you can't get enough of." He replied.

"How do you find out which is which? Is there a way to know?" I ask.

He looked somewhat worried as our conversation continued. "Yes, usually we can take a blood test and find out that way.

Depending on how the antibodies from their blood react to the different blood types, if the antibodies continue to react normally, then that's the blood type that will cure their hunger.

If the antibodies start going crazy and attacking the other cells, then that's the blood type that will make them sick.

If the antibodies begin to rapidly multiple, well that's the blood type that's addictive to them. That comes along with a lot of other issues.

Overall It is different for everyone but for some they can become addicted to the one they're weakest towards by Just smelling that blood type, some have to taste it, and some can even drink it for a while before realizing they're all of a sudden addicted."

I thought for a moment and remember every time someone drank my blood and how he reacted when I offered him to drink it.

"What blood type are you weakest towards?" I ask, assuming I already know the answer.

He looked at me for a moment before saying, "yours, type O negative." He paused for a moment, seeming worried and then continued, "O negative is actually one of the most common ones to be addictive.

Considering the fact that it's also the most rare blood type to have, Im sure you can imagine the extra dangers that come along with that."

A look of shock must've crossed my face because he scooted closer towards me and started to say,

"I promise though Hayven, its not a problem for me. That has no effect on our relationship, and there's things we could do if it ever happened, which it never will."

He waited for me to respond, looking nervous.

"Are you sure?" I asked, feeling worried.

"Yes, absolutely. I would never let myself hurt you or anything. I would rather die than hurt you, Hayven." He replied.

I nodded, feeling myself relax as I let myself trust his words.

"why didn't you tell me before?" I asked.

"I was scared to tell you. I had that moment before where I almost gave in, and then you offered, and it took everything in me to tell you no. After that, I was afraid that you would be scared of me again or think I only love you because of something to do with that."

I understand why he would worry about that.

"I love you, and I know you love me too." I replied.

He looked relieved and smiled at me. "With everything that I am." He said, continuing to smile.

He moved all the way over to me and softly tilted my head up to look at him.

"I never want to go back to a time where I don't know you. Where I can't love you, or you don't love me. I worry every single day that you'll realize that i'm not worthy of your love.

You are truly the greatest thing to ever happen to me and the greatest that could ever happen. I am so in love with you."

I sat up more to give him a kiss. Damien slowly leans back, not breaking our kiss that soon enough turns into us making out while I sit on top of him with one leg on each side of his body near his hips.

As we continue to make out, he puts one of his hands on the back of my head, with my hair intertwining with his fingers, and he places his other hand on my waist.

Each kiss gets more passionate and intense as time goes on. His touch starts to send a tingling sensation through my whole body.

He suddenly grabs me and softly pins me to the opposite side of the couch, where a pillow behind me keeps me in an almost sitting up position.

With both hands holding mine, he starts to kiss my neck softly. Every touch, every kiss beginning to engulf me in this feeling of pleasure.

We start to undress each other in between each touch and kiss as we move to his bedroom, with soft moans escaping our lips and our breathing becoming erratic.

Pleasures over taking our whole being and feeling like we are connected on such a deep level that we can read each others every sound, every movement, every breath.

Afterward, we lay together still undressed under the covers, with my head on his chest and his arm wrapping around my upper back.

He continued to kiss my hand, my head, and every inch of skin he could reach from his current position.

"That was incredible." I said to him as I looked up to make eye contact.

He looked down at me to meet my gaze and smiled, "Yes, it was amazing. You're amazing." He replied as he leaned down to kiss me on my lips once again.

Damien is my first. But he was so gentle, patient, loving, and affectionate. It was easy to get lost in the pleasure.

We both got dressed in pajamas and got back in bed together.

I've told him before that I've never been with anyone else in that kind of way, and how my exes were towards me on that topic.

Needless to say, all my exes are exes for a reason.

"Hey, I have a question." I asked as I rolled over to face him.

"oh no, all your questions make me nervous, Hayven." He said with a nervous laugh and continued, "but what's your question?"

I smiled as I realized that seemed to be a true statement.

"well, I was wondering, how many people have you been with before me? Like, in the way that we were together tonight, I mean." I ask.

"oh, like how many people have I slept with?" he asked for clarification.

I nod my head yes and wait for him to continue.

"Well, to be honest, I don't really have a straight answer." A puzzled look struck my expression.

"It's kind of a long story, but after your dad died, I felt like I had no one else on this entire planet.

I felt alone, resentful, I hated myself for far more reasons than one, and even when there were a few people still around like Daniel and Cindi, I still felt like my existence to them didn't really matter.

That if I were to die, what would it matter to them. I hated what I am, I still do. So there was a long period of time after he died that I just kind of gave up.

I drank until I'd pass out or black out, I felt numb and would do anything to just feel anything but the numbness.

I'd go to bars just to meet women and sleep with whoever would come home with me.

It wasn't the same as what it was with you by any means, with them it was just to feel anything and usually, more often than not, just felt more empty, even more worthless, and I hated myself more and more, and at the time I guess that's what I wanted.

If I didn't do things to make me feel more negative emotions, then I found myself unable to feel anything at all. Nothing but feeling numb inside and out.

That's actually how I ended up meeting Daniel, and I helped him kill a few dangerous people.

I didn't even care at the time that I killed anyone. I almost hoped that one of those people would manage to kill me instead of me killing them.

With you, though, I wanted to take that step with you because you already make me feel things, so many amazing things.

Ever since I fell in love with you, I stopped feeling numb. I've never felt more deeply than when you came into my life.

Part of that time, I don't even remember because I spent so much of it blacked out drunk." He paused for a moment, waiting for me to process the information and respond.

"You killed people? Who did you kill?" I asked, feeling most surprised by that part of his story.

His expression showed disappointment and regret as he didn't say anything for a minute.

"We can just talk about this later if you want, I don't want to make you feel uncomfortable or feel like you're forced to tell me." I said.

"No, no. I need to tell you. It's something that I will have to eventually tell you either way, and if you're going to choose to love me, then I want you to know who it is you're in love with.

I'm not just this hero who has saved you or some perfect person in the slightest. I've done a lot of things I regret.

I've hurt people and killed people. Usually, only people that have put you in danger, myself in danger, or that Cindi needed help handling, but there was a time that I let myself hurt regular people.

Cindi almost kicked me from the program and sent Daniel after me. Thankfully, at the time, Daniel knew my story with your dad and the promise I had made to him to protect you.

I almost killed him that day without a care in the world, but he was able to talk me into going to check on you at least one last time if I was so committed to be on a suicide mission and go from there.

So that's what I did, and that just so happened to be the day I fell in love with you.

I couldn't understand at first how both of us could live our lives, both struggling, both surrounded by the death of those we love most, both unsure of how we're making it day to and feeling like we were in this revolving door of awfulness,

and yet, I was over here feeling worthless, on a suicide mission, didn't care if I died or who I hurt, and you were there, still shining so bright, smiling.

Seeing the goodness in life that remained. It was almost like we were both stranded on the same island, and while I was focused on the ocean around us being undrinkable water and us having no way to get out of there,

you were finding fruit baring plants that grew endlessly on the island and could sustain us both until the day that we die.

It changed everything for me. It was the most beautiful thing I've seen, and I fell in love with you instantly.

After that day I cleaned up my act, Cindi gave me another chance for the sake of your dad and how highly he spoke about me when he was alive and I started working for her and working with Daniel.

Despite me being endlessly irritated by him, I guess I kind of owe him for my life in the end. I owe him for everything. I really hope that none of that changes your opinion about me, though." He explained.

"No, it didn't change my opinion. Who you were during your darkest times doesn't change who you are all the time.

It doesn't change the fact that you do care, that you've saved me multiple times now, and everything good you've done.

Your mistakes of the past don't define who you are today. That's why they're in the past. They've passed. The choices you make now are what define you as a person.

Overall, I think you're doing really great, and my dad seemed to think so, too. Two years of mistakes in your life doesn't erase the good in you." I replied.

He rolled over to hug me tighter, holding his head to the side of mine where I couldn't see his face.

"I don't deserve an angel like you as my girlfriend. I will never know what I could've possibly done in this lifetime to get the chance to have you love me. I love you so much." He says in a whisper.

I hugged him tightly back and replied, "I'm the lucky one, and I love you so much too."

We layed there silently just holding each other until we both fell into a deep sleep.

The next morning, Damien made breakfast and woke me up so we could eat together before he had to go help Cindi again.

"At this point, I'm pretty sure I'm just working for her full time again." He said with a laugh.

"but I don't think I will be there for very long today. oh, and Daniel wanted to meet today and talk about something important he said, so I was going to invite him over after I get home." I nodded, acknowledging that I had no objections to his plans.

CHAPTER 18

A few hours later, I heard a knock at the door, so I went to answer it.

"Daniel, hey, you don't look so well, are you okay?" I asked as I saw Daniel standing there, looking like he might be getting sick.

"Yeah i'm fine. I'm just here to talk to Damien." He said as he walked past me and sat on the couch waiting impatiently.

"Okay, well he's not back home yet. He should be back pretty soon, though." I walked over and sat next to him. He looked uncomfortable even being in the same room with me.

His eyes look bloodshot, and he looks like he's been sick for a few days. Heavy bags under his eyes and that tired appearance to his face. Which made me feel worried, but I decided not to bring it up.

"I... asked about blood addictions. Is that what happened to you? Or what is happening to you?" I asked.

He sat there silent, not responding to me, not even looking my direction.

"Okay... I was wondering, how did you end up becoming a vampire?" I ask.

He gave me a quick side eye look and didn't say anything for a moment.

"When I was 17, I had a girlfriend. She was one year older than me, and she was my first love.

We dated for a year, and one day, she confessed to me that she was a vampire.

At the time, I thought vampires weren't real, and I wasn't sure how I was supposed to react.

One day she was over my house and she sked if I wanted to become a vampire too and I told her I wasn't interested in anything like that, so instead of accepting that answer, she put some sleeping pills in my food.

So much that I came close to overdosing on them. While I was unconscious, she drank almost all of the blood in my body, and force fed me almost every last ounce of her blood.

Come to find out, she took off when she realized I wasn't waking up, and I didn't come to until the excruciating pain hit.

The antibodies from her blood were attacking the natural antibodies my body made until only hers remained, and her vampire D.N.A embedded itself into mine.

It was awful and lasted about a month, I think, before the pain finally began to settle.

When I woke up, I also discovered that she had murdered my whole family as well, and made it look like I did it so that the cops couldn't be called on her once we were all found dead.

She killed my family, turned me into a vampire, and left me to die and go through it all by myself. She ended up having a new boyfriend pretty soon after she thought I was dead also.

So I took every bit of money my family ever saved up, and one day, I went to the library and did some research on vampires, and that's actually how I ended up finding Cindis contact information.

She took me in and made me feel like I was a part of the family. She helped me learn more, helped me get through a lot of the pain that still remained within me, and she gave me a job working with her." He explained.

My heart began to hurt thinking of all the pain he had endured. "I'm so sorry you had to go through all that, Daniel." I replied as I reached my hand up and gently placed it on his back.

He jumped up when I touched him and walked over to a nearby chair to sit instead.

"it was five years ago. I'm past it all now." He replied, trying to hide the real sadness he still showed through his expression over it all.

Our talking was suddenly interrupted by keys unlocking the front door and Damien walking in.

"Oh hey Daniel, you got here sooner than I expected you too. I have to go through some paperwork and do a few things in my office, but then we can talk.

Do you mind waiting?" he asked as he walked over and kissed the top of my head to acknowledge me being there as well.

Daniel shrugged a bit impatiently, and in a monotone voice, he said, "Sure."

Damien gave an understanding smile in his direction, recognizing His impatience and walking to his office.

Daniels pov.

Hayven keeps trying to talk with me, and it's not that I don't want to talk to her. I miss being her friend, but every touch, everything she says, just being in the same room as her. It all just makes me want to act on my impulses more.

I've been hallucinating so much lately, and in every single one, I fight this urge to feast on her and give in to every desire.

I end up kissing her, and then I come to when i'm mere seconds from being unable to hold myself back anymore.

I feel like I've fallen in love with her and simultaneously want to drink every last drop of her blood.

Maybe im not in love with her though, I've considered the possibility that this addiction to her blood is confused and mixed with other emotions and desires.

I miss just being her friend and not feeling this way towards her.

I suddenly start to feel dizzy, and my mind feels foggy. It seems like this is what happens whenever I begin to hallucinate.

I haven't been able to sleep in a couple of days now, either between the hallucinations and this feeling eating at me.

"I'm so sick and tired of these hallucinations." I said in a frustrated tone.

Hayven gives me a look of confusion. "Daniel what are you talking about?" she asks.

"Don't play dumb, you know what i'm talking about. This is all just in my mind again. Just another one. It's not real."

Hayvens pov:

Daniel isn't making any sense. I can barely understand what he's saying. He stops talking abruptly and stands up, beginning to pace around the room.

"Daniel, are you okay? Is there something I can do to help you? What's going on with you?" I ask.

He stops pacing and turns to face me for a moment before walking straight towards me.

"You know what? Yes, there is something you can help me with." He began to say as he quickly walked over to me.

Before I could process what was happening, he put one knee up on the couch beside me and wrapped one of his hands around my throat, preventing me from saying anything.

"You can help me by staying still. I'm so sick of these hallucinations, and if i'm going to keep hallucinating, why bother fighting so hard in every one of them? Why not just give in? I can't stand it anymore." He continued on to say.

Anger and frustration filled his voice, but he spoke in almost a whisper.

My heart was pounding in my chest. I tried to speak out to him and tell him this is real, but I could hardly breathe with his grasp on my neck.

He finally released his grip on my throat as he started to lean his face down towards my neck.

"Daniel stop, this is all real. What are you doing?" I ask, trying to push him away from my neck and snap him out of it.

"Yeah right. It's never real anymore. I struggle and fight myself to not give in, and I'm left craving your blood more and more." He replied while still trying to push my hands away from him.

The look on his face looked cold, and as if he lacked any empathy. It seems like he truly believes this is just a hallucination and couldn't possibly be reality.

"Daniel, this is not a hallucination. Please stop. Think about it!" I pleaded.

He ignored me entirely as he used his left forearm to block my hand and arm from pushing him away and placed his right hand on my head pushing my face away, allowing him a clear opportunity at my neck.

"If you do this, you'll kill me." I tried to reason one last time.

In a deep and emotionless tone, Daniel replied, saying, "I don't care."

I could feel his sharp teeth grazing the skin on my neck, preparing to go all in as I started to yell for Damien.

"Damien! Damien help!" I cried out.

Daniel froze where he was, losing his focus on pushing my face away. So I quickly turned to look at his face.

He looked confused and panicked all at the same time.

"What? That... that's never happened in them before. Is this... real?" he spoke to himself in a whisper next to me.

As I hear Damien running out of the other room, Daniel pulls himself off me and stumbles backward, one leg tripping on the coffee table, causing him to fall back to the ground.

He landed with a heavy thud and lay there frozen, propping his upper body up on his elbows as he stared at me, still confused.

"What happened!? What's going on?!" Damien said as he ran out into the living room, seeing the spectacle that was us, both looking panicked and confused, sitting in odd positions.

"I think Daniel is addicted to my blood. That night that all those guys attacked us here, I seen him taste my blood off of his hands and he said he's been hallucinating and he just almost..." I trailed off as I reached up to touch my neck.

Damien looked mad but calm all at once as he looked over at Daniel.

"Oh no, this can't be happening," Daniel said to himself and stood to his feet, holding his head in one hand.

"That's what I was coming over to talk to you about. I... I can't tell what's reality anymore and what's a hallucination.

It overtook me so fast, I didn't mean to taste her blood, but it dripped into a puddle next to me, and it smelled so good. When I saw it all over my hands, I just couldn't help myself.

I thought if I just kept my distance it'd get better, but it's only getting worse." Daniel said emotionally.

He sounded like he was holding back tears almost, feeling so sorry and regretful.

"Why didn't either of you tell me about this?" Damien asked more curious than upset. Though he wasn't happy about this new found information.

"I didn't think much of it at first. It wasn't until he already seemed like he was going to talk to you about everything that I started to piece together that it might be a problem. I didn't think it was going to be as serious as it is now, though." I answered.

Damien looked toward Daniel, waiting for his answer.

"Because how do you tell someone who is your best friend, who is like family now after everything, what little family you would have in this entire world, that when you look at or think of his girlfriend, who is also one of your best friends and like family, that you want kill her?

That you want to consume every last drop of blood in her body. That your emotions are all over the place about her, one moment you think you might be in love with her and the next minute you feel absolutely nothing except for the cravings and hunger that don't seem to be satisfied by anything else.

How was I supposed to tell you that? I tried, and I really tried to stop it, to keep my distance. I thought maybe if I was away, I would just go through withdrawals and be done with it, and we could all go back to normal, but I feel like I'm dying.

I am really so sorry to you both. I'm so sorry." he ended collapsing back into one of the chairs.

He was expecting the worst. It was written all over his face. He was distraught, I could tell that he was expecting nothing less than Damien killing him or us both never forgiving him.

"You should've told me." Damien sighed and then continued, "blood addictions aren't the same as human addiction to drugs. Where you can go through withdrawals and it be over.

When you consume the blood that you end up addicted to, the antibodies inside you begin to multiply rapidly, and at first, it feels fantastic.

You feel this high, like you'll never come down, and you almost feel invincible.

Everything about you feels amazing, but then, as time goes on without you having access to that blood type or choosing to try and fight it, all those extra antibodies start going crazy.

They're unsure of what to do anymore, so they eventually start to attack everything in your body. Causing you to feel sick, to hallucinate, to have headaches, to not be able to sleep, and countless other health problems.

It's one of the experiments they did on me back when I was in that awful program.

Hayvens' father actually came up with a shot to cure the addiction, at least until you're exposed to it again. It cured me in a weeks time, but I was treated very quickly after being exposed.

So, for you, I'm not sure it'll have the same results. It might help you right away. It might be something you have to take daily and can never be fully cured of, or it may not help at all."

We all stayed quiet for what seemed like the longest few minutes of my life.

"How will we know if it worked or not?" Daniel asks.

Damien walked over and sat next to me on the couch. "Well, I guess it'll all be based off of if you still crave her blood still in general or if it's only when the medicine seems to where off, etcetera." He answered.

Daniel looks over at me after processing everything and asks, "Are you okay? Did I hurt you?" Damien then matches him and looks in my direction, awaiting my answer with a concerned look on his face.

"I'm a little shaken up from what just happened, but I have definitely lived through worse already. I'm okay, I promise." I answered.

Damien then stands up and points at Daniel, "You, come with me now. We're going to go get what we need to make the medicine cocktail shot,

and you're sure as hell not staying here or getting out of sight when i'm not here until we know if the medicine is even going to work on you or not." Daniel stood up to follow Damien, now seeming to be back to avoiding me entirely.

He looked almost ashamed and embarrassed walking by me.

"Hayven, are you going to be okay here by yourself while we go get what we he need after everything that just happened?" Damien asked as he grabbed his jacket.

I nod yes with a forced smile. Truth be told, I don't want him to leave, I don't want to be left here alone right now, but I know that right now, it's best if I just stay here.

I care about Daniel, and it's best that we avoid anything happening in public, especially. Daniel needs Damien's help right now.

Damien walked over and gave me a tight and long hug. I got the sense that he didn't want to leave me here and that he wanted to hit Daniel for what he almost did.

Daniel looked at us with a sad and guilty look on his face and walked out the door without saying a word.

Damien pulled away from the hug and held my face in both hands and said, "I will try to hurry as fast as I can. If this wasn't as important as it is, I wouldn't leave you for even a second. I hope you understand."

I nodded without looking at him. If I meet his gaze then I wont be able to hold back these tears that are fighting for control, and if I cry I know he wont be able to turn around and leave, even though he has to.

With that said, he hesitated to walk out the door but finally left to get everything.

I locked the door behind him and waited until I could hear the car start before I allowed myself to be vulnerable in this moment.

I slid my back down the door with my face in my hand. My knees met my chest as I got to the floor, and I let myself cry for a minute.

I didn't want to be scared, but I was. I didn't know everything Daniel was struggling with after that night and can't help but wonder what would've happened if I had told Damien right away what happened.

I wasn't trying to hide it from him by any means, I just thought it was a moment of weakness or that he maybe needed the extra strength in that moment.

I never imagined it would've led to what happened tonight and to him struggling so much all alone.

Now, because I didn't say anything about it, he might not be able to be cured.

I feel like my emotions are on a roller coaster right now. I pulled myself together and stopped crying after a minute, wiping away my tears and taking a few deep breaths.

I can't stop thinking back to that moment when he was seconds away from biting into me.

I didn't want to have to yell for Damien, I had hoped that something I would say could snap him out of it, but nothing I said mattered.

"I don't care" is what he replied to me when I said he would kill me. It wasn't until I called for Damien that he finally realized he wasn't hallucinating.

I wonder if he really meant what he said or if it was just in the moment.

He also said he keeps going back and forth between feeling like he's in love with me and feeling like he wants to kill me, but is that how he really feels? I'm having trouble getting out of my head right now.

I felt my phone buzz twice, so I picked it up to check what it was. It's from Daniel.

"I'm so sorry Hayven...

I understand if you can't, But is there any way that you can possibly ever forgive me?"

I thought for a moment before replying. It's not that I can't forgive him, but it did scare me.

Back when Damien almost drank my blood, I was scared then too but he never gave in and I guess I kind of held Daniel to that same standard and thought there was no way this would ever happen.

Perhaps that is my fault, thinking that they would both be the same in a moment of weakness and letting my guard down. I don't know, maybe this case is different. I texted him back finally, saying;

"If you had the same opportunity, but knew that it was real life, would you have given in and done it? If you had the chance but knew you Weren't hallucinating?"

The bubbles kept popping up to let me know he was typing, and then he would stop, then he would continue, and then stop again. That went on for a couple of minutes until he replied.

"No, I don't think I would have. I would like to think I wouldn't have even gotten that close to allowing it to happen,

had I realized it was all real and not a hallucination.

In every hallucination I've had so far, I wanted to give in so badly. I craved it so badly that it became painful, but I couldn't let myself do that to you.

It felt so real every single time, and then only to find out I fought so hard not to give in just for none of it to be real to begin with, just made it feel a million times worse.

In that moment tonight, I was just so exhausted of fighting a battle that, in my mind, seemed pointless since none of it was real.

Had I known at the time that it all was real, had I listened to what you were saying, I would never have even gotten close to you.

I truly am so sorry, Hayven, I don't know where to even begin on how to show you just how sorry I am."

I read through his message and took a moment to process everything he said. I replied;

"Then yes, I can forgive you. I do forgive you.

you're my best friend.

But, I do think it will take a little time to feel safe around you again... to not feel scared.."

Daniel didn't reply. After 20 minutes of waiting for a reply and realizing he wasn't going to, I decided to go ahead and try to get some rest.

CHAPTER 19

A few days later, there was no sign of Daniel. Damien finished making two weeks of the medicine for him to take.

"If he needs more, I can make more then, but for now, this will be enough to see if it's going to help him right away or not." Damien said as he placed each syringe in a small padded case.

"Listen Hayven, I'm going to need Daniel to stay over here while we test this medicine.

It's going to be painful to start because this medicine is going to kill off the extra antibodies, and having him around you is currently the only test I will have to know if its working on him and how well its working. There's a chance he might go kind of crazy at first, though. Are you comfortable with that?" He continued.

I thought about it for a moment before saying, "Will it... be safe? Will I be safe?"

Damien stopped what he was doing and turned to me. "Well I can't promise that it will be entirely safe, but I would rather die than let anything happen to you, so I will do everything in my power to keep you safe." He replied.

I sighed and then put on a brave face and said, "We gotta do what we gotta do. I'm okay with it, as long as we can help him."

Daniel showed up an hour later with one bag full of his things. He looked miserable in this moment. Daniel pointed to his room and said,

"I'm going to let you take my bed this time. We're going to have to keep your hands tied up at night, in case you go crazy or anything like that. Just until the first stage of it is over."

Daniel agreed and then went to get settled into Damien's room and get changed into some more comfortable clothes. Once he was done, we met up in Damien's room.

"Okay, i'm ready. Let's just get this over with." Daniel said as he layed down on Damien's bed.

"Okay let's do it then. I don't know when the pain will set in for you. For me, it was a couple of hours before the pain started, but your case is different. It's going to burn a bit going in, but other than that, we are just going to have to see what happens." Damien replied.

I stood by the door just listening and watching as the two of them sat together.

Damien took out some rope and tied one of his wrists up, taking the rope and wrapping around the top of the bed frame and then pulling it to the bottom out of Daniels reach and tying it tightly.

Daniel pulled on it a couple of times to make sure it would hold if he went crazy. Once that was tested and good to go, Daniel held his free arm out, and Damien held one of the syringes full of medicine, ready to give it to him.

Damien counted to three and pierced his skin with the needles. Daniel winced, showing slight pain in his expression.

"Okay well that's it, it's done. Now we wait." Damien said.

We waited, waited, and waited. By 10pm, which was 2 hours later, there was still no sign of anything happening. We all ended up falling asleep in Damien's room.

Around 2 a.m., we woke to Daniel beginning to groan in pain, and the pain seemed to become excruciating within minutes.

He started to thrash around a lot, trying to fight off the pain, but was getting close to hurting himself more.

Damien and I both jumped up and ran to his side to try to hold him down more.

He was so strong that we could hardly stop him from lifting his body off of the bed. I don't know what else I can do to help him.

The only thing I can think of is trying to talk to him to distract his mind, even just a fraction.

"Daniel, it's going to be okay. We're here, were not going anywhere, and it's going to be okay. You're going to get through this, and it's going to work. It has to." I said to him.

He reached his free hand over to me to hold my hand. His whole body was trembling so bad that it almost looked like he was convulsing.

"Keep fighting it Daniel, keep fighting it." I encouraged him, realizing that he was giving his all to fight reacting to the pain.

His grip on my hand was tight and borderline painful, but I didn't dare pull away.

The pain slowly started to die down some at about 5 am. He started to sweat a lot and felt hot to the touch.

"That's normal." Damien reassured. "the natural antibodies start to recognize that the extra ones aren't supposed to be there and start to work over time to get rid of them. It's kind of like when you get a fever when you're sick. Now that the pain is over, the fever shouldn't last too much longer. Can you run to the kitchen and wet a wash cloth with cold water for him? That might help some." Damien continued.

Daniels grip on my hand tightened again. "Please don't go, I don't want either of you to leave. Please stay." Daniel begged.

Damien and I sat next to him on the bed with no further words spoken, and with me still holding his hand. By 8am, we were all exhausted.

"Did it work?" I asked.

"Well, it's at least helped get rid of some, if not all of the Extra antibodies which should help with his hallucinations and any sickness hes been feeling at the very least, but it's too soon to tell if it's going to help with the cravings and hunger.

It's going to take at least a day to start helping that at all, and then we will just have to wait and see if its going to cure it or if it's only going to be a temporary help and see if he will have to take the medicine every day for the rest of his life or if he can stop in a few days." Damien explained.

Daniel was no longer feverish or in pain. Other than being tired and bored, he was almost completely back to himself now.

"Can we at least untie me now and get food or something?" Daniel asked.

"Yes, I think it should be safe to do that now." Damien answered as he started to untie him. Daniel rubbed his newly freed wrists.

"I'm going to go make us all some breakfast." Damien said as he walked out of the room, leaving the door open just in case.

I leaned against the wall near the door and slowly slid down it into a sitting position on the floor.

We sat there in silence for a few minutes, as if neither of us were willing to break the silence.

Finally, after what seemed like so long, Daniel quietly said, "Hayven... I am so sorry for everything. There's so many things I wish I could go back and change, but I can't. I understand if it will take you some time to forgive me, if you will forgive me at all."

He was going to continue talking, but I couldn't let him keep talking without at least settling his mind.

"Stop. I forgive you, Daniel. I never really blamed you or held it against you to begin with, but if you need to hear it, I forgive you." I said, cutting him off.

"but why?" Daniel asked, looking like he just couldn't grasp how I could possibly feel how I feel.

"Because it was a situation that was somewhat out of your control. What happened? You saved me. You didn't know the full extent of everything that was happening to you, and you tried to deal with it on your own.

You kept your distance from me when it was affecting you the worst, even though I cant even imagine how hard it was to deal with it all alone, and when you realized that it was only getting worse you came to Damien for help.

I don't blame you. I care about you, and I might feel a little weary around you until we know for sure if this medicine is going to work or not, but i'm not mad or upset.

If anything, I feel sad that you dealt with it alone and couldn't tell me, and then watching everything you just went through." I replied, making eye contact with him across the room.

He looked relieved and almost stunned. After a minute, he broke eye contact to turn his head and chuckle in disbelief, though i'm not sure what he's thinking exactly.

I tell Daniel that i'm going to help Damien with the breakfast, then stand up and start heading to the kitchen.

Walking through the kitchen doorway, I see Damien standing there from behind.

His muscles stood out through his skin-tight shirt from his back and his arms. His hair loosely laying in a messy style from him not having a chance to brush or comb it after the long night we all hard.

Something about his body language as he stood there cooking and preparing food, something about the way he looked, heck everything about the way he looked really just was so attractive to me in that moment, even more than usual.

He noticed I was standing there admiring him as he turned to look at me and smirked, sending the butterflies in my stomach to rush to my heart and rush back down to my stomach, causing my heart to stop and then speed up with the feeling of my stomach doing flips.

I shyly walked up next to him, all nerve and normal courage leaving my body with that simple look on his face.

He stopped what he was doing for a moment to smile at me, and then he reached out to hold my face and leaned in to kiss me softly.

I didn't want him to stop and I could tell he didn't want to stop, but the eggs and bacon on the stove called to him with a sizzle and pop, so he sadly had to pull away to continue cooking.

"I like whatever you're wearing on your lips. It tastes sweet." He said.

"Oh, my chapstick?" I asked him.

"Yes, what flavor is it?" he replied with his own question.

I giggled as I replied, "I guess you'll have to kiss me more and figure it out yourself."

He looked over at me with a look of excitement mixed with a little surprise for not expecting me to say what I said.

He flipped the bacon and checked the eggs and then grabbed me, lifting me up to sit on the counter playfully.

Causing us both to laugh. "Okay love birds, let's not burn the food, okay?"

Daniel said as he walked into the kitchen and sat down at the island counter.

Damien and I quietly chuckled to each other, almost because it was like we got caught, not that we were keeping it a secret or trying to hide it.

I continued to sneak glances at Damien as we all talked.

I've missed this so much, just all of us hanging out together.

The rest of the day went pretty much like normal, minus just being extra careful since we weren't sure how well the medicine was going to work.

Before we all knew it, it was already nighttime again and getting late.

"Hey man, you can go ahead and stay here again tonight. It'd probably be easier to see how well the medicine is working and keep an eye on you if you just stay here anyway." Damien said as he grabbed a blanket and walked over to the other guest bedroom, which now had a bed and dresser in it.

Daniel smiled. "You stay here enough. It's about time you get your own room." Damien said, half chuckling.

Daniel looked relieved and genuinely happy all at once. "Thank you. It'll be nice not sleeping on the couch when i'm here" Daniel responded, matching Damien's chuckle.

It makes me feel so happy that I have them both. It's strange to think back to a time when none of us knew each other, or even when they disliked each other.

I believe they secretly always cared about each other, but their bond has grown just like it has with all of us.

It feels like I have a family again, and I think that's something we all feel. It feels almost like i'm living an entirely new life, and to be honest, i'm okay with that.

It's not perfect, but I truly wouldn't want to live any other life without them at this point. I never want to not know these people I've met that have become such a big part of my life.

We all decided it was time to head to bed since it was getting late, and we were all running on little to no sleep.

The worst of Daniels blood addiction and recovery should be over since most of the extra antibodies should have died off.

A few hours later, I wake up feeling thirsty, so I get up and head to the kitchen. As I grab a glass out of the cupboard, I hear Daniels door open.

"I can't sleep," he says as he walks into the kitchen and sits down at the island counter, laying his head down in frustration.

"Well, do you want some tea? I can make you some." I replied.

He turned his head while still laying down so he could look up at me and breathe better.

"You do make really good tea." He said, meaning yes.

"I do? I just make tea." I respond with a laugh.

He sat up and chuckled and said, "Yeah but you make it different. You add stuff to it that's like the perfect amount of everything, and then the fact that you're the one who is making it is probably a bonus."

I laughed, realizing he meant when I added honey or when I made milk tea and added honey to that.

"Okay I will make my ever so amazing tea then for you." I said.

I grabbed another cup from the cupboard and decided to make it all on the stove in a sauce pan so there was no loud whistling from a tea kettle.

"I really missed having your around, you know." I said matter of factly.

He watched me as I spoke, then looked down at the counter and nodded.

"I missed being around. I missed our joking and talking to you in general, really." I nodded in agreement, feeling the same way.

I pulled myself up on the counter to sit down still near the stove.

"It felt really lonely being away from you both. Like I was trapped in isolation and stuck away from the only real family I know." He continued.

"I've felt like a very important family member has been gone, and I missed you." I said.

Daniel smiled. He looked genuinely happy for the moment. "Once all this is over and I get better and we know all the details of how this medicine will work on me and everything, we should all go somewhere and do something fun." He said, looking excited at the idea.

I smiled back at him. "That would be so much fun. I feel like it's been too long since I've left this house really in general, especially to do anything fun. It'd be great for us all to get out and kind of forget about this stuff for a while." I hopped back off of the counter to add in honey and milk now that I could see the tea was almost done.

"Well, then I can't wait for us to get out for a while and just forget it all. Focusing only on having fun." He replied.

I smiled at him and nodded as I stirred the mixture and left it to sit for a moment to heat all the way through again.

"Can I talk to you about something kind of serious?" he asked me.

"Of course, you can tell me anything Daniel, you're my best friend." I answered.

"Well, when I was going through all those hallucinations, and they were all about you every time." He started.

"Yeah?" I asked now, becoming curious about what he was going to talk to me about.

The milk tea mixture started to boil so I turned the heat off quickly and went to pour a little into one of the cups so I could sit down with him and give him my full attention while we talked and drank our tea,

but I accidentally spilled some on my finger and hand that was holding the cup, causing me to drop the glass cup and it breaking on the floor in front of me.

A whimper escaped from the pain of burning my finger and hand. I quickly sat the pan back down to grab my other hand freely.

The moment I whimpered, Daniel flew out of his chair to rush to my side and check on me.

"Hayven are you okay?" He asked, worried as he grabbed my hurt hand and examined it.

"I'm okay, i'm sorry." I assured him and continued, "So much for choosing to make it this way to stay quiet." I said, feeling guilty, now worried that I woke up, Damien.

We both lean down to try to pick up the glass as Daniel says,"No, I should've waited to talk. Let me pick up the glass. It's okay."

I shook my head no, now filled with more guilt that I made Daniel feel like he distracted me and interrupted the serious conversation he wanted to talk to me about.

"No, don't. I-" I began to say as I started to pick up a couple of pieces of the glass and stopped because I cut my hand.

I gasped loudly and shot my head up to look at Daniel, who can't be more than two feet in front of me.

He looked at me wide-eyed and dropped the glass from his hands as he fell back and crawled his way backward until he reached the wall in a panic.

My heart sunk into my stomach, and I stood back up speechless as I held my now cut hand. Every logical thought seemed to leave my brain as I stood their almost frozen in place.

"I-I will go get Damien." I stuttered out.

As I started in motion to lift my foot, Daniel stood back up as fast as his body would allow and begged,

"Wait! One little taste wouldn't hurt if i'm currently on the medicine, right? Please, Hayven."

I stepped over the glass, heading around the other side of the island counter, and replied, holding my hand closer to my chest.

"No Daniel, you can't. I'm going to get Damien, and he's going to give you a shot or do whatever it is he does so well that just seems to fix everything, and he's going to fix this." Daniel walked over to one of the doorways to the kitchen closest to the front door. Blocking my way to Damien.

"Come on, Hayven, that was too well done. The world wants me to at least have one last taste. You burned your hand, so I jumped up to check on you only for you to cut your hand when I was right there in front of you." He continued to beg.

"That's just the addiction talking Daniel, don't fall for it. That's not you. Just let me go get Damien." I replied, now feeling the anxiety in the pit of my stomach growing.

He hesitated for a moment before beginning to walk in a fast pace over to me without saying a word.

He grabbed my injured hand and started to pull it up towards his mouth, but just before his lips touched my skin I lifted my leg as high up in front of me as I was able to and kicked him hard, causing him to trip over his own feet and falling through the doorway that was closest towards his room.

I turned to run out the doorway nearest to the front door and down the hall that led to Damien's room.

Daniel jumped back to his feet and rushed after me.

"Damien!" I called out.

Daniel was close behind me as we ran into Damien's' room. Damien was already out of bed from hearing me yell for him as we both rushed in, and he grabbed Daniel almost as soon as he saw him.

With one arm across Daniels collar bone and grasping the collar of his white thin T-shirt and his other hand firmly pressing Daniels chest.

He pushed him up against the wall and kept the pressure on him to keep him there.

"What happened, Hayven?" Damien asked while still looking at Daniel.

"I cut my finger on some glass from a cup I accidentally dropped, and he was right in front of me." I replied.

Damien sighed and said, "In that top drawer, there's a small box. In the box, there's a syringe labeled addiction and a syringe labeled sedate. I need you to grab them both and bring them here."

I opened the drawer, and the box sat there with a number of other things. I found both syringes at the top of the box after opening it and ran over to Damien.

Daniel was trying to push Damien off but didn't seem to have the strength to get free in this moment.

"Okay give him both. Right in his arm." Damien said.

I uncapped them both, giving him the sedative first to calm him down as fast as possible. Next is addiction medicine.

Once he was finally calmed down and had every medicine in his system he needed, Damien took Daniel back to his room and then came back.

"You only cut your hand?" he asked.

"Yeah. It dripped some blood, but it's just a small cut, really, nothing to worry about." I answered as I lifted my hand to show him, revealing the cut on my left hand and the burn on my right finger and hand.

"What happened to your other finger and your hand?" he asked, worried.

"I accidentally burned it when I tried to pour the tea. That's why I dropped the cup in the first place. It's okay, though. I'm fine." I assured him.

"Okay, as long as you're okay." Damien started to say as he sat on the bed next to me and wrapped his arms around me and then continued,

"Well, a small cut like that shouldn't have been enough to set him off like that.

Even when recovering from a blood addiction, you have more self-control when you're taking the medicine, even after the first few hours of taking it. As long as it's working.

So it looks like im going to have to up the dose, and he might have to be stuck taking it every day.

We're going to have to make sure he takes it on time every day, and you're going to have to be careful around him when i'm not with you.

Maybe one day that will change, but for now that's just what he's going to have to do.

Otherwise, he can't be around you. I won't let him even one hundred miles from you."

I nodded in agreement, feeling saddened for him.

"And tomorrow I'm going to make you something that I want you to always keep with you. Something to help you stay safe if anything happens, and i'm not there in time." He continued on to say.

"Okay, I promise I will be more careful." I replied as I leaned into his chest and hugged him.

"Do you want to sleep with me tonight?" Damien asked, hugging me tighter.

I nodded yes without saying a word. He stood up and walked to the bathroom real quick to grab a small first aid kit so he could bandage and wrap my hand.

He then locked the door just in case and lifted the blankets, climbing into bed. Once he was in place, he lifted the blankets on the side I would lay on to invite me to join him.

I gladly accepted his offer and snuggled as closely to him as our physical bodies would allow.

Even when the world seems chaotic, when I feel scared, worried, sad, or any negative emotion that can run through my mind, he somehow makes me better and makes me feel safe.

CHAPTER 20

The next morning, I woke up in bed alone.

It felt so lonely without Damien there next to me, holding me, caressing my skin softly, kissing me gently from time to time.

I look over to the nightstand that's on his side and see a note folded like a card and placed on its side to stand.

"My angel" it read at the top, "I've decided to take Daniel out for the day to try to burn off whatever it is that he has within him that's holding on to this addiction.

We were both worried about your safety, so we thought it would be best that you stayed home this time.

We will be home by dinner time and are always a phone call away. I love you with all my heart and soul." It continued.

I'm very sad that they left without me, though I understand. It feels like i'm being left out of something important. Laying in bed still, I let my thoughts wonder.

"What if Daniel never gets better?" I thought but quickly tried to dismiss.

I would miss him very deeply if he could no longer be a part of my life. I am more than happy having Damien in my life, but something would feel like it's missing if Daniel couldn't safely stay.

I feel weak and tired, like I just can't catch a break from one crazy thing or another.

The more I think about it, the more it sounds fun and sounds necessary to escape this world for a day or two, but at this point, that seems like it's in the far future..

After laying in bed for another hour just thinking about the million and one scenarios that could be my potential future, I decided to get up and get dressed.

The weather is very nice today so I think a soft pink dress with a light sweater and high-heeled boots would be good for today.

I'm going to keep my makeup simple and throw my long hair into a ponytail just to keep it out of the way.

It's been a while since I woke up feeling completely alone, getting dressed with no disturbances what so ever. Seems almost bitter sweet.

My phone dinged, and my heart raced with excitement that it might be one of the two I already missed having around during this short time.

JERAMIAH: Hey Hayven, what are you doing this weekend?

HAYVEN: that's a good question, i'm not really sure, though. Why, what did you have in mind?

JERAMIAH: Well, i'm having another party this weekend and was wondering if you wanted to go?

HAYVEN: Oh. I mean, that sounds like a lot of fun, actually. But i'm not entirely sure if I can make it or not, Can I get back to you on an answer?

JERAMIAH: Yeah, no problem. Just let me know when you can. I would love to have you join my party. And you're welcome to invite whoever you like.

HAYVEN: Okay, I will asap. Thank you for the invite

JERAMIAH: Absolutely

I wish I could say yes, but I don't want to go unless Damien and Daniel can go too, and at the moment i'm not sure if they would be able to go, let alone if they'd want to.

A party sounds like just the type of thing we all need to forget about everything for a while.

Sitting on the couch, I suddenly hear a knock at the door. I was almost worried to answer it since I wasn't expecting anyone besides the two who have a key.

I opened the door to see a younger girl who looked about two years younger than me standing there.

"Hi there, is Hayven here?" the girl asked. A confused look washed over my face.

"Well, I'm Hayven, so yes." I replied. The girl began to giggle and jump with joy.

"Oh Hayven, I've been searching for you everywhere!" she exclaimed as she jumped into me to hug me.

"I'm sorry, but I don't know who you are." I said with an awkward chuckle, even more confused now than ever but trying to laugh it off.

The girl pulled away from me, a smile still painted on her face. Her dark hair gently caressing her porcelain cheek from the soft breeze blowing back and forth.

"Oh that's right, my apologies. My name is Alivia, and i'm your sister." She said as if this wasn't big news.

"My sister!?" I said surprised and then continued, "No, you must have the wrong person, or the wrong name, or you must be playing some kind of cruel joke, I don't have a sister." I replied.

"Well, you do now sister, it's a long story, but to sum it up, we have the same mother." She replied.

I stood there in complete shock, silenced simply from the surprise of it all.

I mean its possible that I'd have other siblings from my mother since she was alive last time I checked and living some where else, but I guess it never crossed my mind that she would abandon me and continue to have any other children.

"What's your mothers name?" I asked curiously.

"Her name is Marree. She has long dark hair, blue eyes, pale skin, and she's 5 feet and 7 inches tall." She answered.

That sounds like my mother exactly. I've only ever seen her photos since I was little and have no memory aside from photo albums, but everything seems to fit.

"I'm kind of at a loss for words. How is this true? Did she meet someone else?" I asked.

"Well, the simple answer is yes. She met a man, fell in love, and then had me." She replied.

"do we have any other siblings?" I asked.

"Possibly, but as far as I'm aware, it's just me and you." She answered.

I invited her to come in so we could talk more. The pain in my chest became more intense as we spoke.

Thinking that my mother went off to have this whole other life without me, not even caring enough to check on me once in a while or come get me when my father died or anything.

Worst of all, thinking that Damien maybe knew about this the whole time and never told me.

"She told me she left you when you were little. She regrets it but never felt that it was her right to step back into your life after leaving." She said.

Those words seemed to sting deeply, but I did my best to hold it together. "How did you find me?" I ask.

"Well it wasn't easy, but I managed to find your last address, which led me to your current address. I've been looking for you for about 2 years now." She replied.

Looking at her now, I can see the resemblance between us. We both look a lot like our mother.

The sound of keys suddenly jingled at the door as someone began to unlock it.

My heart sunk, thinking of having to face Damien after learning that he still didn't tell me the whole truth.

If he knew and didn't tell me I had a sister, what else has he been hiding?

Damien and Daniel both walked through the door and stopped abruptly once they saw Alivia.

She smiled sweetly at them both as they continued to stand there confused.

"Alivia, this is my boyfriend, Damien, and that is my best friend Daniel." I introduced them to her and then continued, "Damien, Daniel, this is Alivia, my newly discovered sister."

Daniel looked back and forth between us with surprise written on his face now instead of confusion.

"uh, yeah. You too look very similar, so it wouldn't have been hard to guess that you're related some how" he said.

"Your sister?" Damien questioned.

"Yes, i'm sure you already know, but she is my sister from my mothers side. " I replied, feeling too upset to acknowledge him fully.

The room turned cold and silent for a moment as I spoke, but quickly softened again as Daniel talked to Alivia.

I'm not sure if she could tell, but I could tell that he was flirting with her.

It seemed like they were going to get along well, and she seemed like a very nice person as far as I could tell so far.

My heart sunk again when she looked at Damien and said, "You actually look really familiar. Have we met before?"

Damien, now looking uncomfortable, replied, "No, I don't think we've ever met before."

Anxiety started tying my stomach in knots as I began to feel like my trust for Damien has been shaken a bit in this moment.

Why would he not tell me I have a sister, and why would he continue to lie and pretend he didn't know about her now?

I decided it was best to try to drop those feelings for the moment and focus on the excitement of having a sister.

"I always wished I had a sister. " I said to her.

She smiled, "Me too. I always imagined how much fun it would be."

We laughed and talked about different things together to get to know one another.

Damien sat down in one of the chairs near the couch and gave her a soft smile before asking the same question I asked earlier, "How did you manage to find her?"

she smiled back at him and said, "It took some time, but I found some records that led me to this address.

I'm so happy to finally meet my sister. I've been dreaming of this day and how perfect it'd be."

Damien didn't say anything back but nodded enthusiastically. I kept talking with Alivia, but out of the corner of my eye, I could see Damien staring at me.

The way he's looking at me is almost like he sees the world in me at this moment, but I can't help but feel like maybe it's guilt instead or regret.

I don't dare make eye contact with him, though, or I will lose my composure entirely.

He can affect me so intensely, just simply by the way he looks at me.

"Well if you don't have anywhere to stay in town, you're welcome to stay here." Damien offered.

"Yes that would be so much fun. You should definitely stay here, and we could have a little sleepover." I said with excitement over taking my voice.

Out of the corner of my eye, I can see Damien staring again. This time, he's smiling at me, though. Almost smirking, and as much as I want to hate him right now, the way he's looking right now catches my attention, and I start to blush.

I can see Alivia notices, too, as well as Daniel, but no one says a word about it.

Trying my best to ignore it and move on, I jump up, grabbing Alivias' arm to pull her to my room.

"You can borrow some of my clothes if you want." I tell her as we both rush away from the boys and Into my room to talk more and go through what she can borrow of mine as she tells me she brought a big suit case of stuff that I can borrow of hers as well.

Damien and Daniel decide to do their own thing and let us have some time to ourselves.

"So you said Damien is your boyfriend, right?" Alivia asked.

"Yes, he is." I said with a smile.

"I seen the way he was staring at you. It was very sweet. What's he like?" she replied.

I couldn't hold back anymore, and for a brief moment, sadness filled my heart and showed in my expression.

"Well, i'm pretty upset with him at the moment," I began to say as I found my composure once again,

"but usually, he's really amazing. Sweet and calm, but passionate and intense at the same time. He's smart, makes me laugh, knows just what to say, usually to instantly cure any bad feelings i'm having. He's just really amazing."

She moved a little closer to me and asked, "is he good in bed?"

I couldn't help but blush again, feeling caught off guard by her question. With a smile, I shyly nodded yes.

"He's actually fantastic in bed. He's my first, but out of all the times I imagined my first time to be, it was a hundred times better with him.

He was rough yet gentle, patient, knew exactly what he was doing and what he wanted, extremely loving the entire time, and it was so passionate that I don't think I could even put into words" I said in a whisper.

"You're first time? Well, that's impressive. I could have never held out as long as you, that's for sure." She said with a slight chuckle.

"So what are you upset with him about?" she continued on to ask.

"Well, it's kind of complicated to explain, but I feel like he knew I had a sister and just didn't tell me." I Answered.

"Not trying to get anyone in trouble, but you're my sister, so I want to be honest with you. I have definitely met him before.

He came and met me in person once about two years ago. That's how I found out I had a sister in the first place, but please don't tell him you heard it from me." She said.

In that moment, with those few simple words, I felt my trust for him start to crumble from underneath me.

My heart once again sunk into the pit of my stomach, causing me to feel nauseous.

I wont even be able to ask him about it since there's no way to tell him how I know without bringing Alivia into it, and since she asked me not to say I heard it from her, I Have no choice but to keep it to myself.

How on earth am I going to pretend that I don't know about this, though, and pretend that everything is normal.

CHAPTER 21

The next few days, I try my best to avoid Damien as much as I can, just making it seem like I needed to catch up with my sister, since that wasn't entirely a lie and the best thing I could think of to keep my distance from him.

Saturday rolled around.

I remembered that Jeremiah invited me to his party, so I told everyone about it and asked if they wanted to go.

Everyone agreed to going so we all got dressed up in our best party outfits and headed over.

Once we all stepped through the door, Jeremiah spotted us right away and made his way over.

He lifted my hand to his lips and gently kissed it as he said, "Welcome back to my home."

Then, he grabbed Alivias hand and did the same as he asked, "and who might this beautiful lady be?" Alivia giggled.

"This is my recently discovered little sister, you know my boyfriend, and the other tall guy behind me is our friend Daniel." I said with a smile.

Damien looked as though he was sulking, Alivia looked like she might be experiencing puppy love over Jeramiah's gentlemanly gesture, and Daniel looked like he was just excited to be at a social event.

We all danced, drank, and were having a good time together. Daniel sat down on one of the nearby couches, and I decided to join him with another drink in hand for each of us.

"how are you doing? Is it really okay for you to be somewhere like this when you're going through, well, you know?" I asked him.

"Damien said I seem completely fine as long as I have enough medicine in my system for now. Even though I'm going to have to most likely take this medicine every single day, I can be back to normal for the most part as long as I have it.

To answer your other question, i'm doing good. I'm having a great time so far. What about you, why are you avoiding Damien?" he replied.

My eyes widened with his question, not realizing it was so obvious to him, and unsure how I would answer it.

"He knew I had a sister, and he didn't tell me. He promised never to keep secrets from me, to tell me everything from the past, and he not only didn't tell me,

but then proceeded to pretend right in front of my face that he had never met her before when he did, and he knew about her either way." I answered while leaning back into the couch.

"That's rough." Daniel began," Are you sure he knew her though or knew about her at all?" he asked.

"Well he watched over me for years. He knew all there was to know, really. I'm sure he even watched extra carefully with my exes and my best friend.

Then I found out that there was a day he actually met up with Alivia, and that's how she found out about me and what started her search for me.

So, at this point, I don't think there's anything else to think except that it's true, and he knew." I replied.

Daniel nodded, unsure what to say. He didn't want to forsake his friend but knew that what his other friend was saying makes sense.

"Now my trust for him has just been completely shaken. What else does he know that he chose not to tell me? Are there details that he left out of stories, things he's lied about entirely?

I feel like I don't know who he is entirely now." I said, feeling the weight of the world fall back on me heavily.

I chugged the remainder of my beer in an attempt to not sober up and just forget everything. Jeramiah came over and sat on the opposite side of me.

"Are you both having a fun time?" he asked. We nodded yes so we could save our voices from yelling over loud noises and people.

"They look like they're getting close." He whispered in my ear and pointed to Damien and Alivia talking and laughing by the drink table.

I paused for a moment, unsure of how I should feel about it. I force a laugh and say, "yeah they're just getting to know each other."

Jeramiah raised both of his eyebrows up and then back down quickly. "I will go grab us all another drink." Jeramiah said.

I've already drank more than I planned, but I want to just have fun and forget all the stress that's been surrounding me.

He came back and handed me and Daniel another drink. We both thanked him. I chugged the beer as quickly as I could and started feeling like it was hitting me finally.

We all joked and laughed together about random stuff, and then Daniel stood up.

He leaned down to my ear and whispered, "I'm going to grab another beer, I will be right back."

I nodded to him to let him know I heard him and watched him walk to the table.

Damien and Alivia were still talking and laughing near there. Once Daniel got his beer, I saw Alivia say something to him, and then Daniel joined them in talking and laughing.

I began to feel so left out and alone that I could hardly hold myself together anymore.

"Wow that's not cool of them. They're all just ditching you." Jeramiah said into my ear.

That was enough to throw it over board for me. I got up and quickly made my way to the nearest empty room I could find that was down the hall and stood there crying by myself.

A few moments later, Jeramiah found me crying in the room. "There you are. Hey, I wasn't trying to upset you or anything. I'm sorry." He said as he shut the door behind him.

"No, it's okay. It's not your fault. I'm just upset about some other stuff. I'm sorry for rushing away upset like that, and sorry if I made you feel like you were to blame." I replied.

"No, it's fine. I just wanted to make sure I didn't upset you." He began, "Hey, are you okay?" he continued on to ask.

I grabbed my forehead, beginning to see the room spin around me and a headache starting to throb painfully in my head.

Dizziness would be an understated description of what I was feeling. I could barely form a coherent sentence at this point and leaned against a wall still holding my head.

"I… don't feel right." I mumbled out before losing my balance and falling to the floor.

The room around me continued to spin with no concern for me, and darkness began to fade in from my peripheral vision until I could barely see anything.

In an almost menacing voice, I heard Jeramiah say "It's okay, I've got you."

As he quickly came over to me and cradled my upper body in his lap.

With the last bit of vision I still had left, I saw Daniel walk in, expression full of panic. Then the darkness finished closing in on me, and I went unconscious.

"Hayven, you need to wake up. Wake up." I heard from a familiar voice.

I felt myself slowly becoming fully conscious again, but my eyes remained closed.

"Hayven." The man said again, shaking me awake.

I summoned the strength to open my eyes to see Daniel sitting down next to me and leaning just above me.

"Daniel?" I asked in a groggy voice, showing how exhausted and confused I am.

"are you okay!?" he asked with stress and worry covering every inch of his face.

"I'm fine, i'm just really tired, and my head hurts a little." I said as I forced myself to sit up off the ground. Looking around, it looked like we were in some kind of warehouse room.

"Where are we?" I asked, confusion still written on my face.

"I don't know, I only woke up a few minutes before you." He replied.

"Well what happened at the party? I remember not feeling right all of a sudden, and I remember you walking into whatever room I was in but it's super spotty and I don't remember what happened after that, or really what happened during that whole thing. " I explained to him.

"I think you were drugged by that guy. I think his name is Jeramiah? I saw you walk off alone and then soon after he got up and followed after you.

I got a bad feeling so I hurried to find you. When I finally found the room you were in, I saw you laying on the floor looking like you passed out, and then he was cradling you on the ground.

It looked like he was smiling, and then when he seen me walk in, he layed you down, and before I fully realized what was going on, I felt something sharp stab into my arm from behind me.

I'm pretty sure someone shoved a syringe into my arm and drugged me too because I passed out soon after, though I never saw who did it.

When I was about to pass out, I heard that guy say that I wasn't supposed to see what happened." He explained back to me.

My eyes widened in shock as his story went on. How could Jeramiah drug me? Why would he do that? I couldn't help but wonder.

"Have you tried to find a way out of here?" I asked, unsure what else to do.

He nodded yes with a frown. "I tried the door, but it's locked. I don't see any other way out." He replied.

I looked around again now that i'm a little more awake. Seems like we're in a small warehouse room. There's one door and no windows.

I can see that the shape of the roof leads up more, which means there's definitely more to the building than just the one room we're in.

The room is empty besides two chairs and half carpeted flooring that leads into the tile floor. A few lights above us illuminating the room enough that it doesn't leave anything to the imagination besides what's outside of the door.

Damien POV:

I don't know why Hayven seems so distant from me at the moment, but I feel like it's better to give her some space right now.

I feel like she's avoiding me, and that's just not normal for her, so all I can really think is to let her have her space until she's ready to talk about what's wrong.

Her sister was curious how me and Hayven met and wanted to make sure I'm treating her well so at the party I was telling her in vague details that I knew Hayvens father who passed away and worked with him, and how he asked me to keep an eye on her.

I left out quite a few details, obviously, but explained what I could to where it would make sense.

I told her about how Hayven is the most amazing person I've ever met. How I think she's the most beautiful woman I've ever seen.

How I think she's one of the smartest people I've ever met, and that if I didn't know better, not that I believed I'm deserving of this, but that it was almost like she's an angel that came into my life, and almost like she's gods greatest creation, made for me.

I don't know if I believe in god, but she definitely makes me think that something bigger than us has to exist.

God, past lives where our souls grew together and met in every life. That something or multiple things beyond our comprehension must exist,

because to think that someone as perfect and beautiful as her could just simply exist in a world like this, just somehow seems to make less sense than a god creating her.

"I'm surprised that I never came across Hayven having a sister." I told Alivia.

She chuckled, "I know! If we ever met, I definitely would've remembered, though. I'm glad we're getting to meet now, at least." She replied.

"Yeah I'm happy to see Hayven enjoying having a new sister. I'm happy to see you both getting along." I said as I looked over to Hayven sitting on one of the couches next to Daniel and Jeramiah.

I really don't like that guy, Jeramiah, and I don't trust him. I've always felt like there's something off about him, but I can't quite place it.

Daniel gets up and walks over to the table next to me, and Alivia says something to him that I can't quite hear over all the noise, but he laughs and walks over to us to talk.

We were all laughing and talking for a few minutes. I saw Daniel walk away, and Alivia told me about a few parties she went to when she was a little younger and that she's always been a partier at heart and loves this atmosphere.

Looking back over to the couch, I see that Hayven, Daniel, and Jeramiah aren't there anymore.

"Hey I have to run to the bathroom real quick, I will be right back." She said as she lightly touched my arm and then crossed the crowd of people, heading down the hallway that's near where Hayven was sitting.

I nodded to her, not fully understanding what she said because I started to worry about Hayven.

I started to look around the crowds, I checked upstairs, tried to call her phone, and couldn't seem to find her anywhere or get ahold of her.

Pulling up the messenger on my phone, I began to send her text after text as I decided to go check the car.

On my way walking down the long line of cars, I try to call Daniel, but I can't seem to get ahold of him either.

I finally reached the car only to see that it was still locked and no one to be found.

My heart was starting to race uncontrollably in my chest, and I couldn't keep my breathing steady.

"Damien!" I heard Alivia cry out from behind me. Quickly spinning around to look at her, I see she's covered in blood.

"What happened!? Where are you hurt?" I yelled out in worry as I scanned over her to see any wounds.

With tears streaming down her face, she shook her head no, and she said, "it-its not my blood, it's Hayvens."

She began to piece together the story of what happened. My eyes widened, and I fell back onto the hood of the car in a sitting position, expecting nothing but the worst.

"When I came out of the bathroom I didn't see you anywhere so I went to look for Hayven and When I walked out into the backyard to see if she was out there, I seen Daniel biting into her neck.

She was drenched in blood, and she fell to the ground because she was so weak from losing so much. There was so much blood, so I ran to her to try and help her.

I tried to help her sit up and was trying to check her pulse to see how faint it was, but then he pulled me away from her and pushed me down, away from them both.

Then he grabbed her and took her away. He took off into the woods somewhere, but I lost them. And--" she paused suddenly.

I jumped up off the hood of the car and grabbed both of her arms, feeling distraught, and like any moment, I would fall to pieces.

"And what!?" I begged for her to finish her sentence.

"and... I think I felt her heart stop..." She continued.

My arms dropped from hers like two heavy weights crashing down, almost taking my body down with them.

Life almost didn't even feel real in this moment. I felt like I was suddenly trapped in one of the worst nightmares I could imagine.

"I don't know, but she lost so much blood." She continued on in a whimpered whisper.

"I have to find her." I said as I ran towards the woods that were near the back yard.

"This can't be real." I thought to myself over and over.

I searched for hours. I called out for Hayven and Daniel until my voice was completely gone, tried to call their phones in hopes that one of them would answer or that I would at least hear it ring, until my phone died.

There was no sign of them. No trail of blood, no foot prints, nothing at all that could lead me to find them.

The sun finally starts to rise, setting the past night in stone and painting the sky a light pink and soft orange mixture with the clouds.

Something in me felt like it was slowly dying as time passed with no sign that there was a chance that Hayven was still alive.

The silence was deafening, even through the sound of birds beginning to chirp as morning was beginning. I started to walk to the nearest road to catch a bus home.

We all took Daniels car to the party and he had the keys still so there was no sense in trying to walk back to the car, not to mention that i'm miles away from there now and probably shouldn't drive right now anyways.

Before reaching the end of the woods, I felt anger take me over. I yelled out as I hit one of the trees repeatedly

"Damn it, this can't be real! No! She can't just be gone!" My knuckles were bloody from the impact.

Finally feeling the weight overtake me, I dropped to the ground, feeling defeated and crushed.

My heart and myself entirely felt like it crumbled to pieces, and tears silently streamed down my face.

"Please, she can't be gone." I whispered to myself.

I wiped my face and tried to pull myself together. I made my way to the bus stop, then got on the bus, heading to another stop near my house.

Part of me believes that i'm going to walk back into the house to see her there, greeting me with that beautiful smile. The world seems so dull and dark without her here.

My mind keeps flashing back to Alivia covered in blood. Hayven let her borrow her house key to get into the house just incase she needed it since me and Daniel have our own, and i'm sure she called a taxi to get there, but I do feel bad for leaving her the way I did.

She must've gone through a very traumatic experience and doesn't have answers or anything.

I'm going to have a lot to explain when I see her, but truthfully, I don't want to care about her or how she's feeling or anything.

I don't want to feel anything ever again if it's true that Hayven is gone. Without her, there's nothing in this life worth feeling.

I let out a deep sigh before unlocking my front door and opened it.

"Damien!" Alivia said as she ran and jumped to hug me. "I'm so glad you're okay!" she continued.

"Yeah. I'm sorry for taking off like that last night." I say to her.

She still held her hand on my arm gently as she said, "I'm just glad you're okay. What exactly did I see happen to Hayven, though? I wasn't sure if I should call the police. Is Daniel like a cannibal or does he do drugs or something?"

I pulled her hand off of me and walked around her to sit on the couch. With another sigh, I sank back into the couch with my eyes closed.

"it's more complicated than all of that." I started to say, feeling uninterested in explaining everything to her right now.

Before I could continue, she asked, "Is he a vampire or something?"

I looked over at her, silent for a moment, and then said, "Yes. Daniel is a vampire, and he was addicted to Hayvens' blood. I thought we had it under control, but obviously, I was wrong."

I tried my best to keep it together while explaining everything. I can't shake this feeling of needing to find her, but I don't know where else to look right now.

"So does that mean you're a vampire, too? Hayven isn't a vampire, is she?" Alivia asked.

I didn't have a good lie about myself and didn't feel like I had enough energy to play it off as any other thing that would make sense so I just replied, "Yes, i'm a vampire too and no, Hayven is human."

she nodded, acknowledging what I said. the anger built up inside of me in the silence again, "God, I should have never left her alone!" I yelled out and slammed my fist on the table.

Alivia jumped from the noise. "Don't worry, if they're alive, then we will find them." she said, trying to console me.

Her voice sounded almost cold as she spoke. I looked at her, and then a laugh escaped through my nose with disbelief.

"Right, if they're alive..." I said non convincingly as I looked down.

CHAPTER 22

Hayven's pov:

We sat there side by side feeling trapped in this room, no way to escape in sight.

"What do you think he wants with us?" I ask Daniel, knowing he probably knew just about as much as me.

"Who knows, blood? money? to party more?" Daniel half joked and then continued, "No, actually I think him and whoever he is working with wanted you for some reason and I just so happened to show up to become apart of this abduction."

"Wow, well, I don't know whether to say you have great timing or really, really awful timing." I joked back and tried to force a giggle.

Daniel smiled back to me and laughed as he said, "Probably both."

I nodded in agreement. "How long do you think we've been here for anyways?" I ask, now in a more serious tone.

"I have no idea. It feels like we've been here for maybe a night. It's hard to tell, though, when there's no way to track the time at all in here." he replied just as seriously.

"I just want to go home already." I said in a sad tone as I thought of where we're at and what Damien must be going through right now.

"By the way, I wanted to talk to you about everything with Damien. Now seems as good a time as any, I suppose, but tell me again how you know him and your sister have met and he lied?" Daniel asked openly.

"Alivia told me that he met her before, and that it was actually the reason she found out about me and wanted to find me, but to my face he pretended like they had never met and like he had no idea I have a sister." I explained.

"What if he just forgot somehow?" he asked.

"There's no way he would just forget something like that so easily. Even if he didn't remember her, he would've remembered that I have a sister out there that I had no idea about, and it really makes me feel like I don't know him as well as I thought I did.

What else could he know about that he just chose not to tell me or has lied about entirely? does he know how my best friend died? what else has he not told me?" I ended with a deep sigh.

Daniel nodded to tell me he understood my concerns and frustrations.

"I understand why that would be so upsetting. I mean, who knows, maybe he knew something about the people in your life and to protect you he had to make a few insane choices, maybe he was even involved in killing your best friend because some how you needed saving or something.

Who knows, but if Damien and Alivia have met in the past and that's what started her journey to find you, why couldn't she have just asked Damien how to contact you?" he said.

"Don't say that. He would have done anything to protect me I'm sure, but there was no reason for anyone to take her from me. She was a good person and a good friend.

He wouldn't have just left me alone like that, and honestly I'm not entirely sure.

Maybe he couldn't risk me finding out about him at the time. I don't know. it's all so confusing. There's too many secrets to keep track of." I replied.

"Hey, I'm just playing devils advocate here a little bit. Damien would do anything to protect you.

He wouldn't have done anything unnecessary, I don't think, but if it was to protect you, then he would've done anything. I'm not saying he for sure did anything.

He did go through that long phase where he did a lot of things that he has openly said he regrets, but whether you want to admit it or not, he's always had the best intentions for you in anything he's done.

You might not be happy with him, you might not like it, but he would go to the end of the earth for you, even if it meant having to survive through hell, and that's a fact that you cant deny. I don't know what's true or not true entirely, or if he has ever met your sister in the past or not.

He's never mentioned you having a sister to me, but if they did meet, everyone has secrets I'm sure and if he has lied or kept certain things a secret, I just hope that you'll allow him the benefit of the doubt and talk to him about it and not punish him for the entire thing before even knowing what crime he's committed for sure." he explained.

We sat there in silence for a moment as we both thought deeply about everything that we just said.

"Do you have any secrets?" I asked.

"Yes, I do have a few secrets." he answered.

"What are they?" I asked curiously.

"Well, they wouldn't be much of a secret if I told you." he replied with a slight chuckle.

"Well, make them not secrets anymore and tell me then. What else are we going to do in here?" I replied with a laugh.

"I'm sure you will find out one day, but I don't plan on coming clean today."

I accepted that answer so as not to make him feel uncomfortable and said, "Well, I hope you know that you can tell me anything, and I will always be here to listen."

he looked at me with the most genuine smile plastered across his face and simply said, "I know."

the door opened suddenly, and we both jumped to our feet in an attempt to prepare for whatever was to come.

Jeramiah stood there in the doorway with a dart gun in his hands and quickly shot Daniel in the thigh with some kind of tranquilizer.

Daniel let out a loud groan from the pain, and the leg that was hit buckled underneath him as he dropped to his knees.

Jeramiah shot another tranquilizer at him, hitting his collarbone this time. He let out another loud pain filled groan as he fell to the ground with one hand holding him up and the other hand on his collarbone area where the dart was sticking out of him.

"Daniel!" I yelled out as I dropped down to try to help him.

"What the hell did you put in these?! Daniel yelled. his voice sounded tensed and like the pain was just shy of being too much to take.

"Oh, these?" Jeramiah asked while holding up another one of the tranquilizer darts.

"It's cows' blood. I've heard that the reason vampires can't just live off of and consume animal blood is because of the different blood types they possess.

Some types can react like a strong sedative, some a poison that can kill you, some that cause extreme physical pain, and many others that cause a variety of fun sounding reactions to watch." Jeramiah explained.

Daniel had panic written all over his face as well as confusion. "Which one did you give him?!" I yelled out.

"Guess you'll have to wait and see." Jeramiah replied with a smirk.

Daniel was beginning to get weaker and weaker and began to lose consciousness.

I tried my best to prevent him from crashing to the ground and guided his body to lay down just before he passed out with his head in my lap.

"What's the matter with you?! what do you want?!" I cried out with tears forming in my eyes.

Jeramiah shut the door behind him and sat down on the floor just in front of it with the dart gun pointed my way.

"You and I are going to have a chat while our good friend here is peacefully sleeping. I like my privacy." he said casually.

"You're out of your mind." I said to him.

"I may be out of my mind, but in this game of cat and mouse, I'm the cat, and you happen to be the mouse." he replied.

"What are you talking about? what do you want?!" I asked.

"You see, originally, I just wanted you to confess your love for me, since as we both know, you've been in love with me for a long time too.

Maybe get you to leave your boyfriend with a few threats to his life and then I'd become your new boyfriend, but an unforeseeable opportunity has presented itself here and for the sake of the game of cat and mouse, I just can not resist taking advantage of it."

he began explaining before I cut him off in anger, saying,

"You're truly a crazy person. There must be something wrong in your head. I have never once been in love with.

I mean, hell, I hated you up until you apologized to me about the past and invited me to that first party. I have never had feelings for you, you psycho. Now tell me what kind of blood was in those darts!"

he stood to his feet and said, "It was only the kind to sedate him, but okay here's the deal. I know all about him being a disgusting vampire, along with your little boyfriend.

Fun fact, my dad worked with your dad when they tested vampires. I also know about your friends little blood addiction and I know that he needs some kind of medicine to stop his vampire side from taking over and losing control because of that addiction, and I know you're in love with me.

You know it deep down but have gotten all confused in the head because of those disgusting creatures and now you've convinced me that my original plan was a great idea and tossing in the opportunity I was given will only serve as more motivation for you to admit it, so here's what's going to happen.

You have up until the time he loses control to admit to me that you've always been in love with me and beg for me to forgive you for calling me crazy and a psycho, to give up on your boyfriend who I will kill after this is all done and over with and you have to kill your friend first so you can start your new life with me, or he's going to kill you." he said.

His voice sounded cold and unfeeling.

"You're completely delusional, Jeramiah. I could never and would never love someone like you." I replied in disgust, the feeling of shock beginning to wash over me.

His face twisted in anger at me, calling him delusional and saying I could never love him.

"The clock is ticking Hayven! I told your boyfriend the first day we met that you would mine one day, so you can either admit it or die lying." he said with anger filling his voice as he opened the door behind him and slammed it on his way out.

My eyes widened at the realization that he was right about one thing. Eventually, Daniels medicine would wear off, and we would both be stuck in this room when it happened if we couldn't find a way out. If it wears off, then it really might just be the end for me after all.

"Damien, please find us..." I whispered to myself.

I realized that Jeramiah seemed to have forgotten the darts in Daniel and reached out to them as they were still stuck in Daniels skin and pulled them out.

They're not huge, but we could possibly use them as a weapon if given the right opportunity.

I hid them behind where I was sitting and started trying to shake Daniel awake. He's still completely knocked out, though, so I guess I have no other choice but to sit here and wait.

Damien pov:

I woke up an hour ago but can't seem to make myself get out of bed. I want her back, and the fact that I don't know how to find her feels like it's eating me alive.

heck, I don't even know if she's alive or where Daniel could possibly be. I searched his whole house last night thinking maybe that's where he would take her, the park, back at that forest, anywhere I could possibly think of.

looking at her phone number seems to be the only comfort I can find right now. I pressed the call button to call her cell and put it to my ear,

everything inside me wishing I would hear her voice on the other end saying hello and telling me she's alive and safe and will be home soon, but my heart shattering when, after a few rings, I reach her voicemail instead.

"Hey, this is Hayven. I'm sure you've noticed I didn't answer, so I will get back to you as soon as I can. Okay, bye!" she says.

This is the 30th time I've tried to call her since that night that I tried to call her phone over and over the night they disappeared.

each time ending with the same outcome as the last, but never failing to make my heart sink from the disappointment.

"Hey, I'm coming in!" Alivia said as she knocked on the door twice real quick. I stared at her silently as she walked in.

"Okay, look, I know you're like super sad, I am too, of course, but you can't just lay in bed all day. Let's get out and maybe go get some out food or something." she said.

"And what if i tell you no thanks?" I replied back in a grumpy tone.

"Then I will drag you out of this house myself one way or another." she said.

"Right, I doubt you could get me to move even an inch." I said with a little chuckle.

She started walking to the front door and yelled, "Wow, I bet the whole neighborhood would love to know that vampires exist and one lives here!"

I quickly jumped out of bed and ran over to cover her mouth. "Okay, okay! Fine, you win. I will get dressed right now, jeez. Just don't be yelling that kind of stuff." I said in defeat and then dropped my hand away from her mouth.

She smiled proudly over her victory and walked to grab herself a sweater.

She was already dressed to go, so I told her to give me fifteen minutes so I could get ready. I took a quick shower and threw on a pair of pants and a t-shirt.

"That's more like it. You look much better now. Very handsome." she said.

"Uh, thanks." I replied, feeling a bit awkward about my girlfriends sister calling me handsome.

We both walked out the door and got into the car to drive to a fast food place.

"What kind of food do you want to eat?" I ask her.

"How about Chinese food?" she asked back.

I nodded in agreement. she tried to talk to me about my likes, my dislikes, what I do for fun, and all the other classic ice breaker questions.

I only replied with short and quick answers since I didn't care much to play this ice breaker game with her to begin with.

Once we parked, I said, "Okay, I will run in real quick and grab us both something to go. What do you want?" she looked at me with a pouty look.

"No, please, can we go inside and eat? please?" she begged.

I let out a sigh and said, "Fine. Let's go." to which she practically jumped out of her seat in excitement.

We sat together in awkward silence for about ten minutes before Alivia said she had to use the restroom.

our food hadn't made it to our table yet anyways, so it was a good time to go, I suppose.

A group of younger girls were seated nearby, and I overheard one of the girls saying, "Yeah, you can track them by their phone, and it will show you exactly where they are in the whole world."

to which a few of the other girls seemed to be amazed by.

I stood up and walked over to them, "Excuse me, I hate to both you, but I accidentally overheard what you were just saying. Is there any way you can show me how you can track someone's phone? I would really appreciate it."

They all giggled, and the original girl took my phone from my hands and looked up this website.

"Find your phone using your phone number!" The top of the page read.

Just below that, it read, "Find the location of your phone any-where. As long as you have your phone number and the location on the phone is turned on, our website can locate your phone anywhere in the world."

I thanked them all and handed them two ten dollar bills. "Here's $20, on me. I appreciate the help so much."

I sat back down just as Alivia walked out of the bathroom, and the waiter who had our food was walking out to our table.

I took a screenshot of the website so that I'd have it just in case I forgot the name of the website.

I typed in Hayvens' phone number into the search bar and clicked the search button.

"Sorry we couldn't find any phones by this number. Check to make sure power is on, location is on, and that you have the right number and try again."

my heart seemed to disappear entirely from the disappointment, and I dropped my head down on the table next to my food.

"Damien, are you okay?" Alivia asked, sounding concerned.

I sat back up and said, "No," in a half angry half upset tone, and then started to eat my food as fast as I could. I wanted to be done with it and get out of here.

Alivia finished her food soon after me, so I put $25 down on the table and said, "Let's go." As I got up and started to walk away.

She followed close behind me. We both got back into the car, and she asked hesitantly, "What happened exactly? Did I do something to upset you?"

I looked over at her, feeling guilt wash over me now to accompany the disappointment and hopeless feeling.

"No, no, of course not. You didn't do anything wrong. I'm sorry for acting like such a douche bag, for acting that way in general lately, really. I just thought that I might've gotten a lead on how to find Hayven, but I was wrong, and I got my hopes up. That's all..." I said to her in my best efforts to reassure her that it wasn't her.

It was that moment that I realized I was distancing myself from her a lot and very inconsiderate of her feelings.

She smiled from ear to ear and said, "Oh no, it's okay. I understand you've been so upset lately. I just wanted to make sure it wasn't something I did since it seemed so sudden that your mood changed."

I fake smiled and felt a little relief. "I'm glad you understand. I'm still sorry for acting that way towards you. I promise it's not you, though." I added.

She nodded, with that smile still across her face.

We got back home and went our separate ways for a few hours. I tried a few more times to look up Hayvens' number in hopes that it'd give me something different.

Then I tried mine to make sure it worked, and it found my exact location with my phone down to the address.

After trying probably one hundred separate times, I remembered that I could try Daniels phone number.

So I typed it in, and his too came up with nothing. This will be the third night they've been gone. I walked to the kitchen and pulled out a bottle of vodka from the back of one of the cupboards along with a shot glass next to it.

They both sat on the counter for a moment as I let out a deep sigh. The last time I drank for the sake of forgetting life, I lost myself.

Hayven was the only one who could bring me back, and that would have never happened if it wasn't for Daniel.

I don't want to feel this pain anymore, though. This feeling that they might both be out there, alive somewhere, but hurt, and I can't find them or help them.

I can't do anything except sit here doing nothing but waiting and hoping that they are alive somewhere.

I grabbed the vodka and poured my first shot, then downed it quickly. One turned into three in less than a minute.

"Hey, if you were planning on partying, why didn't you invite me?" Alivia said as she walked up behind me.

I stood there silently and then poured another shot.

"Hey, hey, i'm all for going extreme to party, but how many have you had so far? I just saw you walk in here less than two minutes ago." Alivia asked.

"This will be my fourth one." I said, very monotoned as I down the fourth shot.

She walked over to me and grabbed the bottle of vodka off the counter, and stepped back again.

"Hey, i'm not in the mood to play games. Just leave me alone, please." I begged.

She grabbed the shot glass out of my hands and with a smirk on her face she said, "All I was going to say is if your planning on getting trashed, at least let me give you some company."

She then poured a shot and downed it, then poured a second and downed that one, too.

I was starting to feel lightheaded, and my body started to relax as the feeling of being drunk was beginning to take over. Alivia walked over to the tv and put on some upbeat music, and turned up to volume.

"What are you doing?" I said with a confused smirk.

She grabbed the vodka, poured another shot, and touched the shot glass to my lips. "Drink." she whispers to me.

I almost couldn't hear her over the music. I took the shot as she held it. Every shot was causing me to slip closer and closer to forgetting life and feeling something more than just sadness.

It was overtaking my whole body. The feeling of relief hit me as I got more drunk. Relief from any guilt, regret, helplessness, from everything.

Alivia and I danced and laughed as we took turns taking shot after shot. By the time I was 10 shots in, I could hardly function properly, let alone remember why I started drinking in the first place.

We both sat down on the couch, laughing at and with each other. "Thank you for accompanying me in drinking." I said as i chuckled.

"It's been my pleasure." She said threw giggles as she leaned closer into me on accident.

Before I knew what was going on, I could feel her lips softly pressed against mine.

Being as drunk as I am, it took me a moment to register what she was doing.

She tried to toss her leg over to the other side of me to sit on top of me as she kissed me, but I stopped her leg and pushed her away from me as I jumped off the couch.

I paced back and forth with stress and frustration filling my entire body, also starting to sober up some but now struggling with the feeling of being overly drunk.

I stopped and looked at her, trying to find the words to say. "Alivia... why would you do that?" she sat forward with a smile.

"Because I like you, and I think you're handsome." she said matter of factly.

"But i'm with your sister Alivia, remember? Hayven? I'm in love with her, and only her." I replied, feeling my frustration slowly turning into anger.

"Yeah, she may be my sister, but I think i'm a much better fit for you than her anyway. Besides, as far as you know, she's dead, and you're never going to see her again. So, I might as well move on when the better choice is here now." She said confidently.

Anger filled me from the words she spoke as well as extreme guilt for drinking when I could be out there at least looking for any sign of her somewhere.

"Hayven is the only one I will ever love, and there's no one on this entire planet who could ever even come close to match her, let alone being better.

You can't beat what's already the best, and you have no idea if she's dead or alive. She is alive. I just know it. I can feel it. There's no way she's not alive somewhere." I replied, anger now seeping into the tone of my voice. disgust was starting to accompany the anger.

"Why wouldn't you want me? I'm great!" she spoke with an attitude.

"Because you're not her! You're not her, and you could never be her!" I yelled.

"Well, maybe I will make it where you can never see your precious Hayven again! Keep her stuck where she is or finish her off for good!" she blurted out in anger.

My eyes widened, and my stomach twisted in knots. "What do you mean Alivia? Do you know where Hayven is? Is she alive?" I asked intensely as I took a step closer to her.

She stood up off the couch now. With regret for her mistake written all over her face. She tried to come up with a lie but struggled to get it out. "What I mean is... I mean, she and I... I don't know where she is, I just mean if I did know, then maybe that would be better."

I grabbed her by the arms and said, "You're lying. I knew there was something off about you since the first day we met. Where is Hayven?!"

CHAPTER 23

Hayven's pov:

Daniel looks like he's started to wake up finally. He had to have been out for at least an hour.

"Daniel," I whispered as I tried to softly shake him awake again.

"Hayven?" he asked, confused.

He then jumped up into a sitting up positioned and turned to look at me.

"Hayven, are you okay?! What did I miss?" he said in a panic.

Everything that was holding me together suddenly crumbled into a million pieces within me, and tears started to slowly drop one at a time.

"Daniel, he's completely insane..." I whispered as I wiped the tears from my eyes.

"He thinks I'm secretly in love with him and wants me to admit it to him and beg for forgiveness for telling him he's crazy. He wants me to give up Damien to be with him instead, and he wants me to kill you..." I continued.

Daniel moved his body closer to mine, hugging me tightly.

"Well that's obviously never happening. What's he think he's going to be able to do if you don't do those things?" Daniel asked.

"He... knows about your blood addiction." I hesitantly said.

Daniel pulled his body away from mine to look me in my eyes. He looked as though the realization had just hit him.

"He said I have to do all those things before your medicine wears off or he's going to let you kill me... So if I want to live, I have to give up and even hurt the people I care about and be forced to be with him, and if I don't, then I'm going to die." I quietly cried out.

Daniel pulled me into a tight hug again, now with one hand placed behind my head.

"I... I don't know how, but i'm not going to let that happen, Hayven. Even if it takes me dying, i'm not letting myself hurt you again." Daniel said, his voice cracking slightly nearing the end of his sentence.

"You can't die. We're going to get out of here somehow. We have to." I replied while pulling away from him.

"I have to tell you something, though. In case we don't both make it out of here..." Daniel said hesitantly as he sat back, crossing his legs.

"You don't need to. We're both getting out of here, just wait until we're both out safely." I replied in an attempt to not admit the possibility.

"No, Hayven. I have to tell you just in case. There's a chance that one of us won't make it or that neither of us will, despite our best efforts to escape. We don't know exactly what's going to happen from here on out. My medicine is already almost completely out of my system." Daniel replied very seriously.

"I can't accept that we both won't make it out together, but I will listen to what you want to tell me if you feel like you need to." I replied.

I looked down towards my lap, trying to distract my mind some as I listened.

"Thank you." he started to say. He paused for a moment as if to think of the right words to say. "I don't really know how else to say this except that i'm in love with you." he blurted out.

A look of surprised must have been painted across my face because he didn't allow me a chance to say anything yet.

"I have been for quite a long time now. I didn't realize it until I started to hallucinate really bad, but i'm very much in love with you.

At first I denied it and thought it was just the hallucinations and the addiction, but then when I got to take that medicine and those things all started to settle some, I realized that what I was feeling for you didn't stop with everything else." he continued.

"Daniel... I," I started to say, but then he stopped me by saying,

"You don't have to say anything to me about it. I know that you're only in love with Damien, and i'm okay with just being your best friend. As long he makes you happy with him and he treats you well, then i'm happy too.

You two are a great together. If I had to pick anyone that I felt deserved to be loved by someone as amazing as you, it would be Damien. So you don't have to explain where we stand or try to spare my feelings. I'm happy just getting to be close to you and a part of your life." he said, sounding very content.

As if he had thought long and hard about this many times. Accepting his place in my life entirely.

"You are my best friend, and I never want to lose you, Daniel." I replied.

He looked me straight in the eyes and said, "For as long as i'm alive, and as long as I have control over it, I won't be going anywhere. Not in a million years."

a smile formed across my face. "Good." I said and then grabbed the darts out from behind me. "I have a plan."

Damiens pov:

"Where is Hayven? What do you have to do with her and Daniel both disappearing off the face of the earth?" I begged as I held her by her upper arms.

Alivia lifted her leg up and kicked me back so hard that I lost my balance and fell to the ground hard, scraping my arms as I slid some on the ground.

"Fine! Yes, they're alive. I can't believe you fell for the whole thing, honestly. No sign or trace of them anywhere in the woods or anywhere I said they were. That's because I lied! I don't see what you see in her anyway. She's a boring normal human. You should be with your own kind!" Alivia said loudly.

"Wait, you're a vampire? How could you do this to your own sister?" I asked, confused as I pulled myself up from the floor to stand again.

"Yeah, our mom is a vampire. Usually, when a vampire and a human have kids together, whether they're human or vampire, is passed down from the mother.

So what the mother is usually determines what the kid comes out as, but of course, little miss Hayven had to be the special one in a million that came out human.

Then our mom got bored of Hayvens annoying dad and wanted to be with her own kind and then had me. Also, I don't know if you've noticed, but we just met.

I actually don't really care about her at all and couldn't care less if she dies. You could go as far as saying I hate her and everything she is. I hate that I have a human sister.

My only goal was to make her miserable. I killed her little best friend and made it seem like a suicide so that she would lose the last person she had in life at the time and blame herself.

Then you came along, and I thought you were cute, so I thought, hey, what better way to make her miserable than her long-lost sister stealing away the man she's in love with.

Nothing else seemed to finally push her over the edge of misery, but it was so funny, you should've seen the look on her face when I told her that you were lying about us meeting and that we had actually met a couple years ago and she thought that you were lying straight to her face and keeping secrets from her. She looked devastated. It was amazing."

my eyes grew wide, and I felt the feeling of disgust seeping out of inch of me.

"Is that why she was distant from me before you took her?!" I yelled.

She laughed and said, "Yes, and it worked so well to keep you two apart. I wasn't the one who took her actually, I got someone to help me. It's sad really, she walked away alone and was followed, and you were too busy talking to me to notice.

Daniel noticed, and he interrupted our plans. Luckily, I had a strong enough sedative on me in case what my little friend drugged her with wasn't enough.

It provided a great cover story as to why they were both gone though, and as far as i've heard, my friend is having a lot of fun with them both and the fact that Daniel is addicted to Hayvens blood."

I struggled for a moment to find the right words to say. "How do you know Daniel is addicted to her blood?" I asked, completely shocked.

She laughed once again. "Oh sweet Damien, I have been watching her for years. That includes her time living with you. Besides, I have my ways to find out little secrets." she replied.

"It's Jeramiah that you're working with, isn't it? Is he the one who took them?" I asked with anger in my tone.

She looked surprised for a moment and then said, "Well, you're smarter than I thought. Just barely." she walked around the couch near the door.

I rushed to follow her and slammed my hands on the wall on either side of her head with anger taking me over.

"I swear to god, if she is hurt at all, in any way, or Daniel, I will hunt you down and kill you in the most tortuous way you could ever possibly imagine. You better hope I find them before he does anything to them." I threatened.

She chuckled. "I'd love to see the look on her face when the man she loves and thinks has been lying to her and keeping secrets kills her newly found sister." She said smugly.

I wanted to rip her head from her body or keep her alive just long enough to find out what they suffered through and make her have to endure every bit of pain and misery they're going through right now, but as badly as I wanted to do something to Alivia, I knew she was right, and I needed her to stay alive in case I needed her to find them.

She suddenly pushed me away and ran out the door and down the road as quickly as she could before I could grab her again.

Knowing she would cause a huge scene if I chased her, I decided against it for the time being and I turned around quickly to grab my phone and my jacket and bolted out the door, slamming it behind me.

I tried to call Hayven again, voicemail again. I'm going to search Jeramiah's house top to bottom and he better hope that I don't find him.

Hayvens pov:

we talked about the possible ways we could use the darts to be the most effective and decided our best options are to either distract him so Daniel can take him down in general, or to stab him in the eye with one of the darts if we get a chance and run out the door while we can.

"Are you cold, Hayven?" Daniel asked.

I was still wearing the dress I wore to the party with a pair of wedged boots.

Whatever building we're in the temperature seemed to slowly keep dropping almost, so I started to shiver slightly.

"Oh, no. I'm fine. I will be okay." I replied.

"Don't lie. You're shivering. I probably should've done this before, but here, take this." Daniel said as he took off his dress shirt that he was wearing over a t-shirt.

He wrapped it around my shoulders and didn't give me the choice to deny his offer. So I slid my arms inside the long sleeves and wrapped myself with it. It was warm from his body heat.

He had a secret pocket on the inside of the shirt, so I put my dart inside of it, and he put his in his pants pocket.

The door opened up again, and just like last time, it flung open, almost hitting the wall. He aimed the dart gun at Daniel, and I jumped up in front of him.

"No! Whatever it is you need to talk about now, you can just say in front of him. If you shoot him with one of those again, then I won't talk to you at all." I yelled.

Jeramiah lowered the dart gun to his hip, pointing downward to the ground.

"What do you want?" I ask.

With an irritated look on his face, he said, "I came to see if you decided to confess yet or if you plan to wait until he rips your throat out."

I looked at Daniel and then took a step forward away from him towards Jeramiah.

"Actually, I do want to confess." I started to say as I took another step towards him.

"Do you?" he asked sarcastically.

"Well, let's hear it then." he continued.

Daniel moved behind me a bit too much, and Jeramiah quickly pulled the dart gun back up to aim it at him again.

"No! Jeramiah, don't!" I begged as I quickly took a couple more steps toward him, standing in front of the gun and gently placing my hand on top of it to guide him to pointing it at the ground again.

"If he shoots Daniel with these tranquilizers again, then there's no way we're going to be able to get out of here. We're running out of time." I thought to myself.

He dropped his aim to the floor once again.

"He won't do anything to you, I promise." I whispered softly in his ear.

I placed one hand gently on his left wrist that was holding the gun and my right hand softly on his chest. I stood on my tip toes a bit so that I could get closer to his ear.

His breathing was slowly becoming more irregular.

"You were right." I whispered.

"I knew it," he said loudly.

"Shhh." I encouraged him to stay silent so I could keep him focused on what I was saying instead of what I was doing. I ran my hands up and down his left arm as I reached inside of my shirt to grab the dart.

"There's just one thing before I leave with you." I whispered as seductively as I could manage. I felt nauseous by my own words to him.

"Anything." he said, fully entangled in my voice.

"I promised that Daniel wouldn't do anything to you, but I never promised I wouldn't." I said quietly as I threw my right hand up holding the dart and stabbed him in the left eye.

He dropped to the floor, yelling in pain and calling me names, and Daniel and I ran out the door as fast as we could. Daniel turned back around to kick the dart gun out of the room and shut the door.

It was too dark to see where the lock was, and we didn't have much time before he recovered enough to possibly come after us.

It was probably excruciatingly painful to be stabbed in his eye, but ever since he was a kid, his anger would over take the pain every time.

I've seen him break his arm and then get back up only a minute after and kick another kid he blamed off the jungle gym, and that was when we were kids. So it's only a matter of time before he comes after us.

We ran down a long hallway that led into a massive room that had multiple doors and more hallways.

"I... I don't know which way to go, Daniel." I said to him, starting to become visibly panicked.

"I don't know either... It's okay, it's okay, Hayven. Try to stay calm. Let's just split up and try different doors." he said, walking to the right.

I didn't feel like splitting up was the right call, but I didn't have a better idea and didn't have time to argue about it, so I ran to the left.

The only light was coming from very high up windows that were near the roof. Only providing enough light to see where we're walking and what's beside us, but the large room was pretty dark over all.

The first door I tried led to a small room with a desk table that was covered in papers and a few filing cabinets and chairs.

I shut it back and stumbled over a few random machines and tools that were scattered on the ground.

Every door I checked led no where helpful, and I was beginning to panic more and more with every hopeless lead on a way to get out.

Suddenly I heard a very quiet ringing coming from somewhere I couldn't quite place.

I followed where I thought the sound was coming from, and it slowly got louder and louder. Before I could find it, it stopped ringing.

About two minutes later, I heard the ringing again, so I hurried to search for it again, and it led me to a small box. I slowly opened it and saw my phone inside, ringing with Damien's photo on it.

My heart stopped with the feeling of relief. I grabbed it as fast as I could and answered it.

"Damien! Damien, oh my god. Thank god you called right now." I said in a hushed yell of excitement as I started to cry.

"Hayven!" he yelled on the other side of the phone with excitement and simultaneously shocked voice.

"Damien, we don't know where we are. Jeramiah kidnapped us, and he's completely insane. We don't have much time before he comes looking for us, I stab him in the eye with an empty tranquilizer dart that he filled of some kind of animal blood. He shot Daniel with it yesterday. It made him pass out." I cried out quickly, hardly taking a breath.

"You have to get out of there, Hayven! Where's Daniel?" he yelled, worried.

"We don't know how to get out of here. This building is so big and dark, and we don't know where anything is. We had to split up to try to find a way to get out." I said, sounding very clearly upset.

"Hayven, listen to me. Turn the location on your phone to on. I might be able to find you if you turn it on. As fast as you can, turn it on." he said, trying to stay calm.

I said okay and pulled the phone away from my ear to turn it on. I pressed the location on and then went to put it back to my ear.

Before I could say anything again, I felt a pair of big hands grab me by the shoulders and slammed me up against the wall.

The phone dropped out of my hands and fell to the floor a few feet away, and I let out a scream from both being terrified and the pain of being slammed against the wall.

I opened my eyes to see Jeramiah standing in front of me. His closed left eye was covered in blood that dripped down his face and was still bleeding and swollen. He put a sharp box cutter up to my neck and looked furious.

"You're so stupid." he said in a growl.

My breathing was heavy as I stood there almost frozen in place. My heart was racing, and I felt sick to my stomach.

"I should slowly cut out both of your eyes to show you how it feels!" he growled out furiously again.

Moving the box cutter up to my eyes, struggling to stop himself from following through with his idea but not touching my skin. I turned my head away from him.

"I'm sorry," I cried out a few times. "Please dont hurt me, I'm so sorry."

he punched the wall beside my head as hard as he could with the hand that was holding the box cutter, causing me to scream again.

Suddenly, I felt him be pulled away from me and look to see that Daniel had wrapped his arm around Jeramiah's neck and was holding him tightly where he couldn't breathe. I was too afraid to move, so I stood frozen.

Jeramiah tried to cut Daniels arm with the box cutter and suc-
ceeded, which caused Daniel to wince and tense up with a pain
filled groan.

Slowly, Jeramiah stopped moving and fighting him. Daniel
dropped him to the ground, and I could see that he was still
breathing, but he was unconscious. I started to cry more again and
ran to hug Daniel. He held me tight.

"It's okay, i'm here." he said in a calm, comforting tone.

"We have to try to find our way out, Hayven." I nodded as I pulled
away slowly and started to try to wipe away some of the tears.

I hesitantly stepped around Jeramiah, fearing that he would
wake up any second and grab my phone or me. I tried to turn it
on, but it died.

I tried to hold in the tears as I said, "I found my phone and
talked to Damien. He said he might be able to find us if I turn on
the location, so I turned it on before Jeramiah found me. I don't
know if Damien was able to find us. It was on for a minute at least
afterward." I said as I put it in my pocket.

"We can only hope and try to find our way out in the meantime."
Daniel replied as he reached his hand out for mine.

I grabbed his hand, and we ran together to search more ways
that we could go to try and find our way out.

After checking more doors and rooms than I can even keep track
of, we finally came across a door that was locked with a padlock.

Damiens pov:

"I can't believe she finally answered. She's alive." I thought to
myself filled with disbelief that this isn't just some sick and twisted
dream that my brain thought would be funny to make me have.

I listened as she spoke to me over the phone and told her to turn the location on quickly.

I can put her number into that website again once her location is on, and hopefully, it'll show me where she is.

"Okay," she replied to me, and I could hear her clicking different things on her phone.

Suddenly, I heard a couple of loud noises over the phone, and I heard her scream.

"Hayven?! Hayven! What's happening?!" I yelled into the phone.

All I could do was listen to the things she was saying and listen to that piece of shit threatening her. Hearing the things he was saying disgusts me.

"When I see him, I won't do something as nice as stabbing him in the eye." I thought to myself as I started to feel unbelievably angry.

I hurried and typed in the website and typed her number into the search bar.

"Yes! It brought up an address!" I yelled out in excitement to myself. I took a screenshot of the address just in case anything happened.

The call suddenly cut off, and the address on the website reloaded and went back to saying no phone can be found.

"Thank god, I can't believe I finally got it. I have to hurry up and get to her. If he hurts her, it will be the last thing he ever does," I thought to myself.

I put the address into my gps on my phone. The gps says it's an hour walk from where I am. I put my phone in my pocket with the gps directions turned on and started to run.

There's no time to search for a bus route, I can't drive because I'm too far from home to go back, and a taxi won't drive out that way. So my only chance is to run there as fast as I can.

"Stay safe for just a little bit longer, guys." I thought to myself.

Hayven pov:

We tried to break the lock off, but nothing we tried was able to bust it off.

"Come on, Daniel, let's go look for a different way out. There's got to be more than one way out of this place, and we don't even know if this door leads to outside or not." I said as I gently grabbed his forearm.

"Yeah, you're right." he said, slightly winded from exerting so much energy into hitting the lock.

We walked back down the long hallway, turning a few times. We checked every door in this area, and the only place to go was back to the big main room and try to find another door that hopefully will lead to an exit.

We made our way back to the big room and as quietly as we could, we checked three more doors and then the third one led to another big room that just wasn't as big as the one we were leaving from.

Daniel carried a big wrench with him that he found when we tried to knock the pad lock off from the other door, and in case Jeramiah woke back up and came to find us.

We slowly made our way through this room, walking around tables and chairs. It was a bit brighter thanks to lights hanging from above.

Around the corner was a short hallway that led to a door that had a red exit sign above it. We both ran to it as fast as our tired and hungry bodies could take us. As we pushed on the door to open it, it wouldn't budge.

We were both looking frantically for a lock of some kind that we could possibly unlock, to no avail.

There was a small spot that could take a key but no other way that we could find to unlock it.

Daniel suddenly yelled out in pain. I shot my head up to look at him and saw that he was hit in between his shoulder blades with a tranquilizer dart.

Daniel was leaning against the door, using it to hold his weight up. I spun around to see Jeramiah stand there with his dart gun aimed toward us.

Daniel turned around and used the rest of his strength to chuck the wrench at Jeramiah as hard as he could, knowing that soon he wouldn't have the strength to use it as a weapon and may even go unconscious and knowing that I cant use it in this moment to protect myself because of how heavy it is.

It hit his leg with a crack and a ting as it fell to the concrete floor. He dropped to the ground, yelling out in obvious excruciating pain.

Daniel dropped to the ground beside me. One tranquilizer doesn't seem like it's enough to sedate him and cause him to lose consciousness, but it was enough to weaken his already much weaker body.

"Hayven, run. Just run anywhere else. Find a room and lock yourself inside if you can, and barricade the door." Daniel said.

"What about you, Daniel?" I asked.

"You're more important." he replied.

"But..." I started to argue, not wanting to leave him here.

"Go!" he yelled.

I hesitantly stepped closer to Jeramiah and then tried to make a run for it around him while he was distracted by the pain from his leg.

The moment I stepped next to him, he grabbed my arm tightly and stood up. He limped on his injured leg as he dragged me back towards Daniel.

"Just let her go." Daniel said weakly.

"I don't understand why you haven't given in yet and drank from her yet. You're addicted to her blood, and you're a vampire who hasn't had any blood in three days." he started to say to Daniel, still visibly in pain.

Before I could react, he cut my forearm with the box cutter he had earlier, saying, "Here, let me help you out. You can have her."

I gasped from the surprise and the pain and then screamed out in agony. I kicked his injured leg, causing him to yell out in pain and buckle over slightly.

I couldn't get past him still because of where he was standing. He stood back up and shoved me into the door hard and then limped over to us. He grabbed my cut arm and pulled it over to Daniels face.

My breath caught in my throat, and I froze. I felt stuck. Even with Jeramiah being injured, I was incredibly weak from not eating and barely sleeping.

Along with already being bruised and sore from earlier when he slammed me into the wall.

Daniel looked like he could hardly hold himself back from drinking the blood from my arm and soon enough sank his teeth into my arm. Jeramiah backed up fast. I let out a little scream.

"Daniel, please remember who I am and what you're doing," I begged, trying to get through to him.

Jeramiah stood back and laughed. Daniel pulled away for a second to catch his breath before pulling me closer to him. He pulled my hair out of the way.

"Daniel, no! Please think about what you're doing." I begged.

"I can't stop myself, Hayven. i'm sorry." he said quietly.

Sounding like it was a struggle to hold himself back long enough to say that even.

He held me firmly so I couldn't pull away and sank his teeth into my neck. I cried out in pain again. He pulled away to catch his breath again. Now, I realized what he was doing.

"God, Hayven I'm so sorry." he said, sounding like he was now getting upset.

He tried to hold himself back for a minute but then gave in again and drank from my neck for another minute and then pulled away again.

We were both covered in my blood. He layed my body on the floor and tried to crawl away from me. I was still conscious but lost so much blood that I was just hanging on to consciousness and life by a thread.

I felt too weak to care to move. It felt like I was in a bad dream, and the moment didn't feel real. The only thing to show me proof that it was real and that I hadn't already died or something was the pain from my neck and arm.

I could see Jeramiah standing nearby still smiling and laughing at our despair.

Daniel kept repeating that he was so sorry and was visibly distraught over hurting me.

Something started to hit the exit door from the outside. Daniel grabbed me and pulled me away from the door and then backing away from me again.

"What the hell?" Jeramiah said.

Damien pov:

I ran up to this building and could hear Hayven and Daniel inside. I could also hear another voice that sounded like Jeramiah, and it brought nothing but the feeling of disgust to my entire being.

I tried to pull the door, but it was locked. I heard Hayven scream and felt frozen for a moment.

I luckily kept some sun pills in my pocket because I always remember the pain I went through from the sun when Hayven and I were both taken the first time.

I needed some medicine, so Daniel wasn't hurt from the sun, and I will have to get another dose of his blood addiction medicine.

It has been days since his last dose, and if I don't get some to him some soon, then it might be too late, and he may hurt someone, Hayven being my main worry. If he hasn't done something to her already, that is.

I try to break down the door that I can hear them behind, but can't seem to get it to budge.

I can't get through the main door, but there's another door nearby, so I try that one and find out that it's completely unlocked.

I quietly open the door and shut it behind me as I sneak in. No one seems to notice, so I slowly make my way around the corner where the first door I found is.

I see Jeramiah standing there laughing, Daniel a few feet away from Hayven fully ridden with guilt and looking visibly shaken to the core and covered in blood, and then as I continue to scan the small hall way I see Hayven laying on the floor barely conscious and covered in blood as well. With wounds on her forearm and neck and shes not moving.

I could feel the rage building up inside of me. My thoughts started to get hazy, and I couldn't focus because of how furious I felt.

I walked over quietly but calmly behind Jeramiah and snapped his neck. He fell to the floor, completely lifeless.

Daniel saw me and started to beg for forgiveness. "I'm so sorry, I didn't give in this whole time, I tried so hard not to hurt her... but he cut her arm and held it in front of my face. I couldn't fight it anymore, i'm so sorry." I didn't say anything in reply to his apologies.

I reached in my pocket and then held my hand out with the medicines Daniel needed, and without looking at him, I said, "Take these before you leave this building. I'm taking her to the hospital."

CHAPTER 24

Hayven's pov:

I could feel the relief of Damien showing up. I wasn't completely sure what was going on, but soon enough, I could feel his arms wrapping around me.

He brought me close to his chest and held me tightly as he whispered in my ear, "I'm here now. You're safe. I'm going to get you help. Everything's going to be okay."

he held me like he never wanted to let go again. Like just a touch of my skin gave him life, and he never wanted to feel life without me ever again.

He was quiet considering all of the feelings he must be feeling, but I could tell he was upset and was just trying to remain calm for me.

I let myself fall to pieces in his arm as he picked me up bridal style, and I passed out as the relief washed over me.

When I woke up again, I was in a bed, warm underneath a few blankets, and could feel someone's arm draped across my thighs and holding my hand.

They were laying there with their head on my right thigh, and I could feel the strongest energy of someone I felt so comfortable with.

I opened my eyes to see Damien laying there holding me. It was as if he was afraid that if he let go of me again. That he would lose me forever.

"Damien?" I asked a bit confused, "what happened? " I continued as he sat up.

"Daniel consumed a large amount of your blood, so I brought you to the hospital. I told them I didn't hear from you for a few days but that I found you on the side of the road near the woods where we hike sometimes and think an animal attacked you." he whispered to me.

"Where's Daniel now?" I asked, worried.

"Don't worry, he needs time to let his medicines work. It's probably a good idea that he doesn't come to a hospital right now anyways considering he almost killed you." he replied with a mixed look of anger and sympathy.

"I don't blame him. He held out a lot longer than I thought he was going to be able to. Damien, I thought his medicine was supposed to wear off after a day." I said, puzzled.

"It is, but there's a chance that it finally cured his addiction, and now between smelling your blood and being starved for days that he gave in because of that and started the addiction all over again, which would mean that the medicine I gave him should work much faster and he may be perfectly fine other than feeling guilty, within the next few hours to the next few days." he replied, very monotoned and emotionless.

"I missed you." I said as I started to tear up.

He sat up quickly and moved closer to me, getting into bed with me as he wrapped one arm around the back of my neck and one across my stomach and held me tightly again.

"I missed you too," he said as he tried not to let the emotions consume him.

"Once you're out of here I have so many things I need to tell you, but would it be okay if I brought a stressful thing up that may relieve some feelings and emotions you still hold against me right now?" he asked.

I was hesitant because I didn't know where he was going to go on this topic but then said, "Yes, you can tell me." he held me tighter again.

"I promise you I never lied to you. Your sister lied to you when she said we've met. I know that brings up more questions and stresses, but I swear to you on everything I am, everything I have, I swear to you on anything that would help you believe me, I never lied.

I have never met her before, and I had no idea you had a sister. I knew you had a mom who left, but I never looked into her or her life because I was more concerned with you, and she was gone. I know what your sister told you, but I promise you, I never knew."

before I knew it, tears began to stream down my face again. "But why would she lie to me about that?" I asked.

"I don't think it would be good for you to get into it all right now. I promise I will explain everything that's happened and tell you everything, but you need to rest right now.

I just really needed to tell you that one thing. I needed you to know that what she said wasn't true, and I'm so sorry.

I wish I would've realized that's why you were being so distant from me, and I blame myself for you getting taken, and i'm so sorry." he replied, sounding close to breaking down.

I cuddled into his chest. I believe him, even though I wish it wasn't true.

"I don't blame you." I said as I kissed his arm that was near my face.

"Damien, i'm so hungry. We're in a hospital, right? Can you call the nurse and get them to bring me some food, please?" I asked him, both because I really was hungry and because I needed to not think about those stressful things for the moment.

"Yes, yes. I will be right back." he said very hesitantly.

I could tell that everything inside of him wanted to stay with me, but he knows I most likely haven't eaten in days and need something.

My body felt sore, and I could feel my stomach growling. It felt like my stomach was almost trying to eat itself. I was so hungry. He told a nurse and then came back to sit next to me.

"What is it that you have to tell me?" I asked.

He layed his head on my thighs facing up at me and reached across me to hold my hand again as he said,

"I swear to you that i'm not hiding it, but there's a time and place that I need to tell you, because you being hurt and weak in the hospital is not the time or place that you should hear it all."

I sighed and then nodded, understanding. I thought back to what Daniel was saying when we were locked in the room and how Damien always has the best intentions for me, even if sometimes I don't see it quite the same way.

A nurse walked in with a plate of food. Here you go hun." she said as she placed the food on a movable table that swung out just in front of me. She picked up my file and looked through it for a moment.

"And just so you know, as far as we can tell, the babies seem to be perfectly healthy. Call it a miracle, but there seems to be absolutely nothing wrong at all." she said with a reassuring smile.

Damien and I looked at each other, both wide-eyed and surprised. "I'm sorry, did you say babies?" I asked with a nervous laugh.

"Yes. I'm sorry, I assumed you knew. You're pregnant with twins." she said, sounding like she didn't quite understand just what we were surprised about.

"No don't be sorry, but are you sure that you're reading the right file?" I asked.

"You're Hayven Davis, right?" she asked just to be sure.

"Yes... that's me." I replied as my heart sank into my stomach.

"What do you mean, babies?" I asked again.

"Well, we tested your blood and it showed that your pregnant so we did a basic ultrasound and found that you're carrying two babies, and it looks like they're measuring about 12 weeks along, so congratulations mom and dad, you have two little ones in there." she tried to explain light heartedly.

Damien and I sat in silence for a moment as the feeling of shock fully submerged us within itself.

"We do have a machine that can do 3d ultrasounds, so we can further check on them and print out a few photos of them if you would like."

I barely registered the words that were coming out of her mouth but could feel myself responding anyway, "Yes, can we please have that done?" I asked.

Damien didn't say a word, which only made me feel more stressed and nervous.

She wrote something in my chart as she said, "Yes, absolutely hun, we will get that going as soon as we can. Would you like to come along to see too, dad?" she continued on to ask as she looked towards Damien.

It seemed like he snapped to reality a little more for a moment, just long enough to say, " Um, yes. Yes, I want to see."

he grabbed my hand and held it firmly as he faded back into his thoughts. The nurse showed herself out to give us a moment alone.

I suddenly felt like I lost my appetite some so I pushed the little table away from me.

Damien looked up and grabbed it, pulling back over. He very calmly and sweetly said, "You need to eat something, Hayven, just start out slow."

he pulled my hand up to kiss it and then grabbed a small bowl of mashed potatoes off the tray and leaned close to feed it to me.

I was a bit resistant at first because of the stress, but I knew he wasn't going to take no for an answer on this since I did need to eat something, for my sake and apparently for our two babies that are growing inside of me.

So I gave in, and after the first bite, I could feel my appetite coming back quickly.

I nodded to him and took the bowl from his hands so that I could feed myself.

He lovingly rubbed my leg as I ate the mashed potatoes and said, "I love you so much.

With everything in me. Meeting you was the greatest thing I've ever done, and being lucky enough to be loved back by you is enough to make up for every bad thing I've ever experienced.

You're the greatest thing to ever happen to me, and I never want to lose you again. I never want you to be upset with me ever again. It's like god made you for me, and I have no idea what I possibly ever did to deserve you."

I put my food down, took a drink of water, and said, "Come here." he moved closer to me once again.

I grabbed the collar of his shirt and pulled him down to where we were face to face.

"God didn't make me for you. He made you for me, and I will stand by that until the day that I die." and then I leaned in to kiss him.

He placed his hands on the sides of my face to lean in and kiss me back passionately and gently, trying to be considerate of me being sore and hurt still.

I could feel that he didn't want to hold back, that he wanted to kiss me and hug me so intensely that breathing would be a pleasurable struggle, but he's holding himself back from the fear of causing me anymore pain.

We both stopped abruptly as we heard someone knock on the door.

"Excuse me, sorry to ruin the moment." a new nurse said while giggling.

Damien and I were both a little embarrassed at someone walking in at that moment, pulled away from each other some, while still holding hands.

"No worries, sorry about that." Damien said a bit shy like and gave a nervous laugh.

"I'm here to take you for the 3D ultrasound." the nurse said, still giggling.

"Oh, okay yeah lets do it." I said.

Damien nodded with a smile. She unhooked me from monitors, IV hook ups, the whole deal, then another nurse came in and helped her guide me out of bed and into a wheelchair and then wheeled me down the hall into a separate room as Damien followed.

They put this warm gel on my stomach and placed the transducer on my skin, and began to move it around.

We both gasped as two little babies popped up on the monitor in front of us. She pointed out baby A and baby B.

"Oh, do you want to see if we can find out the genders?" she asked excitedly.

I looked at Damien, and his face showed pure joy as he nodded yes.

"Yes, please." I said in agreement. I could feel myself getting excited, even though I was equally just as nervous and worried.

She moved around the top of my stomach to find different angles for a moment.

"looks like baby A is a boy!" she started to say, "and baby B is a girl! one of each, congratulations, you two," she said happily.

Damien and I were both in disbelief. We felt happy but almost couldn't believe that this is real life.

After everything that has happened, it's such a scary thought to bring two babies into the mix.

Not to mention the scary parts of being pregnant with two babies, and the fact that I wasn't expecting to become a mom so soon, but at the same time, its exciting because I've always wanted to be a mom, and to have a big happy family of my own and now it seems like that dream is coming true.

Damien leaned down to me. "We're going to be parents." he said happy and nervous all at once.

CHAPTER 25

They're going to keep me overnight for observation but said that I should make a full recovery, and that it's a miracle with how much blood I lost, but me and the babies seem fine overall.

I never thought at any point that I could be pregnant. My stomach is only a little bit bigger than normal, so I just thought I had gained a couple of pounds.

I must have overlooked any other signs or didn't pay attention enough to everything else that's been going on.

Damien stayed the night with me, never leaving my side. The next morning, they checked all my vitals, did one last blood test, and put this band type thing around my stomach to check the babies heartbeats.

Everything came back normal and good so they gave us the clear to go home on the condition that Damien take care of me, not let me lift any weight over 10 pounds, and make sure I take it super easy.

They wheeled me out in a wheelchair and Damien picked me up and sat me in the passenger side of his car, and then finally we headed home.

When we get there, Damien helps me make my way inside, and we see Daniel asleep on the couch.

He jumps up and sees us. He looks almost exhausted as I can imagine I look. I move to hide myself behind Damien, some just in case.

I don't blame him, and i'm not mad, but until I know the medicine is working for sure, then i'm too scared to be around him.

Daniel's face filled with guilt at the sight of me hiding. "I'm so sorry, Hayven..." he said, looking like a massive weight was just placed on his shoulders.

"Listen, i'm not mad. You just can't be around me again until the medicine starts working completely, and we know for a fact." I said to him.

"What if it turns out to be never?" he asked.

"Then I don't know. we will have to figure something out if that happens, but until we figure it out, I can't risk being around you. Not anymore." I replied.

A look of hurt washed over him instantly.

"I understand, I'm so sorry, Hayven." he replied.

I know I should be mad or scared for my life in general, or even just upset, but I just can't be. Something in me tells me that I should be understanding.

He cares about me, and because of a couple of different bad events that have happened, it made him this way.

There was even a time when Damien almost gave in because he was starved, but he was thankfully able to resist.

Though he was never addicted to my blood, unlike Daniel. Not to mention, Daniel seems to have drawn the short stick in getting addicted by just the smell.

"Daniel, I don't think you fully understand." I said as I stepped out from behind Damien just a bit.

"No, I do. This isn't the first time I've hurt you, and I know this is for the best." he replied.

"yes that's true, but that's not the whole reason behind it." I started to say.

"Hayvens pregnant Daniel. It's too risky for you to be around right now because if you can't stop yourself again, then this time, it really may be the last time, and then Hayven and my babies would be gone. I won't let that happen." Damien blurted out.

Daniel jumped up again and walked towards us. "Wait, you're pregnant?!" he yelled with equal excitement, surprise, and even more guilt coming out.

I nodded with a half smile.

"So when I... I'm so sorry, Hayven. I'm so sorry... is the baby okay?" Daniel continued.

"Both babies are fine." I said while waiting for him to catch on that there's more than one.

Daniel didn't say anything for a second as he processed what I said, and I could see the look of realization hit his face.

"Hold on a second, did you say babies? as in more than one baby? The plural of baby?" he asked.

Damien and I both started to chuckle despite the seriousness of everything else.

I couldn't hold back my smile any longer as I continued to laugh and say, "Yes, i'm pregnant with twins. one boy and one girl."

he looked relieved that me and the babies were fine, and once I said there's a boy and a girl, he looked even more excited and happy.

"That's amazing! do I get to be their uncle then?" he asked eagerly.

We nodded yes happily. "Absolutely! That's why you have to get better." I answered.

"But if you slip up even one time or seem to be a danger or any kind, then we won't be able to let you around them. The babies or Hayven." Damien continued to explain.

Daniel nodded, looking like some of the weight was lifted from him even though he still looked weighed down heavily with guilt.

"I understand, i'm going to get better." Daniel said confidently.

He then walked over to me and was about to try to lean in for a hug, but Damien put his hand on his chest, stopping him.

"She's still hurt. Not until you're both better." he looked sad that he couldn't hug me after such big news, but he didn't try to argue it.

He turned to Damien and hugged him instead and said, "Congratulations, my friend, you got the dream."

A couple of months passed since we last saw Daniel. Damien gave him a couple of months' worth supply of medicine at a time to hopefully get back to normal in that time.

We've talked about the babies and how i'm feeling, what kind of parenting styles we want to incorporate into our parenting, and what kind of baby items we plan to get.

I swear Damien would breathe for me if he could. He's been waiting on me, hand and foot, hardly letting me lift a finger.

It's sweet, though sometimes I just want to get up and do things myself.

I've been feeling much better, and like i'm almost healed, despite some bruising that's left.

Money isn't an issue because Damien works and has already made a lot of money that he mostly saved up from before and my father left him and I both a decent inheritance that we will get some time around my 22nd birthday which wont be long from after I have the twins. We also have plenty of room in this house for them.

"Hey, Damien, what should we name them? I would really like to be able to call them by name instead of calling them the twins or the babies." I asked, Damien.

He thought for a minute and then said, "What about Skye and Syrus?" My eyes lit up, and I sat more upright.

"I love those names!" I replied.

"Well, Skye and Syrus, it is then." Damien responded contently.

"Now we just need middle names for them. Whose last name are they taking?" he continued.

"Well, I guess I kind of just figured they would take your last name since I was planning to take your last name whenever we get married in the future." I replied.

"I love the thought of you becoming my wife." He said with a smile as he grabbed my hand.

I smiled back at him and said, "Me too." I thought for a couple of minutes and said, "What about Skye Lee Romaro and Syrus Alexander Romaro?" I asked.

Damien nodded in approval and said, "Yes, I like those names." Damien put his arm around me and held me close.

"Hayven, I think it's time I tell everything. It can't wait any longer." he said.

"Okay, so tell me." I replied.

"Well, to start, your sister and mom are both vampires, and your sister worked with Jeramiah to plan the entire kidnapping you thing." he said.

I pulled away from him and looked at his face.

"What? what do you mean?" I replied.

"She knew Jeramiah felt that way about you. She had been stalking you for years, and she was jealous of you. She set the whole thing up with him." he replied.

My heart sunk to my stomach. "So that's why she's gone? not because she lied about meeting you?" I asked.

he nodded. "She knew where you were the whole time and tricked me the whole time. She made me think that Daniel quite possibly killed you, and that's what I thought for days. She said she caught him drinking your blood in Jeramiahs backyard and that she checked your pulse and thought she felt your heart stop.

She was covered in blood when she told me, so it was pretty convincing at the time, to say the least. Then she said he pushed her away and took off with you into the woods somewhere. I looked all night for you, trying to find even the slightest trace of where you could've been, but I couldn't find anything. She played me the whole time." he said.

I sat there in silence, unsure what to say.

"And then something else happened that i'm not sure how you're going to react to." he continued.

"Okay... tell me." I said hesitantly.

"The day that I finally found you, I tried not to give up hope that you were alive some where, because I just couldn't believe that you could be dead, but I couldn't handle the feeling of emptiness that I felt thinking you were gone.

I looked everywhere, tried to call you and Daniel probably a million times, and tried everything I could to find you. Nothing was leading me any closer to you.

So I gave in and tried to drink away my sorrows. She ended up catching me drinking and drank with me, and I felt numb to all the awful feelings for a while, but then she kissed me.

I didn't realize what even happened at first, but the second I did, I pushed her off of me. That's when she got upset and confessed that she wanted to steal me away from you and everything she did and that her and your mom are vampires.

She ran off, and then I took off and tried to call your phone over and over until you finally answered." he explained.

I pulled my body farther away from him.

"She kissed you?" I asked, sounding hurt.

"She did, but I pushed her away from me. I told her I love you and that you're the only person I will ever love." he replied as he tried to reach out for my hand.

I stood up, trying to gain a little space to process all this new information and try not to cry.

"Hayven, please believe me. I did not want that, I was stupid to give in to drinking when you were god knows where at the time.

I felt so broken with you gone, but I never wanted something like that to happen." Damien tried to explain more, feeling nervous as he stood up.

"But my sister kissed you." I said, feeling my heart break not only at the thought of everything she did entirely, but the thought that another woman's lips got to kiss his.

Not just any woman, but my sisters of all people, who I was so excited to find out about, and who betrayed me in so many ways and had nothing but the worst intentions towards me.

"I know." he said sadly, realizing that my reaction wasn't meant to be directed at anything he did.

I turned away from him in an attempt to hide my tears.

Damien stood up and wrapped his arms around me and held me in silence for a long few minutes before saying,

"I'm so sorry any of this happened, and I wish I didn't have to make you stress out over it all, but I felt like you deserved to know. I know we can't pretend that it never happened, but let's try our best to focus on the good things in our lives right now. I do have a good surprise for you that I think you're going to love."

I nodded my head in agreement as I started to wipe away my tears.

"What surprise?" I said with a little laugh because of the random timing to tell me there's a surprise. I turned around to face him.

A smile grew across his face as he held up one finger and said, " Okay, you wait here and close your eyes, don't open them until I say."

I could hear him quickly go into one of the other rooms and start shuffling around some things.

"Okay, remember, keep your eyes closed until I say." he said as he walked back into the living room with me. "Okay, open your eyes." he continued.

I opened my eyes to see him down on one knee in front of me, holding out a beautiful diamond ring.

"I've loved you for so long, and I feel like my life can't even possibly be real every time I look at you. I'm living in a dream, and i'm terrified that any second, i'm just going to wake up and find out that none of this is real.

I am very nervous for us to be having two little babies here before we know it but I know you're going to be such an amazing mother and I know your dad would have been so excited to find out that were having twin babies and i'm excited for the day they're born.

I have been thinking and planning to ask you for months now, so I promise this is a genuine question, because I love you with everything I am, and not just because were having babies now, but will you marry me and officially call this your home?

No more separate rooms, no thoughts of you ever moving out or only being here because there was nowhere else for you to go, but instead just us both in our home as husband and wife with our two beautiful babies.

I promise you that I will be the best father and husband that I possibly can be, and I promise that I will love you all forever, through anything and everything," he asked.

My hand was covering part of my face as the surprised feeling hit me like a huge wave crashing down on me.

I couldn't find the words to say, so I just nodded yes and held out my now very shaky hand. He looked so genuinely happy as he placed the ring on my finger.

He stood up and placed both hands on the sides of my face and kissed me with a new-found passion, like something inside of him was changed in that moment.

His kiss was even more gentle and noticeably filled with love in every touch. Everything in that moment felt more right than it had in my entire life.

Another month passes by, and we do some of our own research together on the animal blood.

Looking into Jeramiahs father, we found some studies listed online explaining things they had learned by testing animal blood on vampires in a newer study that happened after the one Damien was a part of it.

They tested the way human blood types react with the vampires and then realized that animals have different blood types as well and found that they could use animal blood for a variety of different things and it affected majority of the vampires the same way.

The study further explained that they got this idea from the fact that the first vampires recorded in history could not hold down animal blood, some would get sick, some would fall asleep, some would die, and at the time they had just thought that the blood from animals didn't have whatever it was that vampires needed to survive in it, and with them being the first ever vampires that anyone knew of, there was nothing else to compare it to.

Later on in the study, it explained that the first vampires were actually created because of a medical study gone wrong.

They secretly tested on pregnant women, and that led to a mutation in thousands of children.

This mutation was precisely the reason that vampires need blood to survive, why they age at a slower rate, and why their bodies function with more antibodies.

Some secret organization working with the government hunted down over half of them and killed them but lost track of or just plain couldn't find the rest.

After a hundred years had passed, they found out that vampirism was highly likely to be hereditary if the mother was a vampire and that they could somehow change the DNA of normal human beings as well.

That's when they decided to create the program that Damien was in, and they changed multiple humans in multiple locations into vampires so they could study them and have a way to learn more about vampires.

Many of the locations are still open, but the information was not originally shared upon the first few trials of testing.

We explained to Daniel a lot of what happened while we were being held by Jeramiah and keeping him up to date about what we've learned, how i'm doing, and everything through texts and calls while he's getting better.

While we are deep in our studies, Damiens' phones starts to ring.

"Hello?" he starts off. "mhmm... okay... alright, thank you very much, I will be in touch with you." he ended as he hung up.

"That was doctor Cindi, I told her what happened with Alivia and was trying to find out if she knew any information about her like where to find her, if she's in the program, or if anyone knows anything about her or your mom." he said, frustrated.

"Okay, and what did she say?" I asked.

"She does have them in her system but doesn't have a current address for them." he said with a sigh.

I just nod, trying not to think of what that means for us since we can't find the person who had me kidnapped and would've had me killed by Jeramiah.

"Do you think Daniel is better now?" I ask Damien so that I can change the subject.

"Well, i'm still nervous about having him around, but I've done all the tests I can, and he seems to be his normal self and has been for three months.

So I think it's safe to say that the medicine worked really well and quickly this time, thankfully, and I think he's fine now." he said, nodding.

"Then i'm inviting him over!" I said with a smile as I stood up to go grab my phone.

Damien turns around to grab me around my waist softly to stop me from leaving just yet. I look down at him from where he's sitting and wait a moment for him to say something.

"Just promise me that if anything seems off, if anything at all happens, that you will tell me so I can have him leave or just do something to make sure you're safe. I can't stand the thought of ever losing you or our babies, okay?" he begged with his eyes as he spoke but tried hard to sound calm and not at all actually worried, and then he placed his hand on my now very visibly showing baby bump.

"I promise. You will never have to live without us." I said with a smile to try to reassure him and leaned down to kiss his head.

His hands slid from my body as I pulled away. I called Daniel and asked if he wanted to come over and told him how much we've missed him. He said yes, of course, and seemed very excited.

"Do you think you're better now? No risk of anything happening?" I asked him hesitantly but had no other choice but to ask just to make sure. I would be lying if I said I wasn't at all concerned.

He stayed quiet for a second and then said, "I'm good now, I swear. Never again." So I tell him to grab something for us all to eat on the way over and that we will pay him back.

"Tell him to grab some Chinese food, and I will pay for his gas too." Damien yells from the other room.

I couldn't help but laugh as I repeated what he said to Daniel over the phone.

I could hear the smile through his voice as he said, "Don't worry about paying me back, I got this one. Chinese food it is. Text me what you guys want, and I will head over to get everything right now."

I felt the excitement welling up inside me at the thought of us getting to hang out like we hadn't done in so long.

"Okay, see you soon, bye!" I said excitedly. My stomach has gotten a bit bigger since Daniel last saw me, I wonder if he will be surprised about that, I thought to myself.

Damien walks out of the other room into the one I'm in currently and reaches for my stomach for a second.

"I bet he's going to be shocked when he sees your baby bump." he says as he just barely misses my stomach as he continues to walk towards the kitchen.

I laugh out loud and tell him how I was just thinking the same thing.

He gets a glass of water and walks back towards me, chuckling and takes a drink of his glass of water and then leans the cup in my direction as a way of asking if I want to take a drink, so I nod and take a drink of it.

He sets it on the table and starts to play around with me, poking and tickling me all over, causing me to laugh even more and try to wiggle away from him.

"Stop," I playfully beg in between giggles.

The tickles and touches quickly turn into intense touching and deep kisses.

"How is it that every moment can feel so unreal with him even now?" I thought to myself as I kissed him back.

My lips met his, and soon enough, our tongues were connecting. I tug at his shirt, and he pulls it off in one smooth motion over his head, and he falls right back into to kissing me.

Before I knew it, we made our way into the bedroom, and forty-five minutes had passed.

I checked my phone and saw that Daniel had texted and explained he was running a little late because of traffic and the Chinese food place being very popular on this particular night.

"Oops," I say, giggling as I realize how much time had passed.

We both get out of bed and throw our clothes back on, pretending nothing has happened but sneaking touches and flirty glances at each other as we get a few things ready for our company to arrive.

All of a sudden, we hear a knock at the front door. "That must be him." Damien said as he walked over to the door while I was finishing up getting a couple of drinks ready for all of us.

He opened the door.

I heard a loud bang and saw him fall to the ground with a loud and pain filled groan as he was holding his stomach.

EPILOGUE

The blood poured out over his hand, confirming that he was very clearly hurt and that it definitely wasn't just my imagination.

"Damien!" I yelled, the feeling of fear and worry already overwhelming me as I started to run over to him.

Alivia stepped into view just in front of him, blocking my way to him and stopping me in my tracks.

She held a gun in her hand up in the air like she was proud of what she had just done.

"Alivia," I whispered, with fear hitting every nerve in my body.

"Hi sister. Nice to see you again." she said with a sarcastic and sadistic smile.

"What are you doing here? What do you want?!" I yell out anxiously as tears start to well up in my eyes from what I just witnessed happen to Damien.

"Oh sweet sister, I heard from a little birdie that you were pregnant and had to come see for myself. Aren't you excited to see me?" she laughed out loudly.

"Listen, i'm sorry that you feel jealous of the life i'm living, but doing this kind of stuff is not going to give you a life like mine. The only way to do that is to get out there in the world and be nice, meet someone kind, and go from there." I said,

trying anything I could to make her think about what she was doing so that I could hopefully escape this situation unharmed and can get Damien some help.

Her fake smile dropped, and a look of irritation painted every inch of her face now.

"I don't want a life like yours. That would be extremely boring, but I also don't want you to have a life like you have. It's all too easy, and it's not fair. I would much rather see you dead, and it looks like i'm going to have to do that myself since no one else can seem to do it." she said so coldly.

My eyes widened with fear. She held the gun pointed toward me so that I had no choice but to stay put or else I'd risk being shot instead.

"You know the sad thing about you regular humans? The only thing I actually do feel bad about is that you're so weak, physically and mentally.

You die so easily, you can't ever seem to defend yourselves. You're really only good for entertainment from time to time and a good meal." She continued.

"Alivia, we're supposed to be sisters. We have the same mom. We could've gotten to know each other and always had someone to count on.

You could have been an aunt, and we could have been so much more than just two strangers who happen to share one parent and have nothing else in common." I said back to her, still trying anything I could to get her to change her mind and think about what she was doing.

She laughed in response to what I said but didn't say anything back. Damien was still holding his stomach on his knees.

Very obviously in too much pain to move despite the look in his eyes that he would give anything right now to stand up and help me. To stand up and kill her so she can't hurt me.

Alivia glanced back at him and pointed the gun at him, quickly pulling the trigger and shooting him once again, this time in his side just a few inches away from the first wound.

He yelled out in pain again, calling her all kinds of names in a whisper with what little energy he could manage to speak with.

He tried to pull himself to his feet but couldn't push past the pain to move much at all, let alone to stand up.

"Now you're going to stay still, or i'm going to keep shooting him and then shoot you right there." She ended pointing the gun at my stomach.

I froze in fear, unsure what to do at that point. Feeling stuck in what felt almost like a small bubble that prevented me from moving much at all.

She walked over to me, with the gun still pointed at my stomach as her way to keep me and Damien in check as much as possible.

she pulled the hair away from one side of my neck, telling me what she was going to do next.

"Don't touch her, Alivia!" Damien managed to yell out and then collapsed completely to the ground in more pain from the strain his muscles put on his wounds.

She laughed and looked back at me to see me standing as still as a statue with the gun still to my stomach.

I can only hope that some how, some way we make it out of this, but if I try to run, I know I wont get far before i'm shot, or she kills Damien, or purposed aims for my stomach and we lose our babies or who knows what.

She covered my mouth with her free hand to muffle my screams as she bit down hard into my neck. The pain was excruciating, but she continuously reminded me of the gun points at my stomach so that I would suffer through it.

Damien tried to crawl over to her to do anything he could, but she kicked him back and shot him two more times, once in the leg and once in the chest just shy of his heart.

"No!" I yelled. "Alivia, please stop. Please don't do this." I begged.

She ignored me and covered my mouth again as she went in for another harsh and extremely painful bite. My scream just barely muffled under her palm.

My blood is now streaming down my body, soaking my clothes. It was all over her face and shirt and was dripping to the ground just beneath me.

I saw Damien glance out the door, and his eyes lit up for a moment with hope, and Daniel quietly slid into view beside him.

He saw Damien hurt on the ground and what Alivia was doing to me, and rage visibly and quickly washed over him.

Alivia hadn't noticed him yet since she was so focused on me.

Daniel snuck up behind her as silently as possible, pulling out a pocket knife and stabbing her deep in the back all the way through to her heart.

She let out a small yelp of pain, and a look of pure shock and surprise fell over her face as she fell to the ground away from me, very obviously in intense pain of her own now.

Without hesitating, Daniel grabbed me to make sure I wouldn't fall, and we all seemed to realize the gruesome scene that was at hand.

He looked down at me, completely covered in blood, and seeing that he too was covered in my blood now. He breathed heavily for a moment as the realization was fully hitting him.

"Daniel?" I stuttered out, worried for a moment that this truly might be the end for me.

"I'm okay, i'm okay." Daniel replied.

He helped me over to the couch so I could sit down, and he stood back up. My eyes never left him as I continued to worry.

He wiped his hands on his pants and said, "No, i'm good. I swear. It's different this time. I exposed myself to bloods that I would be addicted to so I could try to overcome it, and to be honest, your blood seems kind of different now. So i'm good. I swear nothing is going to happen. I won't allow it either, never again." he reassured me.

I allowed my body to feel relief finally, believing that I was safe and that we were in good hands. Hopefully, the nightmare was over, and we wouldn't have to worry anymore.

Daniel quickly ran back around the couch near the door and helped Damien stand up.

Damien let out a loud pain filled groan again as he was moved from the floor over to the couch.

"Damien," I quietly cried out as I could finally get a better view of his wounds.

"Don't worry, i'm here, i'm going to help you both. It's going to be okay." Daniel said as he sat Damien down on the couch beside me and pulled out his phone.

He was hiding it well, but I could tell he was worried and scared himself.

"Hey, I need your help. It's an emergency. I'm at Damiens, and we have two injured and one dead." he said and then paused for a second to listen to the person on the other side of the phone.

"Okay, see you soon." he ended and hung up the phone.

Damiens' head fell back on the couch, and the cushion beside me felt like it had become so much more weighed down.

Daniel and I look over at Damien, as he's lying there unconscious now. His seemingly lifeless body just collapsed there next to me on the couch.

I started to call out for Damien, becoming scared that he wasn't going to make it and trying to shake him awake.

Panic swelled up inside of me, and I couldn't control myself.

Daniel reached over to me and grabbed me quickly and began hugging me tightly, forcing me to not touch Damien or move him and forcing me to not over do myself with movements as well since I probably wasn't too far away from the same fate.

He continued hugging me silently as I tried to push him off, and screamed and cried until I gave into his hug and buried my face into his shoulder and reached farther underneath his arms more to hug him back as I sobbed.

He held me tightly, not saying a single word. To be honest, I don't think he knows what to say in this moment. I don't know if he thinks Damien will be okay or not, and either way, it's probably best that I dont hear what he has to say.

What felt like an eternity later, but also somehow only mere moments later, doctor Cindi walked through the door with a big bag and started working on Damien first.

Currently, he's the one who seems like he needs the most immediate medical attention.

She cuts open his wounds and pulls the bullets out one by one, cleans the wounds, and then sews him up, all without him waking up or flinching in the slightest. She then injects him with a few different medicines.

"There's no way to know what will happen for sure from this point, but I think he's going to make it." she says as she walks over to me and starts to clean and stitch up my wounds.

I felt relieved, even though it was too soon to know for sure what the end result would be. She pulls out some fluid in a bag and hooks me up to an I.V. while she checks the babies heartbeats with a fetal doppler.

"They seem to be okay as far as I can tell. Their heart rates are completely normal, which tells me they're not in any distress, and this fluid should help your body replenish the blood you've lost.

It seems like you've lost a lot of blood, but thankfully, you didn't lose too much surprisingly. Plus, being pregnant, your body has a lot more blood running through it, so you should be completely fine." She explained to me.

It all felt like it was passing in the blink of an eye. Before I knew it, she was telling Daniel to take care of us, and Daniel was helping take Alivias' lifeless body out of the house.

A couple weeks of Daniel helping us day and night, and we were completely back to normal.

Damien healed over time, but he admits that he truly believes he came close to actually dying.

Me and the babies healed quickly. Soreness was the longest lasting bit I had to experience as usual.

We couldn't thank him enough for his help and felt even more like we were all a big family.

His blood addiction seemed to be nothing but a problem of the past now since my blood has changed, according to him.

We told him about our engagement, which was the only thing we left out in our updates to him, and asked him if he would be the twins God Father in case anything happened to us. He agreed and was so thrilled for us.

Doctors' appointments showed that the babies were both as healthy as ever in there somehow, despite the struggles they've already had to face.

Damien felt guilty that he couldn't be the one to save me when I needed him most, but we all felt happy that some how, some way, were always there for each other to save the day.

It seemed like all the bad things and people that once tried to hurt us were all in our past.

Everything felt right again, and it felt like we were all on our way to much better days, together as a family again.

I get to wake up every day now, with people I love, who love me back, and I've never felt better.

I'm looking forward to all the things the future has in store for me.

Milton Keynes UK
Ingram Content Group UK Ltd.
UKHW020315021124
450424UK00013B/1254